Book Two of the Rostal

Dan

The Queen's

Dragon

Enjoy! ☺

Emma Barrett-Brown

The Queen's Dragon

First Published Independently
Dec 2020 ©Emma Barrett, Plymouth UK

Cover Photography:
    (C) Jay McKinnon, www.facebook.com/MckinnonImages

Chapter title custom font:
Griffy by Font Diner, licenced for commercial use(c) www.fontdiner.com

Printed and Bound by KDP – Kindle Direct Publishing

This is a book for the wonky people! They know who they are!

It's also for Ash, without whom I would likely not have written this series!

One

The first scream was agony to hear, it always was. A long thin wail as stinking hot tar splattered down over grey stone to embrace the foot-soldiers waiting below. The scream was one not just of pain, although that must have been great, but defeat too, a submission to a known demise. Fear too, although few would admit to it even in the presence of death. Then came the rest, the din of screams and the roars of a united battle-cry; men about to put their lives on the line for another person's game. Those roars were bestial, putting those disciplined soldiers more in line with their wilder counterparts, The Woldermen. Those roars would soon turn to a din of weapons upon weapons if the walls were breached. The keep really could not stand much more of this! This was the third attempt in as many months to take down her defences, and Queen Niamh's strength for battle was fading.

'Draw!' a voice to her side shouted, and suddenly the noise was turned to a shing of arrows being placed into bows. Niamh glanced sideways, her lips pressed, to take the eye of Josynne Shale – her second in command and long-time friend.

'Fire!' he completed the command and a sea of sharp, pointed death crashed out like a wave on the men below.

Niamh's belly hurt, her shoulders were so tight from standing upright for hours on end that her entire back ached. Her leather breastplate dug into her hips, rubbing so she knew that her skin would be blistered and sore when she came to take it off – presuming she didn't die in it, that was! Her hands were warm in fur-lined gloves, clenched so hard that had she not worn the thick coverings over her fingers, her nails might well have pierced her own skin. Her aching shoulders too were wrapped in furs, she'd never really gone back to the fashions of court. Besides, in war-time, the leather armour and fur felt safer than any hard plate. Niamh pulled in a long steadying breath. Speech was beyond her now, the panic gnawing her gut, but she need not speak, not yet, just observe as Josynne led the archers and Kilm, another old friend and the last of the Wolder Lords to remain at her side, manned the lighting of the tar barrels and oil.

'Draw!' the cry went out again. Niamh watched, not interfering with the work which her commanders knew better than she did, and then inadvertently put out her hand to the boy next to her. Alistair, her son. Still a babe really, at just thirteen years old. The boy took after his father, dark hair with the tell-tail blue streaks of dragon-blood in his veins. He was a handsome lad already and Niamh was already sure he was going to break hearts once he fully grew into his skin. He had Helligan's eyes too, despite that his face was more like hers, a little chubby and with a few odd freckles when the sun was high in the season. His shoulders too were tight, but then this was his first battle - no more could be expected of any boy! His eyes darted about, not calm and experienced like Niamh and her commanders, but anxious, frightened. When Josynne had suggested the boy join them, during the emergency council meeting earlier, Niamh had challenged the idea of bringing her son into battle. She'd been overruled though and her advisors had managed to persuade her that she was reacting on a mother's caution, and that as her heir, the prince should be allowed to witness what it took to keep the kingdom. Alistair had, of course, not been consulted but had he been, Niamh was sure he'd have jumped at the chance despite his tendency towards a little shyness. Alistair was a boy born to be king, and even at thirteen, he took that seriously. The boy pressed her fingers gently but then dropped her hand. Niamh could not help but smile – what boy *would* want to be seen clinging to his mother's hand in the midst of battle? Especially the future king! Alistair gave her his smile though, the one which was like hers, and then looked back out over the ramparts.

It seemed an age that the battle remained in the first step, a siege locked into the early stages of tall walls and desperate breech attempts. Her enemy were not so well-situated as she was, safe within the walls of the once again restored Anglemarsh Keep. They had the advantage of supplies, though, fed to them from the villages to the south which they had taken on their journey upwards through the mountains. Anglemarsh had been burned out by her father's men many years earlier after her war of ascension, but she'd made it one of her first decrees as queen to have it rebuilt, and quickly. The fortifications were better than they had been in her father's day, she'd insisted upon that, with a new portcullis and heavy wooden gates in the walls surrounding not just the keep, but its associated town too. The Golden Keep – the traditional home of the kings of Rostalis – would have been easier to defend, but Niamh had never felt at home there. Anglemarsh was better; nowhere had ever felt so much like home. To the north, the Golden Keep stood empty but for a handful of servants who maintained it, just as it had for the past ten years. Niamh would not make her home under watch of the ghost of her father. Never! It was bad enough that she'd been forced to lodge there the three years whilst Anglemarsh was restored.

Niamh wet her lips again, the battle grew louder and louder, and from her vantage point, she could see the forces marching ever closer, hundreds of them this time! Why would so many turn to the opposing side? Had she not ever been a fair and just queen? Beloved and kind? Her brother's son did have the better claim though. He, of an age with Alistair but led by his desperate grandmother, Niamh's stepmother of old, Queen Magda. After the final battle where her crooked father had fallen, Niamh had been left to piece together what had happened to the rest of her family. Her brother Lauren, of course, had died under Helligan's flame, and in the aftermath of that his wife Lady Kyran had fled, already heavily pregnant with his son – the boy now Niamh's enemy. When the king fell, Queen Magda had taken her other daughters and fled too, going into sanctuary in the temple of Octavia, in the south. This Niamh had heard from Jedda, the only one of those girls to return and beg her pardon, swear fealty to the new queen. She'd told of how Lady Kyran had joined them, baby in arms, and of how almost at once, Magda had begun her plotting to crown the child as his father's heir. It had taken ten years for those plots to develop, but now here they were, at war again!

'Mother, are you well?' Alistair asked, his hand touching her arm.

Niamh nodded, then, in true need to at least do something, fingered her own bow. The weapon was ornate and delicately carved, not the elven bow she'd used in her youth, that had been burned up by the same dragon-fire that had ended her brother's life, but it was specially made for her hand, sturdy and capable of ending lives just as her old one had been. She gripped it and glanced to the archery platform which they'd had built into the side of the rampart.

'Don't,' Josynne said softly, putting a hand on her arm, 'If you go up there you are too sweet a target!'

Niamh sighed and nodded; she knew he was right but she felt so helpless stood silently watching as her men fought for her. At least she was there though, she told herself, not fleeing away through the tunnels as once before she'd had to. That was the day she had met Helligan. Niamh's stomach churned even at the thought of him. Helligan, her hero. Lord of the Wolder, mage and – as they had later discovered, Draconis – a dragon in human form. At the end of the war he'd gone back to face his own people and to answer for crimes he'd committed in leaving the draconis, in revealing their kind to humanity… and in marrying her. Even their son's birth was a crime against him.

He had never returned.

Niamh fingered the little shard of dragon glass about her neck, now dull and black. Helligan had given it to her with a glimmer of his essence within – as long as it glowed, he'd told her, he lived. It no longer glowed. It hadn't for years. Alistair seemed to see the movement as her fingers caressed the necklace. He put a gloved hand onto her arm.

'Father would have been proud,' he said – ever he'd been old for his years. 'He is with us now, I am sure!'

'I am sure,' Niamh whispered the first words she'd spoken in hours. Her mind, too busy for singular thought, though, moved back to the battle. They were making more ground now, the tar not quite enough to keep the men from the stony walls. Niamh could smell the battle, that dizzying stench of blood, death, and the overwhelming, cloying tar. She wondered what it must be to die such a death and, as ever, she wondered why men did such, fighting for a cause not even their own! Was it for coin? For glory? She'd never understand it.

Niamh forced her back straight again where she was beginning to slouch and glanced behind her, at the door through which the softer of her subjects hid. If the walls fell, then they too were all at terrible risk. The maids, the womenfolk, the sisters readying their bandages and salves, none really able to swing a sword, to defend themselves. Further back, in the dense part of the house with good access to escape through the tunnels should it come to it, was her other child too, her daughter Jessaline. Jess was in the care of Jedda and another of Niamh's oldest friends – Sister Dora of the order of Herodite, high priestess. Jess was the child of Niamh and Josynne Shale, the result of a night or two spent in comfort in the years after Helligan's demise. Those were not times she regretted, but times she had put a stop to with the conception of the child. With her ever growing belly, she'd been unable to hide the fact that another royal bastard, just like she'd been, was in her belly.

Josynne had taken her rejection and the ending of their night-time trysts, hard at first. She'd ever known that he loved her and for a time she thought that she'd lost him for good in the pain of her withdrawal. That pain was something she held deep within, along with the shame of having given him false hope in her efforts to stem the grief in losing Helligan. The years had worked their healing magics, though, and after the initial conflict, their bond had begun to regrow, blossoming to a friendship almost as strong as it had once been. Niamh's mind rested on the little girl locked away inside for a moment, remembering how her own royal siblings had died. There were no orders to end Jessaline's life though, no matter how the battle went – surrender and merciful death was not an option when escape was possible. Niamh was not her father, not one to order the massacre of children!

Almost angrily, Niamh forced her attention back to the battle, stilling the anxieties that churned her gut and made her belly ache. Josynne's archers were doing well at keeping the larger army at bay, but Kilm was looking more stressed, the tar and oil supplies low now – not through lack of the substances themselves, but the ability to heat them fast enough. Below he had a wife too, and several favoured whores. Niamh watched his old features carefully, wondering if he felt the same stresses she felt. He paused, seeming almost panicked and she knew she had to intervene.

'Kilm,' Niamh managed to call through dry lips, 'give that up and begin to ready your men!'

'Aye my queen, getting on it now!' Kilm said. 'If your mages could…'

Niamh nodded and clambered down the wooden stairs to the battlement walk, leaving her son to man the battle.

'Be careful Niamh!' Josynne's cry, but she merely waved a hand at him as she made her way along the thin corridor. A volley of arrows flew, somebody had seen her, but Niamh ducked her head and moved to the nearside wall with its curved overhang to avoid them. Overhead, a thin drizzle began too, the type which could soak a person right through. Once the arrows ceased, Niamh ran the distance on the slippery stone, to the far tower, her hunting boots slapping on the slimy boards which had been put down in places to try to make the floor less treacherous. There she took up one of the still-lit torches and waved it above her head. At once, another cascade of arrows came her way but Niamh was prepared for them, ducking behind the pillar and letting out a few pants of both fear and exhilaration.

From the other side of the keep, out in the guard tower to the east, suddenly there was a flare of light, and a bolt of green chaos-fire lit up the evening sky. Niamh smiled. Her mages might not be to the calibre of Helligan and the old council, but they were improving at least. The reinstatement of the mage council had been one of Niamh's primary objectives when she'd taken the throne. An ancient order of men, the ancestors of the half-fey or half-dragon who had, through the generations, maintained control of their ancestral magical ability. It had not been an easy task to gather those who were left. Most hid their talents, or were so undisciplined with them that they were dangerous. But the kingdom needed mages, and Niamh needed at least some link to Helligan, some memory of him, and so she'd persevered.

From the first it was a difficult task to train the children too. Niamh had only herself and her book knowledge to guide her. Niamh's father had murdered all of the old council swiftly after the first war, a series of executions so that the blame for the conflict might be swiftly imposed on those poor innocent souls. It was the very first thing which had made Niamh doubt her father's goodness. She watched as the magic in the air brewed and as ever, it made all the hair on her neck prickle with its tingling mists. The spells, whilst lethal, were beautiful too and as Nervoria, the pretty little female mage who was making quite a stir amongst them all, sent out her ice-fire, Niamh's heart pulled again. As a blue dragon, Helligan had favoured ice-magic. If she shut it all out, she could almost believe he was there, fighting with them. Time dulled the overwhelming grief somewhat, but still she wished for his presence daily. Another bolt of blue streaked out towards the invading army, and Niamh allowed the smile to form. Despite the hardships, forming the new mage council was another thing she'd never regret, nor her pilgrimage to gather them all up and bring them to the new academy.

Nervoria they had found in the remnants of a burned-out inn out in the countryside south of the marshes. She'd been the only survivor of the fire she'd inadvertently started. Of the others there were four, all male – traditionally the magics were stronger in males and so they were more likely to show early traits. Elenni was the eldest at twenty-two. It was he who used the grey magics with air as his catalyst. Niamh had high hopes for him and young Jessaline adored him openly in the manner only an eleven-year-old girl can. The brunette beauty, Nervoria's ice-fire was created from the element of water, as was the nineteen-year-old Friggan's feeble blue magics. The younger two, Maven and Genn at fourteen and fifteen both used the more usual elements of fire, thrusting their poor still child-like hands into the flames of candles and lanterns in order to create the bright orange magicka. Niamh lived ever in fear that she would be called to the infirmary and met with burned hands and faces, but as of yet, the fire seemed to leave no marks on their skin. She was yet to find an earth-mage in her travels, and none of them showed Helligan's aptitude to use all four elements in their casting. Maybe once they made their focuses, but Niamh still wasn't really sure how that was done.

With the assault of the mages, the army turned to the east tower, freezing Niamh's heart. They had expected this but still it was painful to watch the masses turn on those she considered her children as much as the two of her own blood were. The magicka seemed to rattle the tower almost off its foundations and Niamh was certain that she did see a tile or two slide free, a pane of glass shatter.

'Work together!' she whispered, heart hammering. 'Don't be afraid! You are stronger together!'

Almost as though they heard her, the bolts stopped for a moment, then the crackle of magic in the air intensified, the power grew. The explosion from within, whilst also expected, was terrifying. Niamh glanced back around the pillar to witness as three of the four elements seemed to blast out of the tower all of a sudden, a wave of energy, so hot it warmed Niamh's face even at a distance. Beautiful, that wave of green, blue and red fire which leapt from the window of the tower and washed over the soldiers in a deadly wave. Two thirds of Magda's army were incinerated in an instant, the rest left screaming and howling, turning about as panic set in. Niamh heard their screams, felt the pain of the sobbing of men in her heart too. After all, they *were* still her subjects – just misguided. She closed her eyes against the sight and sound of it all and had to force calm not to drop and cover her ears. She had not been the one to start this war, had never wanted to see another war in her life, but she could not allow them to massacre her people either. The tower dimmed and the magic in the air dissipated. That would be it now. The children, to have created such a spell would likely all have fallen, wiped out and exhausted.

Niamh moved, more shakily, and turned back to where Josynne and Alistair stood. She felt dizzy and sick. A glance over the battlements showed her Magda's men regrouping after the wave, a much smaller army now but being drawn back in. Amazingly, some seemed to have survived the magic too, stumbling back to their feet in jerky, broken movements to re-join the throng. How? Niamh let out a long breath. The siege weapons which were pointed at her home still stood in the most part, and after the few moments of panic, those too seemed to be being manned again. She'd thought that such a blow might win her the battle, but she was wrong.

Niamh regathered her wits, then glanced up at her little group by the steps. Josynne was back in command, starting another volley from his archers whilst Kilm was gone, readying the men, she supposed. She didn't have much of an army anymore, but Kilm's Wolder were men of war, always ready and willing for a fight. Niamh wiped her face and then took a swig from her water bottle. Another chunk of stone flew from a trebuchet towards them and hit the wall before her squarely. The stone crumbled and half of the slate part of the battlement fell in a heaving thud. Goddess! They'd not need too many more hits like that! Niamh panted and then raised a hand to the frenzied Josynne as his head snapped around to her. Then she froze in panic and her heart leapt into her chest. Her boy was moving, clambering down from the shelter of the dais with its heavy stone protection and down the slippery wooden ladder.

'Alistair No!' Niamh screamed, but the boy stepped free, putting himself into view of the army. Niamh had to hope that they were too preoccupied to notice such a prize. Alas, they were not. More arrows suddenly flew, clinking and clanking about her son.

'Josynne!' she screamed, appealing to her friend in a last-ditch hope that he could catch the boy and prevent him from getting to his target, which looked to be the edge of the battlements. Josynne ran and seemed to try to grapple the boy, his face showing him as confused as Niamh, but to her horror Alistair shoved him aside and continued on. At the edge, leaning so that he could look over, Alistair paused, arrows coming so close that some at least must have nicked his arms. Niamh couldn't breathe, couldn't even run to him for the stone and clutter blocking her path. Alistair let out a roar that was almost primal and then ripped off his gloves, opening up his palms. A blue light formed around him and once again Niamh felt the prickle of magicka. Her breath left her body, her heart picked up pace to thud even more-so in her chest as her son, her precious baby, used the latent gifts his father had left him for the very first time. With a moan that Niamh could hear even from across the parapet, Alistair raised up both of his palms into the air facing the rain which gushed down, and then made a grabbing motion and pulled something invisible down towards the ground. At first Niamh didn't understand, but then she froze, her jaw dropping, as massive hailstones, some the size of boulders, formed from the very air and began to rain down on the crowds of the army below.

Two

Helligan Darkfire opened his dry tired eyes and blinked. The darkness remained. He groaned and rolled over, his body aching much as it did every morning, for lack of even a bedroll to sleep on. The ground was dirty and dry, hard. Helligan barely even noticed anymore, his fingers scrabbled in the dust as his vison began to adjust once again to the dark empty void of his windowless cell. It could have been any time of the day or night for all he knew in his black prison, but in an attempt to maintain some semblance of normality he had to at least presume that it was morning. His hands moved to push under him in an effort to move to a sitting position. It was a struggle even to do that, his arms weakened now as was every part of him, wasting away in his imprisonment. The floor below was of a dusty natural slate, the prison cell one of the old ones dug into the hollows of cave below the dragon city of Zaikanis. Helligan shuffled again, feeling the pull of steel at his ankle, the chains of the bondage he faced every morning upon waking. His chest hurt and his stomach growled. Eating was not an easy decision. Not just for the scarcity of food, but also that it was one of the highlights of the day. To waste it so soon after waking up would leave little to look forward to until the next sleep. His stomach growled again though and forced the decision. Helligan felt around at the edge of the room where he kept his stash. It took a minute to locate in the darkness but then his fingers found purchase, right where the rough slate gave way to wet stony walls. There wasn't much left, just the tiniest noblet of bread. Sometimes Helligan worried that he must sleep twice or three times a day, either that, or they did not feed him regularly – for it was now three sleeps since his last plate was delivered. The bread was hard and stale, an indication that perhaps it was not his sleeping pattern which was skewed. He once more half-considered saving the food but the hunger suddenly overwhelmed him and he put the morsel into his mouth and chewed slowly. It tasted like mould and dust, but then everything in his prison did. The food brought back some of his senses a little though. There was water too, some in a jug and more to be had by putting a tongue to the walls where the rains seeped in, undignified but then Helligan had not known much of dignity since his imprisonment.

'*An example must be made*,' his father had said, standing up on his dais before the rest of the blue dragonflight. 'Helligan might be my son but his crimes are heinous and too many to be ignored. He must stand trial before the council.'

Helligan bit and chewed another piece of bread. Perhaps one of the blessings of being stripped of his true form was the ability to eat such small amounts of food and still live. He could not starve. His body aged though, he could feel it now, moving ever more away from what he had been. Again, without his dragon-form, he could not die of old age, but he could not stop the aging of the human form either. At least his youth could be restored, he thought, once he was whole again this would all be just distant painful memories.

When he was released.

His sentence was 100 years.

Helligan's head rang, as ever it did, with those words. He had known when he'd left Niamh and his son, that he might never be able to return, but he had feared death, not this slow powerless rot. It was worse than death.

And yet the sentence had been given in mercy.

The room in which they'd held the trial had been one of the amphitheatres. Not open air, but a vast chamber within one of the tall sky-buildings. It contained a platform surrounded by a sea of seating which was rarely used aside from the row in the front centre – there were not enough dragons left now to fill all the seats, and Helligan doubted there ever had been. It was for intimidation alone, a show of grandiose and supremacy which was not supported by the facts. Much the way with his people. Once within, Helligan had been thrown to the ground before the attendees of the court, some twenty in total, chained so that he could not stand, and there left on his knees before them all, humbled. This too was the way of things with his people, all pomp and ceremony. The trial would have no witnesses to call, nor a defence as such, unless the friendly clans present were counted thus. All the clans. Helligan recalled still how his gut had twisted in anticipation. In this era, it was rare to call a full meeting of the draconic council. Not all of the different clans particularly got on, and even those who did, many of them disliked matters of state such as this. However, for Helligan's trial, an elder of every family had stood, if not the leaders themselves. Helligan hadn't been surprised, it was not every day they had the chance to witness the trial and sentence of another clan-leader's son.

Helligan chewed another mouthful of bread, lost in the memory, replaying it over and over as a form of torment to himself. It was something to do in the darkness, at least.

All of the attendees of his trial had been in humanesque form. This was standard, their true forms were lesser used, in a world where communication through words was easier than the more bestial manner of the animal they became, intelligent or no. The docile emerald dragonkin leader Oris had stood for his family. He was ancient, nearly 900 years – an incredible age even for a Dragon! He was an intelligent creature who showed wisdom above most of the others. Helligan had always liked the man, but then the blues had always got on well with the emerald-skinned clan.

Next to Oris had sat the elderly leader of the blackflight kin, Ariane, beside two of her cousins from the greyscale. Both clans were hot-headed, but then they patronised Helston – the goddesses face of battle – and so it was in their blood. Helligan had held Ariane's eye for a moment but she showed no softness on her hard, pointed features. He'd received more sympathy, though from the old woman who stood for the richly clad Bronze flight. Not their leader, Gern, but a female who probably rivalled the old man in age. Her fair hair was immaculate as was her gold-thread purple gown, her hands adorned with jewels. These were the clan who had spurred stories amongst the mortals of dragons hoarding wealth, and they had little time for politics. Their companion clan, the Crimsonskins were represented by two princely males, both young, both handsome, but then weren't they all? Vanity prevented them from allowing their human forms to age, and so Helligan could never be sure if he were talking to an ancient or a child of that clan unless he knew them well. Both were dressed in the same sumptuous fabrics of red, black and gold which showed off their fine forms. Helligan had nodded to them and one of them had nodded back. He knew neither of their faces, though and so there was little hope of leniency there.

The kin of brown scale – those patient and perseverant – had sent one of the younger-looking ones too rather than old Jakin. The girl in his spot had big eyes and pressed lips, she was pretty but unfamiliar. Finally, standing back, were the shy and quiet white dragons, the master healers of the draconis. Korbyn had not come himself, but had sent the only two others who remained of the clan: his two daughters. Both girls were albino beauties, with red eyes even in their human forms. Of all the dragonkin gathered, the whites had looked the least comfortable with the proceedings, but then they must all know the truth of it – that it had been their father, Korbyn, who had sent Helligan through in the first place.

Then to his own clan.

Helligan's memory brought him the ghost-images of his father and mother sat in the front of the chamber, dressed in robes of state, with his younger brother, Argosus sat at his mother's side due to his close family tie to Helligan. Family ties were unbreakable bonds to the draconis, even if siblings were not brought up to be close as humans were. Argosus was very young though, still a foundling at a mere hundred and fifty years or so… a full fifty years Helligan's junior. He had a look of his brother, with the same black and blue hair, higher cheekbones and the eyes which shone with ice-fire. He cultivated facial hair though, which Helligan did not, and his locks were clipped to his chin rather than the long braids his clan favoured. Helligan loved him as dearly, just as any Draconis loved a sibling. He hated that the boy had been there to witness his downfall. Argosus had watched with intrigue though, as his brother sat chained before him. Helligan was naked, as was the nature of draconic trials, but he'd held his head high despite that, his eyes skimming still from person to person as they debated his case. Helligan had broken three fundamental rules, it was never going to go easy on him.

And so the charges were brought: He had left the sacred forest, that was the first strike. He had revealed himself to humans, showing them that the dragonkind existed still. Worst of all, he had sired a half-breed child on a human wife.

Finally the verdict came: 'Death, by the rite of Paxion' – an ancient ceremony for draconic execution, where the offending dragon was stripped of his essence to prevent changing form and set out onto the spire of the tall tower to be eaten alive by the Gurrans and Swigs – mighty birds of prey which lurked only in the darkest recesses of the forest.

On the passing of his sentence, Helligan had bowed his head, accepting of his fate. He had not expected to escape with his life, even despite that he had also retrieved the ancient and lost artefact, the crystal sphere the humans named as Guul. This sphere was an artefact designed in the ages of the first war to give humans dominance and control over the dragons. As the sentence was passed, though, Helligan's mother had fallen prone before the council.

'Please, spare his life! He is young still, impulsive but he has also worked in our interests! He went to save us, not to damn us!'

And so the council had moved to whisper together, and a general murmur in sympathy had forwarded his mother's pleas. Not a one had voted for his death, in the end. Once discussion was done, Helligan's father had stepped forward

'We cannot go lightly on him,' still that voice echoed, 'my son sits before us all as an example. He will live to know that his human wife ages and dies, that his son will grow without him. When he is returned to the light of day, everything he knows in the world of the humans will be gone, and with it his temptation to flee back there. There is no room, at all, for these types of affairs between us and them!'

The darkness stifled as Helligan lay in silent contemplation of his fate. How many years had it been now? Time did not pass as it should within his dungeon and it could have been a mere matter of months, or it could have been as many years. Endless, drawn and dark. The removal of his dragon essence would have clouded Niamh's necklace. She probably thought him dead — they all probably did. His human hands fidgeted with the stones, finding a piece of rock loose. Once, when they'd first thrown him down there, first chained his foot into the manacle which still held it, Helligan would have saved up those loose bits of rock and stone, ready to attack his jailers in a hope for escape, but time had shown him how fruitless these endeavours were. Besides, without his dragon form, he'd never escape the city anyway. Zaikanis was way up above the forest and there were no paths for human feet to reach it.

As Helligan sat lost in memories, the clattering echo of footsteps sounded without. His eyes tried to see through the darkness but he did not stir, did not move. To his left, the old iron and wood door which formed the barrier between him and the living world creaked on its hinges and opened, revealing a humanesque figure by the light of a dim candle. Helligan knew well enough to know it was not human, though, just another of his kind. A grey-scale by the looks of him. Helligan did not react. This was a familiar drill.

'Your jug,' the man said.

Helligan lifted the empty silver carafe and flung it towards the door. The chain about his leg would not allow him to walk there anyhow. The figure lifted the container and put it to one side behind him, and then produced another, filled to the brim with water. Once, in the early days, Helligan had flung a full jug at his jailer. Three days without any water but the thin layer which lingered on the damp cell wall had taught him not to try that again. The figure moved a little closer and set the water down so that it would be within Helligan's reach... after a struggle at least. It was ever the same. Then he moved back to the door and flung in a loaf of bread and some cheese. Helligan focused his eyes on the food. Yet another lesson learned, if he lost sight of the food once the darkness closed in again he would not be able to find it easily.

The jailer paused, and then – something of an anomaly, he spoke soft words, 'Your brother sends his regards, Lord Helligan,' he said, 'and those of your mother.'

Helligan had not spoken since they'd thrown him into the cell, well, other than the odd strained day when he found himself muttering aloud in the darkness. His tongue and lips were very dry but he managed a gruff word of thanks before the door was closed again and the darkness was once more complete. Helligan moved to retrieve his food and lay it down in the spot he had designated for it, food for another few days, most likely. Then the bigger challenge as he reached for the jug of water. It was just in the reach of his fingertips, if he lay flat on his belly with the chain about his ankle pulled tight, and there could be inched closer and closer by tiny fumbling movements. Every now and again, the icy liquid splashed onto his hand but Helligan had become adept at the sport, and so no longer spilled so much as he had when he was first imprisoned. Once he could get his fingers around the handle, he did so, pulling it closer and indulging in a long cool swig. It already felt like hours since the jailer had left, and so Helligan closed his eyes and laid his head against the hard rock of his dungeon. He knew he was sleeping too much again, but really, there was little else to still his troubled thoughts.

Three

'I didn't know that I could do it, until I did it!' Alistair insisted again. His young lips were pressed and his eyes filled with the tears of anguish which had remained since the battle. In the aftermath, Niamh and Josynne Shale had grabbed the boy and all-but dragged him away from the battlements. Still the melting ice-boulders littered the pathways leading up to the keep, some with the bodies of dead soldiers still trapped beneath. The rest of Magda's army had fled and with the combination of Niamh's mages, and then her son's magic, who could blame them? Niamh sat very still, her eyes taking in the frame of her boy. Still so young and yet still so very much the image of his father. Would Helligan have known – suspected at least – what his son was capable of? Somehow Niamh doubted it, she'd not even seen Helligan perform such a devasting spell. Alistair looked exhausted though. His skin was grey and his eyes were rimmed with dark circles. Niamh had seen Helligan thus, after a battle; depleted and in need of replenishment. It was easier to stomach witnessed on the face of a man, though, than on the features of a thirteen year old boy. She put a hand on her son's in gentle reassurance.

'Nobody is angry with you, Alis,' she said.

'Angry? M'lad, you won the bloody battle!' That was Kilm – somehow he'd abstained from his whores in the aftermath of the skirmish for long enough to sit in on the conversation.

'And yes, whilst that is true,' Josynne interrupted, 'It is dangerous to use magic untrained! If you had guidance and…'

'And if my father were still alive,' Alistair interrupted, 'then you would condone it more, my lord?' Ever it was a bane to her son that he'd never met his father – or not in his memory at least.

'Yes, if Helligan the mage were still living, then perhaps you could have had the training to control more properly, this untamed magic in your veins…'

'Tell us again, how it came upon you,' Niamh said. She was the only one kneeling, sat beside her son with her hand on his. The boy was seated in a hard wooden chair by the fire and the two commanders both stood like some sort of inquisition, albeit a kind one, for both men loved the young prince almost as much as she did. Kilm and Josynne had both taken it upon themselves to help her raise her boy and so he'd received education from both – the polite manners of court combined with the wildness of Wolder living. As long as Kilm didn't see fit to introduce the prince to the brothels and whorehouses where he spent a lot of his time, Niamh encouraged the dual upbringing.

'I said it before,' Alistair was not usually peevish, and so his tone indicated the strength of his disquiet. 'I was standing watching as Mother ran to signal the mages, and then something within me began to burn. As I watched their magics fly and felt them in my core, I knew, somehow, that I could… that I could touch it too. Then they fired at Mama and a rage filled me. I had no mind for my safety, nor for anything other than calling down the rains.'

'But your rains were of ice – great big bloody boulders of it,' Kilm said with a chuckle, 'good lad! Bit o your father in you indeed!'

'Indeed, but a lack of caution! Had you mis-aimed, you could have tumbled our walls and let them inside!'

'I knew that not! Nor the devastation I would cause. It was almost a compulsion.'

'A compulsion, as though you knew not what you were doing? Josynne asked, his face suddenly serious.

Niamh could understand the worry. In the last battle of the last war, Helligan had been put under the control of a magical sphere wielded by her father. Whilst thus controlled he had murdered a dear friend and nearly taken her life too, as well as decimating half of their own army. Helligan had taken the sphere back to their own people but if somebody other had managed to clone the magics somehow, had been controlling her son…

Alistair shook his head, he'd heard the story enough times to understand the worry too, 'No, not… not like that. Just, like I needed to do it, like I knew it was the only thing which would work…'

'A compulsion from within, not without?' Niamh asked. She tightened her fingers on Alistair's arm, a caress which betrayed her nerves, and her son glanced up at her with eyes that shone out older than his years. Her heart melted a little at the worry in those eyes.

'Yes. I am sorry, Mother,' he whispered.

'Don't be!' that was Kilm again, firmly on the boy's side. 'if it weren't for what you did…'

'If it wasn't for what I did, Mother's mages might have turned the tide anyhow.'

'Aye, or maybe Magda's army would'a pulled down that tower an killt em all.'

'Either eventuality is unknown now, and for the better,' Josynne said, moving to Niamh's side and putting a hand on her shoulder. 'Go and get some rest, son! You look like death warmed up.'

The boy nodded, then looked up at his mother again, 'Perhaps I should join your mage training classes?' he asked.

'I'll ponder on it. Goodnight Alis.'
'Goodnight mother, My Lords.'

Once Alistair was gone, Niamh sagged down into the chair he'd just vacated. She pulled in a deep breath and then let it out slowly, pulling the chair a little closer to the fireplace. The night had turned chill and the fire was burned to embers, casting only a feeble glow of heat. The drapes at the windows – a new addition to the furnishings of the old keep – helped to keep in some of the heat but still, Niamh shivered. Today, even aside from her son's new-found prowess with magic, had been draining. Magda had come too close to victory, far too close! Niamh glanced to Kilm and then to Josynne. She had other lords too, those who had joined them at the end of her father's reign, driven to her by his cruel deeds and barbary at the end. Lord Shelby and Lord Glenn, as well as Lord Nightingale who had come since and Lord Carver – the son of one of her father's men who had begged forgiveness for his family's actions upon the death of his father. Josynne had been hesitant but something in the boy's open and smiling face had won Niamh over. In an unexpected turn, Lord Lorne's son had come over too – his price for loyalty being the hand of her step-sister, Jedda. Niamh had asked the girl first, she was not her father to make unwanted matches in the family no matter what it might gain her, and the one remaining member of her family who was loyal to her had nodded with full eyes. Niamh could understand that, Jedda was young and impressionable, and Lord Lorne was a hedge-knight of the old chivalry; handsome with his chestnut curls, young enough – about Niamh's age – and brave in both battle and joust. She'd agreed the match despite that the man was poor as a picker, and made him a member of her council with a good salary. Loyalty was hollow sometimes but his gratitude would keep them at her side, Niamh knew enough of simple politics for that. Jedda and she had grown closer for it, too, almost like true sisters and Niamh was glad of that connection too. It was a lonely world with a dead husband and no family at all but for her son and daughter.

Niamh was half-tempted to call the lords now, an emergency council meeting, but the memory of her father's court and of his own midnight meetings put her off. There was no threat that night, it would wait until morning.

'Niamh, are you well?' Josynne asked, pulling up another chair beside her and bending so that his forearms rested on his legs. He was obviously tired too; he'd been at her side for hours commanding his archers.

'I am as well as I can be. We always knew that this might happen.'

'We did. I find myself asking what would Helligan do, now… if he were here. His son is so like him… I miss his insights even after all these years.'

'I can imagine, and what do you think is the answer to that? What would Helligan have done?'

'He would o trained him,' Kilm butted in, 'sure as my name is Olaf Kilm!'

'He would,' Niamh agreed.

'And yet you waver?' Josynne probed.

Niamh looked at her hands, trying to find the right words. It was a habit she'd never lost. 'I… I think Alis is more powerful than any mage I have ever seen. The others I can barely teach. I am out of my depth with all this. I don't think I can…'

'And there are no others, you are sure? None of the old council remain?'

'No, none that have come forward these past thirteen years, at least.'

'None the less, if ye stifle that boy's gift, ye do a disservice to his father,' Kilm said, his grey eyes dark, 'He is the spit o Helligan the Mage, and he could be even more powerful… if ye let him.'

'But…'

'Nay, Niamh, I've said me piece, act on it or don't as ye please!' Kilm swigged the last of whatever was in his goblet and put it down on the table, 'I'm done in, I'm to me bed,' he said and then took himself from the room. Niamh smiled at his back as he left; she was well-used to his straight to the point advice. When she'd first arrived at his little humble house in the marshes as Helligan's hostage, he was the one she'd feared most of the marsh lords, he'd been the last to accept her too, as queen, and yet once he'd done so, he'd been more loyal than any she'd known, except maybe Josynne.

'Wife... or whores?' Josynne said, nodding after the old warrior with a smirk.

Niamh finally found a smile, 'After a battle – whores, definitely.'

Shale shook his head, 'One day his good lady will take his head off with that battle-axe he leaves lying around here there and everywhere!'

'The Wolder are a freer people than us. She does not mind his indiscretions.'

'Ever you were indulgent of them,' Josynne said. 'It is no wonder they love you so much! Do you ever hear of any of the others? Morkyl and co?'

Niamh shook her head, 'No, Morkyl returned to the Wolder when Helligan left. He resides in Havensguard with Mother Morgana now.'

'Ah, the Wolder queen!'

'Don't let the old lady hear you call her that!' Niamh smiled. More a witch than a queen, Morgana was the "mother" to all Wolder, an ancient hag with a firm grip on the other world.

'Aye, I suppose,' Josynne said, and then sighed and looked Niamh in the eye. 'And what of Helligan?' he asked, 'last we spoke of him, you said you still do not believe he is really gone. I know that this might well be the last hope of a bereaved wife but you were ever a woman who knew your own mind well.'

'I cannot put a finger on it, but I continue to hope,' Niamh said, her voice dropping to a whisper. 'I thought him dead once before and he was not so. Perhaps if the bead he gave me,' she pulled out the necklace on its chain, 'if it had turned clear, turned to normal glass… but it is not, it is black… perhaps I am clutching at straws…'

'Perhaps,' Josynne murmured, and then stood and kissed her brow as he was often wont. 'Goodnight my queen, be sure to get some rest soon. I will cast an eye over the children to ensure they are sleeping on my way up.'

Niamh nodded and patted his hand, but then moved to pull aside the drapes and look out of the set-in window at the town below.

Mainly seeped in darkness, the town sat in the shadows but for the few lights which flickered in the windows. Anglemarsh was more a keep than anything else, but like all keeps, the few dwellings at its feet thrived and were offered the security of its walls in times like these. With the gates closed, most of the livestock was trapped in with them, a food source in case things got desperate. Niamh's eyes skimmed the scattered and broken chunks of ice about the walls. She'd think it a good bet that Magda would not try again, not soon at least. It had been six months now since they had lived with the gates open, Niamh hoped that this at least meant a return to those better times, before the bitterness of Magda's hate twisted her people against her.

Four

Helligan put up a hand against the sudden brightness which surrounded him, blaring in through the doorway of his cell, no dim candle but a torch of bright white dragon-flame. His human eyes felt feeble, his limbs weakened from years of captivity. He blinked a few times, and clenched his hands into fists. For half a minute he wanted to hide but pulled himself to calmness with the whispered meditations he'd taught himself whilst locked away and alone in the dungeons. Her face too, as ever, helped with the calming, and so he brought that too, imagined her soft lips, her golden hair – his princess, his queen.

Once his eyes had adjusted to the light, Helligan looked about himself. As ever, there was little of note. The chain which bound him was tightly secured to a ring in the wall. The floor was clear, the walls rough stone and damp.

Then the person stood at the door spoke:

'Helligan Dericaflae of the House of Marcandis, Son of Edius and Eyona… you are to come with me.'

Helligan raised his eyes to look at the figure. One of Ariane's, of course it would be… another of the greys who tended to take on the roles such as jailor which their blackflight counterparts found beneath them. It was not his usual jailor though, a stranger, tall with broader shoulders, older too, if human form was anything to go by.

The figure was speaking again but Helligan was struggling to follow, his addled brain flying from tangent to tangent. The figure paused and then moved into the cell to release the chains that bound him. He put up a hand to assist Helligan to rise. There was a hint of something in his eye, could it be sympathy? Helligan didn't know. The figure led him from the prison cell, up two flights of stairs and then into a chamber which had – bless the goddess – windows! Helligan stood and stared for a moment at the soft yellow light seeping in and inhaled a few more times. He was coming back to himself now, the strength he'd once had surging in this holiest of places. He was back in the tower of inquisition, where he'd faced his previous trial. Once more he was led up to the podium, locked into human form still and naked before the jury. The other dragons, much as before, sat in stony silence from their human bodies, ready to cast *impartial* judgement. Helligan doubted that they even understood the word. He repressed the anger which bubbled under the surface of his thoughts. About his foot was the chain which had been re-secured there, and other than that he had nothing but for his own form, his long hair falling down over his chest.

Helligan pressed his lips as his eyes flit over the faces of the front row. His mother and Argosus, his brother, sat in silence with the rest. His mother's eyes washed with tears though, and his brother sat in his father's seat. Was his father dead then? How long had it been since last he saw daylight? Surely it had not been a hundred years yet? He was aged but not to ancientness, his skin still firm and tight. It could not be! Time was difficult to track though, in the hold, and he could not be sure. If so, that meant Niamh was dead – long dead probably. The thought ripped a hole in him, hardening him even more so.

'Bow, brother,' Argosus said, his tone commanding but gentle.

Helligan fought the urge to spit in their faces and instead managed a slight incline of the head. He felt vulnerable, exposed in his nakedness, and humbled for his filthy form and matted hair. He stank too, he was sure of it, and his skin felt greasy suddenly unclean. Helligan forced a calm, forced himself not to care. Let this council – and his family if they must – look upon what they had forced him to become! It was their shame, not his.

His brother stood in his father's stead and turned to the council.

'I present the case of my brother, Helligan, to the high council,' he spoke in his sharp tone, and then turned so that Helligan could see his eyes, brimming with sympathy and anger.

'Thirteen years ago, our father decided to make an example of you,' Argosus began. Thirteen years! So it was not yet the century gone. Relief and worry in equal measures flooded Helligan along with another, almost lost, alien, emotion – hope. His son would almost be a man now! His wife – what? Remarried? Lost to him? Or patiently waiting. He did not know which thought broke his heart the most.

'…He sentenced you to rot in human form for a hundred years,' Argosus continued, his black eyes running over Helligan's face, 'to shame you and to break you. To allow you to live knowing that the human you had come to love perished whilst you remained locked away and powerless.'

Helligan took and held his brother's eye, steady and feeling able to meet what was to come next, whatever that might be.

'Our father is now dead, and I stand in his stead. The wheel has turned and now the Blues take the rein of clan rule from those of the white scale. This makes you the Lord of Draconis in the normal state of things, for the next ninety-seven years.'

'What…' Helligan murmured. His tongue barely worked, his lips dry and parched.

'A title none of any of the seven houses is comfortable to bestow upon a criminal,' Ariane spoke from in the pews. Her voice was coarse and gravelly with age.

'Indeed, and yet one which is yours by right and blood...' Argosus continued, 'thus posing a dilemma…'

Helligan wet his lips. The leadership of the clans was a complex and fragile system, which gave each clan a hundred years of rule through their appointed clan leaders. His father had been the next in line, after Korbyn. Helligan had known that of course, but it had never even crossed his mind that his father could die and leave the burden to him.

'What… what happened to father?' he managed through the thickness of his dry mouth.

'That is a matter still being investigated.'

'And so you wish to… to what?'

Argosus's expression softened, he seemed to have aged immeasurably from the boy who had shed a tear at Helligan's trial. 'I have a proposition for you, brother, one discussed and agreed to by all of the members of this inquiry.'

'What proposition?'

'There is a rite which would allow you to stand down, leave your clan to become without, and pass on your position within it to another. If you announce before one and all, that you will not take up our father's mantle… that you renounce us blues, then another might take up your role.'

'And for me?'

'A lesser sentence. Banishment from our realm.'

Helligan looked to the silent faces of the high council, moving from one to the other, 'and all have approved this?' the hope built even more so.

'They have. Our people cannot allow you to go without punishment with the magnitude of your crimes, however they have agreed to my terms. Banishment is for life, though, brother – you know this. There will be no return when your wife and son are dead and you live on in the human realm!'

'I… I understand.'

'My clan have agreed to this,' Ariane spoke again, from the silent crowd, 'only on the proviso that you *cannot* return. Do you understand?'

A coldness touched Helligan's belly. Yes, he knew what that meant. The dragon city lay not on the ground or even in the forests but high up in the mountains, unattainable without the power of flight. True banishment meant the removal of that ability. Without wings, a dragon *could not* return home. It was a custom which was told in the storybooks of old, but not something Helligan had ever seen done.

'You wish to amputate my wings?' Helligan asked, his tongue struggling to make the words.

'A harsh prospect I know, brother... but this way you could go home, back to your wife and child before they are lost in time to the ether. Is that not what you want?'

'And if I decline?'

'If you decline,' Oris spoke from the stalls, 'then you will retain your birth-right, but also must finish your sentence. You will serve the remaining eighty-seven years, and then come out of imprisonment as our leader for what remains of the century. In the meanwhile, we will be without a leader and will group a council to rule in your stead.'

Helligan's head reeled. Freedom, home, Niamh! All at his fingertips! He cared not for the loss of position; he had never wanted his father's place as leader of the Blue Dragonflight anyhow, but to lose his wings? That was a true sacrifice indeed. Helligan tried to think, tried to use reason and logic, but in the end, the overriding motivation which pushed him to nod, even above the image of Niamh's face, was his inability to face even one more moment of darkness down in the pit.

'Do it,' he whispered.

Argosus's eyes showed compassion, despite how his lips pulled into a tight smile.

'Was that agreement, brother?'

'Yes,' Helligan whispered.

'It will take more than a simple yes,' another of the elders – a bronze male – spoke up, 'This is a serious rite, Helligan. You must knowingly and willingly renounce your blood-right now. Say before us all that you give up your position in the clan of the blue and become nameless… and of course, you must choose your successor.'

Helligan glanced to his mother. The older woman sat as was tradition with a serene and unbiased face but her eyes seemed to be pleading. For what? To comply, Helligan supposed, to do as he was bid.

'I…' his throat hurt, badly, and speaking did not aid it well, 'I, Helligan, give up my… my birth-right as the new leader of the… the Blue Dragonflight, and name my brother, Argosus, as my heir.'

'And renounce the clan,' Argosus said, gently.

'I… I re-renounce my clan, and agree to never more be… be a part of any decision or… or rite by which they are involved. I… I give myself to obscurity. There – will that do?'

The other clan-leaders stood and for the very first time, Helligan realised that they were all present in person aside from Korbyn who was once again represented by his daughters – allowable, as he was so very old! The gathering of them all could only mean one thing though, the kin had anticipated his agreement.

Helligan's belly hurt, suddenly.

The elders linked hands. Oris to Ariane, Gern of the Bronze to Malina and Joryn – the twin leaders of the crimson. The Rustscale leader, Jakin took the hand of the first of Korbyn's daughters, who then linked with her sister. Finally his own brother, Argosus completed the chain. Together, they began to chant. As their voices swelled, something seemed to snap within Helligan's chest. He coughed and then doubled over, a fleck of blood came to his lips, the coppery taste burning there. Something growled, hurt and angry, within his form but then it was gone. Helligan fell to his knees, reeling.

'There, it is done, release me,' he whispered as the swell of voices suddenly ceased.

Argosus came forward to kneel before his brother. He put his forehead to Helligan's in a gesture of solidarity. 'I thank you, brother,' he said, and produced a vial from his embroidered silken sleeve. Within was a thick blue mist. Helligan held out a shaking hand for his essence and Argosus gave it to him, closing his fingers about the vial in a gentle gesture. Helligan felt the anguish within lash at him again whilst Argosus's face showed the required decorum and serenity, his eyes veiled but not unkind.

'Change form,' Argosus whispered so that the others in the room could not have heard him, 'I will do the deed myself as to ensure it is done as quickly as possible.'

Helligan looked down to the bottle in his hands. He'd heard tales since boyhood of dragons stripped of their wings. He'd never thought to be one, never thought to be seen as the ultimate traitor, banished and maimed, a half-thing. His fingers caressed the smooth glass, no longer Morgana's vial, the one Niamh had helped to bind for him, but one of the draconic ones, a smooth tube with the three runes burnt into the top. He pulled in a deep breath. The amputation of a wing was much like that of any other limb, and he did not suspect for an instant that he was going to be given the mercy of any numbing magics or potions.

'Make it quick,' he said to his brother, 'and don't make Mother watch.'

Argosus glanced back at their mother as though the barbarity of making her watch as her son was maimed had not occurred to him.

'Agreed,' he said, still magnanimous, 'Mother, you are excused. Helligan would not cause you the pain of watching this.'

Helligan's mother stood. She moved as though to come to him, to the dais, but then thought again of it and turned about, fleeing the room. Everybody was polite enough to not acknowledge the sound of her sobbing as she fled. Once she was gone, Helligan uncapped the bottle and allowed his essence to flow through his limbs. Argosus said nothing as he took back his true form. His limbs at once felt fluid, his claws sharp and his wings, his beautiful swishing blue wings moved for one final time to flap – not enough to lift him, just to give him the feeling of it, the memory.

'Chain his feet,' Argosus ordered of somebody lingering in the side-lines, and then Helligan felt the shackles go about his hindlegs at the ankles. He steeled himself, and closed his eyes. Argosus put a hand to Helligan's chest, he patted the scales there, a brotherly caress, and then moved out of his sight. Panic tried to set in them, sheer blind fear but Helligan repressed it, pushing it down inside. Argosus murmured something, and then suddenly a pain worse than anything he'd ever known in his life washed through Helligan's form. The fire of the blue dragonkin did not so much incinerate as it did to burn cold, flames of ice. They enveloped first one wing and then the other in a brilliant blue agony. Helligan squealed in panic, rearing up and trying to flap the wings, to remove the pain, but even that merely caused the flames to burn brighter, colder. Helligan squealed again, screaming blindly, and then felt consciousness dipping as his wings froze into a blue arc of shimmering ice. Again and again he cried out as the fire moved from the tips right down into his back piercing him and causing a jet of his own flame to roar free of his lips into the back of the auditorium.

'Enough!' a voice shouted from the ranks of the watchers, serene demeanour broken in the shock of Helligan's torment, Helligan felt the gratitude even through his pain.

'Stop this at once. Shatter the wings and let this ungodly business be done.'

Helligan did not witness it, the burst of agony was too great as the tissues and sinews, the fibres and skin suddenly exploded in a spattering of blood and bone. He roared again, this time more a whimper than a real roar, and then fell, his head striking the floor and his body tumbling down after.

'I'm so sorry,' his brother's voice came in the midst of the fever, drifting in, panicked, 'I thought it would be quicker…'

'Take him to the forest and call for the Wolder healers,' another voice spoke, that of the black-flight leader, Ariane.

'Lord Helligan is one of us no longer, take him back to his new people to be cared for, let us forget this incident now. Long live Lord Argosus.'

'Long live Lord Argosus,' the crowd chorused.

Five

Niamh entered the great throne room of Anglemarsh and, after a brief and formal greeting of her son and Josynne, moved to the edge of the room where her throne stood. The dais was not overly raised, Niamh hated to be above them all, but as a compromise, three marble steps had been added so that when the room was full, people could still cast an eye on her. That chair was an ornate thing, but no golden throne, tall-backed and carved from the trunk of an ancient Wolder oak. It had been a gift, and a sign of acceptance, from the Wolder people who shared in her rule. Niamh sat down and caressed the smoothness of the carved oak arm. She had used no other chair as her throne from the minute it was delivered to her with the restoration of Anglemarsh, finding the plainness of it much more to her tastes than the garish ornamentation of her father's old throne. The curves of the chair which had once fit her body perfectly, were now snug for the extra bodyweight that childbearing had brought. It was not enough to be uncomfortable though, her body had recovered well enough from the birthing of her son and daughter. Her gown rustled about her body as she moved, a deep green silk with golden embroidery and long white drapes of flowing swishiness from the arms and about the skirt. Niamh had always loved beautiful clothing but now her tastes followed a more earthy kind, a trend which had been taken on by the ladies of the court led by Jedda.

Once comfortable, Niamh poured herself a glass of water and a glass of mead. The mead because she enjoyed the taste – especially because it reminded her of Helligan – and the water to prevent her drinking too much and clouding her senses. She sipped the mead, a sharp infusion of honey and wine, and then stood both goblets beside her on the ornate golden table and looked up at the room. For the first time in weeks, the gates of Anglemarsh were open, the enemy retreating back to The Whites, the wide mountain-range in the south where her brother's family resided in hiding. This had meant a reinstatement of Niamh's court, as well as the allowance of visitors to call again. Anglemarsh did not have the hugely decorated and ornate great hall that The Golden Keep boasted. Instead it was of grey rough-brick, with six tall white stone columns which spanned the room in pairs. The musician's area, down in the far corner, was deserted, Niamh allowed festivities only in the evening unless it was a feast day, but still there was a murmur of background noise and several lords and ladies milled about.

It was an audience day, and so most of the multitudes of people about were there on business of one type or another, but some of the courtiers came every day too just to loiter – or so it seemed to Niamh. She cast her eyes over them all. Sister Freya stood quietly by the arch which led to the stairs as ever she did, really to offer spiritual guidance or healing to any who required such. Of her courtiers, Nessa Firebrand and Huxley Jome were probably the most ornate, friends since childhood but denied marriage to one-another by their families. Niamh took great pity on them and turned a blind eye when hands touched, or when they occasionally vanished together. She was tempted to make Jome part of her council, as he was good friends with her sister's husband, Lord Lorne. Nessa and Huxley were sat talking on one of the benches, alongside some youthful boy of about sixteen who Niamh half-recognised as one of another courtier's sons. Jedda was in the corner looking as princely as ever she did. Her belly was recently emptied but she had not the hollow cheeks of motherhood. Her hair was still thick, braided in over her shoulder with colourful wraps and her face so like Queens Magda's, the solemn reminder that their enemy was this girl's mother. She smiled at Niamh as she settled herself down but did not approach; work came before leisure and her courtiers knew that. The rest of the council were closer to hand. Lords Shelby and Glenn, different enough in age to be father and son, but none-the-less, good friends, sat at a game of sticks, whilst Nightingale and Carver were more solemn in their chairs of state. Lord Lorne was stood by the fireplace, his eyes were on his wife although she did not seem to notice, never had Niamh seen a man more besotted. Josynne was, of course, in his seat close by hers, in the role of her first advisor. There were more too, sitting, talking, laughing, happy just to be here at Niamh's court, despite that she'd greeted none of them and didn't remember half of their names.

Alistair, on the other hand, was making his rounds, chatting quietly to people as was his way, holding a hand in his here or there, bestowing favours – little trinkets like scarves and pins – to the ladies, making them coo. He was a good boy, Niamh thought, and would make a better king than she had a queen. As a girl she'd been beloved by her people but as time had eked on, the commoners had grown wary of her quietness, her lack of entertaining and reluctance to put herself over for the feasts and whatnot. Alistair was more beloved now, and likely one of her saving graces. He'd kiss the hand of courtier or commoner alike, always finding conversation no matter to whom he spoke. Niamh knew Josynne Shale was largely to thank for Alistair's considerate manner. He'd taken the boy under his wing and had taught him everything from how to fight, to how to speak to people. Niamh could not help but wonder if she'd have been as good, if she'd been given the same tuition. As one of the king's bastards, she'd never even in her wildest dreams, expected to sit on the throne herself.

On the other side of the room to the normal dignified attendees stood the commoners. Those who had come for a boon or favour, perhaps to have her help to resolve a dispute. There were many of them, but since the gates had only just reopened, Niamh was not overly surprised. The first few were fairly standard. An old farmer who had lost his crop to the invaders. Niamh compensated him for the lost value and sent him on his way to buy new seed. The next was an older woman, widowed, who had been driven from her home by her deceased husband's family. Niamh gave that one over to her advisors to investigate. The next was a man who was barely more than a child, the orphaned son of one of her brother's soldiers. He came on the hand of an older woman, maybe an aunt, to beg her forgiveness for his father's desertion and to ask to return to his home.

Niamh looked to Josynne Shale, who sat in his normal place just below the throne platform. He raised an eyebrow. This was new, perhaps Magda's army really was broken. Perhaps so, for the next and then the next were much the same. Men begging her forgiveness, asking permission to return to their lands and homes.

Niamh stood. 'How many more of you?' she asked, her voice not quite ringing out, but at least audible, 'how many more of my enemy's army stand before me to beg forgiveness?'

A few more moved to the front, making a gathering of fifty or so men, all ragged and tired-looking in torn armour, some wounded. Niamh looked at every face, especially the wounded, taking them in to her memory. The men shuffled and Niamh felt sympathy pull. What must it have been, to have witnessed the devastation her mages – and her son – had caused, to be in the midst of it?

'Y-you are all forgiven,' She said, trying to make her voice gentle. 'Let Laurie and Magda's defeat be the lesson enough. Many of your houses will have fallen though, I am sorry for that. If they stand still, go back to them and rejoice. If they do not, seek out the sister, Freya, who stands yonder and beg the charity of Herodite. She will ensure you are fed and housed!'

Sister Freya inclined her head. She was a young girl, younger than Niamh, but an initiate from birth to the mother face of the goddess. Niamh trusted her more than most, considering she was new to the kingdom but then she'd been sent by Sister Dora, upon her return to the temple just a few days prior and Niamh trusted Dora completely.

The citizens who had come to the front all began to move away, mainly towards Freya. Niamh watched them go, concerned, and then beckoned Josynne up. Lord Lorne joined them, appearing from the corner behind the pillar but he did not approach the throne, merely sat in Shale's vacated chair.

'Hmm?' Shale murmured, crouching beside her so that she could speak to him without rising and confusing everyone into thinking the session was expiring. Despite that their love had fallen to a platonic state, Niamh was still ever glad to have Josynne about her.

'What do you think this means?' she murmured.

'At this stage, I would not like to hazard a guess, but perhaps it is hopeful.'

'I have allowed them forgiveness; do you think that wise?' her voice was barely a whisper.

'I think it kind,' he allowed.

Niamh nodded, still unsure of herself but then put her eyes back over the handful of people who remained. 'I'll finish here and then perhaps a ride out to the shrine to give thanks again to the goddess?'

'Of course.'

Josynne retreated back to his chair and Lord Lorne, leaving it, moved to kneel before her.

'My lord?' Niamh spoke fondly, then glowed more so as Jedda made her way to join them, 'Sister?'

Jedda was quite some years younger than Niamh, still in the trusses of youth really, despite that her belly must sag after giving her husband a child every year or so since their marriage. Jedda curtseyed but then straightened and demurred to her husband.

'My Lady,' Lord Lorne said, 'I wish to announce that upon the reaching of three months, we have decided to go ahead and announce our son's name,'

A little early, but Jedda's children were generally strong and she'd not yet lost any of them. 'I think that a fine idea,' Niamh smiled.

'Good, my lady,' Lord Lorne turned to Jedda and then back to her, 'My lady, we wish to… we wish to name him Alistair, for his royal cousin.'

A true smile lit Niamh's features and she nodded eagerly, 'Oh, he will be thrilled,' she said, 'we will arrange a small celebration and perhaps a joust when you pick a date for the naming!'

'Thank you, my lady,' Lord Lorne said, and then took Jedda's hand, 'We will disturb your day no more, but I thank you for your kindness to us.'

'May the goddess go with you,' Niamh smiled, and then beckoned forward the next man, she was now in somewhat better spirits. From the corner of her eye, she watched as her son approached the couple and took Jedda's hand in his. They spoke for a moment and then he beamed. Niamh's heart eased up a little more and the odd realisation took her that her son looked more like her when he smiled, than usually he did.

The next commoner was a rotund man, a little red in the face and dressed still in torn mail. Obviously a soldier. Niamh knew not his face, or if he was one of hers or one of Magda's, Josynne too was sitting a little more upright, his hand moving to his waist where his dagger would be accessible.

'Well met,' Niamh said, 'What can we do for you today, good sir?'

At once the man knelt at her feet, bowing his head low. When he raised it, Niamh was surprised to see water in his eyes.

'My lady, my dear queen,' he began. 'My name is Josha Barder. I am the leader of the west defence.'

Niamh nodded and motioned for him to rise up. She disliked when people knelt.

'Welcome, and I thank you for your service to me.'

'I come to serve, my queen,' he said, 'and to warn you of a terrible thing which we – my men and I – fear you are not yet privy to.'

Niamh's eye caught Josynne's again, he was listening intently. 'What thing?' she managed. Fear and worry were drying out her lips, making her stomach knot tight. Alistair too had moved to the foot of the throne but did not climb the three steps to his own seat in respect for the man stood before her. instead he took a chair next to Josynne, listening intently to his mother keeping court.

'That of your enemy's mage, my queen…'

'I… what?'

'Spit it out, man,' Josynne snapped from below.

'Magda has… has no mage?… to m-my knowledge at least?' Niamh stammered.

'Tis as I feared, you are not aware,' Josha said, then, 'It was apparent on the battle, and after it my queen. Before your own mages attacked, my men and I, from the tower above, saw a strange light on the edge of the battlefield, a deep off-red, purple magic.'

'Purple? I have never seen purple magic…'

'No, nor I. My men… my men took to watching for it. We were committed to defend but they were… we were spooked, My queen. I said to send the arrows forth, despite that we had no order for it, and to focus on a strange figure who stood on the edge of the battleground. He was tall, hooded and hidden, but it was he who was controlling that purple lightning. Magda herself appeared then, and stood at his side but our arrows could not find her form, missing and firing off into the darkness around her… I…' he broke of and then looked from her to Josynne, and then back again. 'My queen…' he said, his voice was very low, frightened, 'My queen we… we took out a wave of men, thirty or so, and watched as they dropped to the ground. They was dead, my queen, I saw it with my own eyes… but then that purple magic crawled across the ground, dragging through like lightning on the ground and… and those men… my lady… they stood back up again.'

The room fell to silence. Some of Magda's men were looking over, as were the others still waiting to be seen. Alistair was frowning but Josynne looked more curious.

'Surely you must be mistaken?' Niamh asked.

'No, my queen, I vow it no.'

'You say that they were definitely dead?'

'There was one, I saw him for sure, he was hewn by four, maybe even five arrows. They pierced his body every which way and one went through his jaw where his helmet was not fast. He stood back up at the touch of that magic, jerking and swaying, with the arrow still jutting out of his face. I could not take my eyes from him! He was grotesque, like a mummer's puppet show, as he began to drag himself along again. Oh, they were dead, my queen, I am sure of it.'

'Aye!' one of Magda's turncoats spoke from where he stood on the other side of the chamber, causing everybody to turn. 'We've seen it too, my queen! In battle, the men will fall and then Magda's stranger comes and the dead begin to walk once more. They don't last long, five – ten minutes – before they fall again, but for a time they walk.'

Niamh let out a long breath, suddenly she was exhausted, and frightened too. 'What you speak of is necromancy,' she said, 'I've heard no tell of such outside of storybooks!'

'I don't know much about that,' the first man, Josha spoke, 'but I know what I saw – what we saw!'

'Dragons too were once only of the ilk of children's tales!' another voice spoke, one of the younger courtiers. 'and you showed us that they too were real, My Queen!'

Niamh felt dizzy suddenly, her stomach churning. Josynne and her son were looking up at her, Josynne looked as worried and as flummoxed as she was, and Alistair just looked lost.

'I… I…' she began with a stutter but pulled herself back together again and spoke, 'I thank you for your council, and I offer you now an invitation to remain here in the keep for this night and to tell it all again to my military advisors. The… the rest of you waiting, I apologise, but I must… I must close this session now. If your matters are of… of finance, or of land, then please speak to Lord Shale before you leave and he will… will resolve them for you.'

With that, Niamh stood and forced herself to remain calm as she moved away from the throne and swept past Sister Freya to take herself up the stairs.

Once out of the glare of all the people below, Niamh made her way to the library chamber above. The room was up in the north tower, a fair large chamber in the rafters where she had placed all of the books she'd had sent over from The Golden Keep. As a child, Niamh had spent more time amongst books than she had people, and so some of the old tomes were like childhood friends. She sat herself down in a splintery wooden chair with a soft hand-embroidered cushion which sat closest to the one window. For a long moment she just sat, her hands unconsciously rubbing together. Niamh had always been frightened of the idea that the dead could rise again. The old tales of necromancy, death-magics and blood sacrifices had terrified her as a child, rendering her cold with fear. Despite how well-read she was, how she loved to absorb folklore and stories, ever she had skipped those and once when her maid, Maggie, had picked up such a tale to read, she had climbed under the blankets and refused to come out until the book was away. Niamh still remembered it, still remembered the title. It did not take long to locate.

"Oliah and Oasha"

Niamh held the book in trembling hands and took it back to the table. She opened it and began to read.

Six

Oliah and Oasha
The corruption of the Dusk King

In the early days, there was a land which was forgotten, lost in time and glorious to behold for its lush forests, it's fine lakes and rivers, and the mysts of a civilisation older by far than man. That world was what we now call Rostalis. It is said that this is the birthplace of the goddess herself, a many coloured land of summer. Here, the magical beings of myth made their homes: the playful fae, fauns, centaurs, fairy folk and mischievous pixies. Graceful elves built up their majestic treehouses in the branches of the world trees and the fearsome and ancient dragonkind patrolled the skies from their mountainous cities. Deep in the hillsides, the dwarven kind made up villages of stone, and there they herded mythical unicorns, feydragons and mellicats. A tranquil and untorn land, troubled only by the monstrosities which dwelled in the densest forests, but which kept much to the trees, hidden and peeking through branches, murderers of the occasional unwary fae, but still part of the goddess's natural order.

Then came the humans.

They came slowly at first, sailing to the fair shores in boats carved from the trees of foreign lands, the golden kings of Kopper and the darker ones of Jel. They set up on the shores and then settlements appeared, villages, towns!

For a time, the elves, dragons, and other fae lived in harmony with the humankind, allowing them the edges of the land, so long as they stayed out of their forests, but humankind was greedy and pushed further and further in, stealing more and more of the land for themselves. The harmony of the newly formed Rostalis was almost at its end. The humans wanted the land, but the Fae refused to leave, horror-struck as the world trees were felled for firewood, and the arboretums which had stood for generations as temples to their goddess fell to make way for new villages. Their unicorns and feydragons were slaughtered for food or skins, and their Mellicats domesticated, bowed like simple Kretch.

Then came the wars, three hundred years of fighting for supremacy, for freedom. Nobody knows who threw the first blow, who began the fighting between the races, but after time, it became that a stalemate formed. The fae-kind could not equal the technological advances of the humans, and the humans could not match the magical advances of the fae-kind. This stalemate could not be broken, no side was strong enough to win. The fae-tech changed that though. Artifacts were created by the humans using the captured magics of the fae, items to bind and control them. Most of the little folk fled into the forests and there began the preparations to depart to the other realm. The Dragons and the Elves fought on though, in fury at their own magics being turned against them. One of the elven generals, a dusk elf named Oliah set out to bring about the final conclusion to the war, using a new form of magicka. His plan was to use the human's greater numbers against them, by raising up the corpses of the dead in order to create an army of walking mindless zombie soldiers.

The great Zenna, the last united queen of the Dragonkind, forbid such an act, claiming it was unnatural and against the goddess. Zenna's interference and her taking up the mantle of overseer of the fae caused a great rift to form in the elven clans. The wood elves, forest elves and water elves all acquiesced to her rule, but the older clans of mountain, fire and dusk were furious and thus a rift split them, a rift led by the self-proclaimed dusk king, Oliah. In time, the elves of the mountains were made to see sense, and after them the elves of fire. The elves of dusk, however, refused to follow the leadership of the dragons and hid away instead, going into the root bases of trees to dig down underground and make their homes in the darkness below Rostalis. In time, even they too began to give up, and to cross over to the other realms.

Oliah was one of the last to resist. He continued on with his plans and schemes, alone, but one night, as the moon turned full, a beautiful wood-elf came to him from the forests. Her name was Oasha, and she was the youngest daughter of Hogbria, king of the wood elves. Her father had sent her, the weeping maiden whispered, as an offer to be Oliah's bride, should he give up his evil magics and return to the forest. Now, Oasha was very beautiful, with hair of gold and a waif-like figure lost in the spider's silk gown in which she was dressed. Like all wood-elves, Oasha's magics could cause the flowers to seed, the spark of life to birth forests and as her tears fell they wet the hard earth around her, causing white blooms to flower at her feet. Oliah was spellbound by her beauty, by her innocence. He took her into his arms, kissing her sweet face and wiping her tears. In a state of pure lust, he agreed to the terms and stripped Oasha bare. Her virgin blood spilled on the very ground and in the morning, Oliah called the last clan, the dusk elves, back to the forests. There he was apprehended by the draconis and his magical focus was stripped from him.

True to oath, though, Oliah and Oasha were wed the very next moon, and then made their spells and portals to follow the rest of their kind to the new realm, leaving Rostalis for humanity. The new world was lush and rich, a utopia, but Oliah could not bear to see it, when his own home was stolen from him. Rather than cut out a new home for his clan in the lushness of the bright new world, Oliah instead led his people to the roots of one of the ancient world-trees just as he had in Rostalis. Lost and becoming consumed by anger, he dragged his people further and further below ground, so deep that the sunshine could no longer reach them and the light they wore in their chests turned to shadow. All but for Oasha, who every day would make the trek back to the surface to refresh herself, to welcome back the light. Oliah, twisting and withering, could not be at peace. For a hundred years, his bride pleased him well-enough, but as time passed, he found her beauty faded for him, and his anger at the humans who had stolen his lands grew. At the anniversary of one hundred years, Oliah decided to return and to exact his revenge.

Zenna's dragons patrolled the portals – to return to the realm of humans was now a crime and death was its sentence – Oliah, however, extended his tunnels past them, and so was able to bypass their patrols. The dusk elves, all now feeble and twisted creatures, led by a half-insane shadow king, spilled back to the world of humanity, with the beautiful Oasha dragged behind them, trussed like a prisoner. As the army gathered, Oliah took his bride back to the spot where first he'd seen her, on the outskirts of where a great golden keep had newly been erected. There he slit her throat and allowed her ruby scream to echo throughout the forest. A dribble of her blood he took into a vial, which he fixed about his throat. A new magical focus. As Oasha's blood hit the ground, there suddenly sprung up a flurry of red flowers, amidst the white which still grew there from her tears. The little white and red flowers which line the banks of the moat around The Golden Keep are still called Oasha's Tears even still.

With a vial of Oasha's blood as a focus about his neck, Oliah set about visiting the burial grounds of the dead, raising them up as skeletons, zombies, ghouls, and monsters. With his army of the dead, he began a march across the human lands as once before he had planned, allowing the beasts to tear apart any man or animal in his path, and then raising them up too, to follow in mindless obedience.

Oliah's rampage lasted seven days. In that time, his magics had wiped out two thirds of the human population of Rostalis.

On the seventh day, the great dragon queen Zenna returned and cleansed his path with fire. Oliah tried to turn his minions upon her, but even the might of his army could not match the queen of the Draconis. Oliah breathed his last breath in the agony of the black dragon's flame, the very last creature in this world to die of such.

Victory was Zenna's, but in their hatred of all creatures fae, the humans captured her upon her retreat, and put her to torture using the magical artefacts they had developed a hundred years earlier. On the very brink of revealing the location of her people, Zenna drove her head onto the spiked gatepost of the Golden Keep. Her dying scream echoed so loudly that it was heard by her own people in the other realm, where it was decreed that nevermore would the draconis venture into the world and affairs of humanity. It is said her bones are buried still under the keep, a monument to her sacrifice, although their exact location is lost, as are the artefacts used to torture her.

In retaliation, the draconis enslaved the remaining dusk elves, and took them up to their city in the mountains. One final spell was cast upon our world, then, a spell which clouded the memories of humanity, and which put the fae firmly into the world of the mythical. The spell of forgetting. It was the only way a true peace could be achieved.

The next page showed an ink-drawing of the great Zenna's final battle with the necromancer, his body bathed in the flames of her fire whilst his undead army fell behind him. It was gruesome to behold.

Seven

Niamh closed the book and wet her lips again. There it was, the dusk elves, now known as the drow or the withered, were all-but prisoners and as far as she knew, the only creatures who had ever known the secret of necromancy. Oliah was no longer the last creature killed by dragon-fire though; Helligan had done his fair share of that in his time amongst them. Illegally, she now knew – likely why he'd never come home to her. The draconis were not known for letting criminals off lightly, and for a dragon to even return to Rostalis was a crime. That brought up more questions though – who had sent him, then? If this was true, even his coming to Rostalis was a crime, but he'd claimed to be sent. That's if it *was* true; some of the facts of the story were obviously incorrect. She now knew that the dragons and fae had not retreated into another realm at all, but had remained in the last dregs of the enchanted forest, protecting themselves with befuddlement and cloaking spells. The writer of her old book had not known that though, nobody had!

Niamh sighed, her fingers caressed the cover, that old fear still flooding her limbs despite that these were mere children's stories. She flicked through the book one last time, shuddering at the images printed onto the pages in harsh black ink, and then shut the book and put it away. She dallied a moment longer, but then moved to the door, whispering a thank you to the old librarian, Tarren, who kept the books for her.

Without, Niamh went not back down to the great hall, but across the corridor and out through a big wooden door onto the battlements of the keep. The door was sagging a little on its hinges since the last battle. Niamh made a note to mention that to somebody, and then walked out and paused to glance over the view. From this side of the castle she could see right out to sea, sometimes when the mists were not so low she could almost see the outlines of the ice isles above. They were not a part of her kingdom, in fact uninhabitable aside from a few yeti and snow-ettin. Niamh allowed the rhythmic swish of the waves and the call of an occasional Gic to calm her frayed nerves, despite how she shivered. The wind blew away the cobwebs and the icy air made her skin tingle, bringing her back to life once again.

As she watched, Kilm appeared around the other side of the wall, a large barrel in his hands. He must be still gathering them up after the assault. He paused when he saw her, his eyes running over her in surprise but saying nothing.

'Kilm?'

'What you doing up ere my queen? An without a cloak too!'

'Just thinking, Kilm. How goes the repair?'

'No worse'n it ever is.'

'This door wobbles too.'

'Aye, I have somebody on it already.'

'I suppose you must think us foolish, defending these old stone keeps thus?'

Kilm, Wolder through and through, paused to ponder but then shook his head. 'It's good to have a solid foundation,' he shrugged.

'I suppose.'

'You seem pensive, Niamh?' Ever Kilm tended to drop into informal speech when nobody else was about. At least he used her name now, rather than just "girl" or "child".

'I am…' she paused and then glanced up at his old warrior's face. The Wolder knew far more of magic than the common folk did, 'What do you know of Necromancy, Kilm?'

'Necromancy – you mean death magic? Only that it aint been done in centuries…'

'Yes, that's what I thought,' Niamh said, then put a hand on Kilm's arm, 'but if what I have been told is correct, I might be needing the advice of your kind, Kilm… I fear that something dark indeed is brewing, and it's not something the common-folk can help me with.'

'Ever you have my axe,' Kilm murmured, then patted her hand on his arm and moved away, leaving her to gaze out over the still ruined and boulder-strewn land alone. It was bliss to have the gates open again but still Niamh's eyes could not help but scan the horizon for some evidence that Magda's army were still there, hidden from sight but ready to attack. She sighed and put her hand to Helligan's necklace as was her habit when in thought.

The necklace was warm.

Niamh froze, her hand shaking a little on the item but almost too scared to look. As she held it, it pulsated slightly, just as it had thirteen years ago when he had put it about her neck. Niamh exhaled, her heart speeding up, and forced her hand to pull the pendant up to her eyes. It was still very dark but there was definitely a hint of blue in the depths.

'Oh goddess!' Niamh breathed, then clutched the necklace again, the warmth of it travelling through her like a current suddenly. 'Oh… dear goddess! He's alive?'

Josynne Shale was sitting on the edge of the archery practice yard when Niamh found him. It wasn't an unusual pursuit since the new war had begun, she knew Josynne felt the burden of being her head of defence keenly. He was growing ever older too, his hand still the steadiest in the kingdom and his eyesight still sharp, but with the pains in his joints which age brought, that and the creaks and clicks when he moved too quickly from sitting. Josynne must be past fifty now, Niamh reckoned, an old man by non-Wolder standards. His long hair showed darts of grey but still his eyes smiled, his broad shoulders stayed solid. He had been a man before she was even born, and had known her mother before she died, shortly after Niamh's birth. Josynne was eating, half a loaf and some Jagger-cheese with a handful of sharp Jummel berries beside it. His bow was on his back, but his quiver was only half full and several shafts littered the targets.

'Niamh, what is it?' he said as she approached. Like Kilm he only addressed her formally in public, especially since their brief affair ten years earlier.

'I… I need your counsel,' Niamh said.

'About the necromancy?'

Goddess! She'd all but forgotten that! 'Yes and… and something other.'

Josynne patted the wall beside him and Niamh clambered up on the rough crumbling surface. His eyes ran over her face, then showed confusion.

'You look like you are repressing tears, my sweet?'

'I am. Jos, I think Helligan's alive,' she whispered, then pulled free the necklace with its cloudy blue tint. Josynne took it in his hand and held it up to the light.

'The blue, within?' he asked.

'Yes.'

'Are you sure?'

'Yes! I always knew he wasn't dead…'

'Will you tell Alis?' Damn Josynne and his logical questions!

'I… I am not… not sure. Not yet, I s-suppose. Not until I am sure, I mean. You know how he idolizes his father… the memory of him, I mean.'

'I do.' Josynne sighed and then cupped her head to kiss her brow, 'I suppose when he returns – if he does – I shall have to get used to sharing in your affections again!'

'D-do not be jealous, Jos! Please… I…'

'I am not being jealous, just cautious of losing you completely. You are dearer to me than you know… or at least acknowledge.'

Niamh frowned. Josynne had never hidden how he loved her, not before Helligan, nor after. During their brief affair he'd never spoken the words of a sweetheart to her, but the joy in his face of a morn after they'd lain together had been enough to break her heart. More-so when she'd had to end it, when Jess had been born.

'W-we will ever be the same!' Niamh said, her words were usually easier with Josynne than most, and her stutter almost gone even in times of wrought emotion but in that moment she felt the words refuse to form. 'N-n-now be… be happy with me? I have had so little hope in the past years that this is a glorious feeling.

'I am happy for your happiness at least,' he smiled, somewhat wry, 'now what of the other? Do you believe these tales of necromancy?'

'I think I must at least entertain them?'

'I agree. If they are false, there is no harm in heeding them and if they are not and you ignore them the consequences could be dire. I've never heard of such a thing, though!'

Niamh nodded, too choked up to argue and to explain the book she'd read. If there was a necromancer, he was likely no more human than her husband, and that thought was troubling. If the fae folk came out of hiding, she'd have more on her plate than her nephew and his army.

Eight

Helligan had little memory of anything but the pain as he forced consciousness back into his body. The agony had not abated with the severing of his wings, but instead spread throughout his form, shearing off nerves and making his whole form ache. He opened his eyes, but then shut them again. The council chamber was darkened, and somebody had put a blanket over his now once more human form. Helligan had no memory of changing back, no memory of being covered and left. His hand grappled for the bottle at his throat, half believing that he'd been robbed of it again, but the vial was there, protected against his skin with the stopper firmly pressed in. Had they forced him to change to this form in order to stop the pain? He did not know. It hadn't worked, his whole back felt as though it was burned, raw.

Helligan lay still for a long while, listening to the silence. He couldn't move, could barely stand the tiny movements that breathing brought with it. The floor beneath him was cool though, hard and soothing to lie on. He put down his fevered cheek to the coolness of it.

'He's just through here,' a voice came to Helligan's ears after what must have been an hour or so. He struggled to open his eyes again and saw two figures approaching. One – by his recognition of the voice – was Argosus and the other was a stranger. Together the footsteps came closer, and then Helligan felt a hand on his arm. He looked at the blurred shape. Short –

about four foot tall, dark skin, a curtain of dark hair and the haze of shadow about her. She was one of *them* – the dark elves who now worked in the service of the draconis as a punishment for the murder – by proxy at least – of the last of the great dragon overlords, Queen Zenna. The figure gazed upon him for a long moment, then moved the blanket and rolled him over onto his front. Helligan went without resistance. He could not have prevented it if he had tried. The elf poked and prodded at his back, her long fingers pressing down hard enough to make him groan in agony.

'Can you do it?' Argosus asked, kneeling beside Helligan and placing a hand on his shoulder.

'Yes.'

'Good… do so.'

At once a warmth washed through Helligan. A magical glow which was so hot it burned. Not a drow then, a fire elf. Her hands on his skin seemed almost to vibrate as her energy washed through him, spreading to each limb, to every inch of him, even his long hair. Helligan sighed as the pain abated in a wash of honey-sweet energy, but then as she moved her hands, it rushed back again, crushing him with disappointment.

'It is done.' She said, her voice lilting like a song.

'How long…' That was his brother again.

'Weeks, months maybe.'

'But it will…'

'Yes.'

'Thank you Ledara.'

Helligan felt himself pulled upright again. His eyes met his brother's.

'Are you awake, Heligan?'

'Yes,' Helligan rasped.

'Brother, can I ever give penance enough?' Argosus whispered, 'I knew not! You must believe me, 'I knew not what I did! I thought that as another blue, the fire would burn with less fervour, that ice would not shear as it did. I tried to save you pain and caused you worse!'

'For-forgiven.'

'Thank you, brother. It has been so long since one of our kind was banished. I had no idea… no idea…'

Helligan said nothing, consciousness was slipping away again, everything blurring into the pain.

'This is Leandra,' Argosus said, 'one of the fire healers. She has stopped the decay of your flesh but she predicts it could be some time before you truly recover. I mean to have her give you something to make you sleep now.'

Helligan nodded and then the elf returned, placing her hands on each side of his head and then muttering in elvish, a chant of sorts.

'Rest well, brother,' Argosus whispered, 'and when you wake you will be with those you love once more.'

After that, very little remained clear, just fragments, blurred visions and half-remembered snippets of conversation. At some point, somebody lifted his form, making him scream out loud in the shooting pain which bounced up his spine. He gritted his teeth but then there was the whispered incantation of the fire-elf Leandra again, and once again he drifted away as his form was carried outside and wrapped in the leaf-hammock which would be used to transport him down from the mountains and into the forest.

Helligan awoke next as his brother held him in his clawed feet and then gave out a swish of blue wings, lifting him and carrying him over the earth. Helligan had never been afraid of heights, it made no sense for him to be with the dragon-form ever close to hand, but suddenly the sheer height from which he could fall put a terror in him and he clutched a hand around the edge of the hammock.

Then nothing until he was laid in a bed of moss, the sound of pipes in the distance and the giggle here and there of the little folk. Helligan ignored their laughter. Fae were neither cruel nor sympathetic, not good or evil, and so their giggles were nothing malicious. Helligan thrust his hand into the damp springy moss and pulled some up to examine it. The smell was musky and almost overpowering in its sweetness. Harrenmoss – renowned for its healing properties. Whoever had left him thus, had given him a bed of healing magic to lie in. Argosus was nowhere to be seen though. For a few long moments which might even have been hours, Helligan lay still, but then attempted to sit up.

'Don't!' a female voice warned.

Helligan lay back down but allowed his eyes to open and scan the forest about him. The faun was hiding behind one of the trees. Her hair was long, tresses of caramel, but her eyes were grey and wary. Where her body tapered down to the goat's legs and cloven hooves, she was darker, covered in a course dark beige fluff.

'W-Where…'

'Almost home,' she replied. 'Your sister has been called for.'

'I-I have no sisters… only…' Helligan broke off though, he had not the words to continue the thought, that he had not a sister, only a brother.

The faun came a step or two closer, her eyes wild and her body tense. Ever the wild fae were a nervous breed. She moved one step at a time, and then knelt and kissed his brow. At once, Helligan was rushed with a strange tingling magic, the glow of it softer than the fire-elf's had been, but more potent. He tried to resist the sleep which came over his form, but he could not and drifted back out of consciousness.

And then there was the white of marble.

A bumpy road leading to a monument of sheer brilliance. Tall white towers with accents of green at the fixtures. The sound of waterfalls and the scent of fauna. Helligan barely registered it all as he was taken to the front of the building which seemed to reach higher into the sky even than the Golden Keep and then the cart he was in was unhitched and female hands lifted him onto a thick wolfskin to drag him into the temple. His fingers clutched at the sides, allowing them to move him thus. Then, finally, a familiar face.

'Go back to sleep, Lord Helligan,' whispered Sister Dora. 'I've sent for the queen.'

Nine

The temple of the face of Herodite was up in the hills behind the capital. All around was serenity, quiet, broken only by the call of a guc or the chirping of insects. The forest was present on both sides of the dusty old road, lingering dark boughs and thicket, but it gave way to the much used path to prevent Niamh having to ride through it. The sun shone overhead, it's gentle beams soft for winter's smile, rather than sharp and biting. Niamh could feel her limbs lightening as she rode, could feel the presence of the goddess's healing face smiling upon her in the unclenching of her shoulders, the loosening of her jaw. Despite Josynne's insistence that she was not safe, Niamh was glad she had travelled alone. The disguise had been the idea of her mages, a little test for them, as well as safety for her. Niamh had wrapped herself up in a scarf and old cloak borrowed from the stable hand's wife, and her mages had come together to glamor her skin, making her appear fifty years older, a bent and broken old peasant. The glamor was good, good enough to stop Josynne fussing, and Niamh found that the freedom it gave was invigorating.

She'd left Alistair in command. Not a decision she'd have made readily but it was Josynne's suggestion… and he'd be there to guide and advise the boy, he promised. It had been weeks then, since the opening of the gate and so they were somewhat relaxed now, happy in the knowledge that Magda must have fled with the dregs of her army.

For some time the road remained the same, twisting here and there, with a few parts partially blocked by stone where the road was falling into disrepair. Not a cost for Niamh's coffers to bear and yet as she rode, she contemplated whether the crown should make a donation to the pauper sisters who ran the temple. If they had found Helligan, as had been implied in Dora's message, then Niamh owed them everything.

The message had come a week after the glow had started up again in her necklace, just one simple line of a piece of paper, signed by Dora.

"*We have Lord Helligan at the temple*"

Seven short simple words which had turned Niamh's whole world upside down and thrown her into a frenzy of preparation.

After three or four hours of riding, the path opened up to show the temple. It was beautiful in the now dying light of the day. The main tower looked to be of old elven design, tall enough that it seemed to be reaching into the sky, with white marble and green glass – or maybe that was emerald? – fixings. Niamh felt as though her breath was taken away, her stomach tightening at the beauty before her. There were no gates, no fences or walls for protection, the sisters merely lived here in the knowledge that their goddess would protect them, which ever she had. This temple was something personal to Niamh too. Back before she'd left her father's court, she'd overheard her father's men discussing an attack on this very temple and the sisters within. It was this which had made Niamh finally defect to Helligan's army, a move that had led to everything which had happened since. Niamh dismounted her horse and led it towards the entrance of the temple. There was a ring there for purpose and so she tethered the horse and approached the entrance.

'State your name and business?' a male voice spoke as she entered the main door. Niamh blinked, the drastic flit between sunlight and the dark interior of the entrance hall had rendered her blind momentarily, but surely there were no men at the temple?

'I am Queen of Rostalis,' she said, but then paused, 'Niamh Darkfire, that is – wife of Helligan Darkfire who resides under your care.'

'Do you come as Queen or wife?' the voice asked, still without the softness that Niamh was accustomed to from the sisters.

'A-as wife,' she whispered.

'Then you may enter.'

Suddenly the blindness lifted and Niamh was able to make out a door before her. There was no other person in the room. Clever magic, it seemed the sisters were not unprotected at all.

Niamh approached the second door and laid a hand on it. A small tendril slid out of the wood and wrapped itself about her wrist, gripping her. Niamh forced serenity, this must just be the next level of security.

'Which of these is most important,' that same booming male voice questioned, 'Honour, candour or loyalty?'

'Candour,' Niamh answered without hesitation.

'Why?'

'Because the other two are not innate. Candour is to speak a person's truest honesty. Honour is a person's own code and might be broken or flawed, and loyalty could be to a tyrant.'

The door opened, the tendril releasing Niamh's hand. She was quietly pleased with her answer, telling herself that most monarchs would likely answer loyalty. As the door opened, the disguise fell away, and so Niamh stood once more as herself, the grey hair regaining its blond and her skin once more smoothing and de-wrinkling.

On the other side of the door, Niamh was hit by a wall of scent – the medicinal aroma of herbs and botanical life growing from every spare piece of ground or wall, outside of the walking paths. She found herself in a vast open chamber. In the middle were more orderly flowerbeds, fed by the green light of the windows all about, in which grew every manner of healing herb or plant one could conceive of. These were built into the same white marble as the floors and walls without. The walls were green with sap from the grasses and other wilder climbers which adorned them, and the floors were mossy and fresh out of the marble. Niamh felt a deep sense of peace enter her form, sinking right into her bones. As she stood, a member of the order finally appeared. A little like Dora in appearance, but then the habits and the sanctions which prevented them from cutting their hair meant that they did all look somewhat alike. As Dora did, this woman wore her hair loose past her shoulders, but cinched in and braided behind her back. She was younger than Dora though, and her hair was still clinging to auburn, although speckled with grey. Even as she approached, Niamh saw two other girls peeking out from behind one of the vast flowerbeds, eyes agog. They had not yet the serenity of the sisters and so must still be initiates.

'My Queen,' the older sister said, taking Niamh's hand in both of hers. 'My apologies for your greeting, we had no idea we were expecting you so soon, nor that you would wear a disguise!'

'It is well!' Niamh paused, her mouth drying up. She felt somewhat overpowered by the splendour of her surroundings and so talking became difficult again. The sister was still looking at her somewhat expectantly though and so Niamh took a deep breath and added, 'I gave no indication of my plans so that none would know I travelled alone and unprotected. I am rather a target lately.'

'Your brother's family are ungodly in the extreme,' the sister said, a glimmer of fire in her otherwise serene eye, 'you are most welcome here. You say you travel alone?'

'I do.'

'Would you like something to eat? Some rest?'

'No, please, take me to my husband?'

The sister nodded and then inclined her head. 'As you wish it, my queen,' she said, 'but please steel yourself, he's been quite unwell.'

'He is recovering though?'

'He is. I will take you to him but perhaps you and I could speak later?'

Niamh nodded.

'My name is Sister Alicia,' the sister spoke again, her eyes softening at Niamh's obvious anxiety, 'I am the matron here for this turn, so if you require anything, remember my name.'

Niamh nodded. 'And Dora?'

'Is at prayer, but I will send her later.'

'T-Thank you…'

'It is well, follow me.'

Sister Alicia led Niamh past the flowerbeds, and the two young initiates who could barely contain their happy shock at having been so close to the queen. Most likely commoners, the sisters of Herodite rarely took on those from wealth as they looked most for humble quietness and a calm manner. The sisters were not a celibate order though, despite that they did not marry, and so the girls might even have been daughters of the temple, initiates who were born into the life. Outside of the main chamber, the temple reverted more to how Niamh had imagined it would look, grey stone walls, slate floors and wooden furnishings and fixings. Here and there stood an old statue or idol, and there were flowers and herbs literally everywhere giving off a bouquet so fragrant that it made Niamh's head a little giddy. Sister Alicia ignored all the other wooden doors which littered the corridor, and led Niamh instead to a grand old staircase cut into the stone in a square shape. Niamh followed but her heart was pounding more and more so with every step. Half of her still believed that there had been some mistake, that the man within the chamber to the right, where she was led, would be a stranger. At the door, Sister Alicia paused and put a hand to her arm.

'Are you well, my queen?'

Niamh had no words and so merely nodded, then pulled in a deep breath.

'Shall I come in with you?' Sister Alicia asked, her voice softening and her eyes shining with worry.

'No, No, thank you. I will… I just… I need a moment.'

Sister Alicia 's grip on her sleeve tightened slightly, a gesture of comfort, and then she nodded. 'I have my duties to attend to. When you are done, ring Lord Helligan's bell, and I will come to collect you.'

Again Niamh nodded, and then was left blissfully alone. Her eyes stung with repressed tears and her heart was hammering so hard that it was making her breathless. She swallowed, and then again, and then put her hand to the handle and turned it.

The room within was pleasant indeed. The scent of healing herbs was overwhelming, but not overpowering as it was in the corridors. There were different bouquets all over the room, some in vases, others laid on shelves and tied to the posts of the bed. The bed itself was a four-poster, huge and wooden, with what looked like soft blankets and throws. It looked comfortable at least, and that warmed Niamh. Helligan was asleep in the middle of the giant bed. From the angle at which she stood, Niamh could just about make out his hair and the shape of him under the covers. She took another step in. The rest of the room was well-furnished too, a shelf full of books, a wardrobe carved in solid oak with the pattern of trees and ivy upon it. There was a chest too, for clothing, a washstand and a table which held a cup, an apple, and an unopened bottle of honey-wine.

Niamh paused again. Thirteen years. Too many. Where had he been? What had happened to him? Why had he come to the sisters and not home to her? Her stomach twisted, her hands shook, but then Helligan stirred in the bed and Niamh's feet took her the few steps to close the gap almost involuntarily.

Helligan was almost unchanged, but for the greyness of his skin, the slight gauntness to his cheeks. The sisters had obviously shaved his face, as the skin was freshly smooth with the hint of a shaving rash on his cheeks from the blade. His hair was braided but the braids were knotted about him, loose and tangled where the jet black locks spilled free – still with the striking darts of blue with indicated his heritage. His eyes were closed still, his lips pressed. Niamh's tears spilled, hot tickles down her cheeks to see him thus. Ever Helligan had been her rock in the early days, her hero. To see him so ill, something within her cracked. There was an old wooden chair by the table and this Niamh took to the edge of the bed and sat down. She lifted his hand and held it in her own, flooded with the memories they'd once shared, memories she'd repressed for years because they were too painful. The way he'd taken her out to dance at one of the Wolder celebrations. Their first kiss, that awkward youthful love-making which had led to the conception of Alistair. Still her eyes brimmed over as she recalled how he'd insisted that she be queen, had declined even to be her king, despite that they were married. Nobody had understood why, not then. Later when he'd shown his dragon form, then they'd understood, a dragon cannot take the throne of the humans.

'Helligan?' she whispered, the tears falling unchecked and unheeded down her cheeks.

Helligan stirred and murmured, but did not open his eyes.

Niamh leaned forward to brush the hair out of his face, but did not speak again, allowing him his rest. She put up the back of her hand to wipe her face, and then sniffed back her tears.

An hour or so passed. Niamh sat in silence watching Helligan toss and turn in the blankets. His sleep was anything but restful and seemed less so still when he lay on his back. He did not fully awaken though, not enough to register that she was even there. Niamh didn't care, she could barely believe that he was even alive, not after so long believing the opposite, that time gave her a space to allow it all to sink in, to process.

By the by, the door creaked open and Niamh looked up to see Sister Dora at the door. The old lady smiled a smile of empathy and then held out her hand, beckoning Niamh away.

Niamh leaned over to kiss Helligan's brow, and then gently released his hand. Her thudding heart hammered in her chest, but she pushed on, standing and moving away from the bed. One last glance, just to reassure herself it was truly him, and then she moved to the door.

Outside, Dora embraced her like an errant child, an embrace of rosewater, sage and other sweet perfumes which brought life to a million memories. Dora smelled of healing, of the temple, and of the sweet sandalwood soap that the sisters made for themselves in the workrooms of the temple. Niamh felt all of her worries dull and allowed herself to spill a few more cleansing tears on Dora's perfect white habit, the shoulder of another absent friend.

'My Queen,' Dora finally said, pulling away and running a thumb under Niamh's wet eyes.

'Please, just Niamh…'

'Niamh. Sweetling, how tired you look, even aside from these tears! Come with me, you need to rest.'

Niamh allowed Dora to lead her back down the stairs and into one of the anti-chambers. Within, a table was laid with bread, fruit, cheese, pomples and what looked like a leg of chuck-meat, despite that the sisters normally ate only simple fare and never meat.

'Eat – you must be starved and exhausted after your journey!' Dora said.

Niamh sat at the table and pulled a small piece of meat from the bone. Even the act of eating such fare reminded her of Helligan, of her first night at Kilm's house – Helligan's hideaway – in the marshes. She'd hidden a chuck leg then, worried that she'd not be properly fed in her captivity. How little she'd known them all then, how far past it all seemed. Niamh felt the damned tears brewing again and despite how she forced them back, her eyes burned. Dora moved to stoke the fire, making it crackle and send up a spray of sparkling embers. At once the room felt hotter.

'Tell me how… how you came to have Helligan here,' Niamh whispered, 'After so many years…'

Dora pulled the drapes across the window with a swish. Thus done with, she sat herself down beside Niamh at the table and put a few grapes and some cheese ono her own plate.

'It was the strangest thing, in fact,' she said. 'We were at evening prayers, a week and a half since, and were interrupted by a knock on the door. It is unusual for any to knock here, especially an unexpected visitor. I wanted to answer it myself but Alicia is the matron for this turn and so she sent me inside too but just moments later called me back. There was a man without who claimed he had a message for my ears only. I went, of course, and there stood a man – a boy really. He looked somewhere upon twenty years, maybe a little older and yet I had but to look into his eyes to know he was but a glamour, an older beast in a lad's body. He had hair of black to his chin and on his face, and in his hair was a streak of blue…'

'Not Helligan, then?'

'No, my queen, but a family member surely.'

Niamh nodded, processing. She'd had no idea Helligan had family! 'And what did he say, this boy?'

'He said that should I wish to recover Lord *Dericaflae*, he slept in the faun-wood, close to Lokenswold, to the east. He gave me a parchment on which were written coordinates… a place which did not seem to exist.'

'A place you found only when you entered the forest?'

'Indeed. The boy turned after that, and walked away not down the road, but into the trees and there he vanished. I discussed this with Sister Alicia first. The surname *Dericaflae* is a loose translation, you see, of Darkfire… in the tongue draconis and so it seemed that it might be he but we were not sure. We agreed that it was best to investigate first, before we informed you….'

'A decision with which I do not agree, but which I understand.'

Dora inclined her head, 'Helligan was laid in a bed of Harrenmoss, and draped with various herbs tied onto chains,' she continued. 'I had taken a horse and cart so I loaded him in – a tedious task for he was unconscious for most of it, and is quite a lump to move…'

'And he has been sleeping since?'

'He is in a lot of pain, Niamh, we are helping him to sleep – by that I mean, we are keeping him asleep. In the morning, I will delay the dawn medicines so that he will awaken and you might speak to him but I warn you, he's… he's not in good shape when awake! The pain is dire and last we allowed him to wake, he could barely string together a sentence.'

'Niamh's heart skipped a beat but she nodded, 'what is his injury?'

'Well, that's the thing. None that we can see…'

'None?'

'No. He arches his back somewhat, but there is no mark on his flesh, and his bones are unbroken.'

Niamh pulled in a deep breath, 'Something magical then?'

'I fear so,' Sister Dora replied, 'I fear so, my queen.

Ten

The sun shining in through the drapes was very bright, blinding almost. Helligan didn't quite grasp where he was, squinting but not opening his eyes at first. The scent of herbs and flowers about was overwhelming, a haze about the bed in which he lay. A bed? Helligan's eyes flew open, his lips parted to pull in oxygen. The ceiling was high above him, white and with a small amount of green and gold décor, the bed was large, wooden and warm. A sheet of red embroidery with gold leaf covered his form – he was naked beneath. Helligan pulled in a deep breath and tested movement. Still his back smarted, but without the previous agony he remembered. His eyes moved to his hand, not quite registering, and found there that it was held in another, a little white hand which was adorned with rings of silver despite how the nails were bitten and ragged. His eyes followed the hand to its slender wrist, a cuff of silver embroidery attached to a dusky linen gown. His eyes moved up further, his heart speeding up still as he recognised the collarbone, the yellow hair falling down onto shoulders unbound. He pulled in a deep breath, and then found her eyes.

Niamh smiled. 'Hello my love,' she whispered.

Helligan felt his lips half-smile, felt the warmth suddenly break free. He could not speak yet, he didn't have it in him, but his breathing eased and he allowed his eyes to skim her face. Older – of course, it had been a decade! But still beautiful, still the golden princess, despite how she despised the nickname. She put a hand on his brow and it was blissful, cool.

'He's waking up,' Niamh said to somebody on the other side of the room, somebody he had not yet seen, and then smiled again. Helligan took in the redness of her eyes where she'd obviously been sobbing. His heart thudded again. He hated the thought that his beautiful wife had sobbed for him. *And likely not for the first time, these thirteen years past,* his mind interjected, pushing lower still his spirits. He sighed and tried to let the darkness take him again, but now that the light had him, he could not sink down again. His back itched too, as well as the pain, like a thousand fliggerbugs had burrowed into his flesh. Helligan pushed up, trying to get an arm behind to scratch at it but the effort made his vision swim again, his head spin. He groaned and lay himself back down, forcing his mind to repress the itch that he could not, and probably should not, reach.

'Gently does it, my love,' Niamh murmured, then stood and slid an arm about him, helping him to sit propped up against the pillows.

'There,' she whispered.

Helligan wet his lips. He'd used his voice so rarely in the past thirteen years that forming words was no longer something which happened naturally and easily. Much like Niamh had been as a girl, he realised. Was she still thus? His heart ached again, what a crime that he should not know.

'T-thank… thank you,' he managed.

'You are very welcome my love,' she said, her eyes glowing with sympathy and affection, her cheeks dimpled with her tight smile. She was obviously worried about something, but her worries were repressed.

'Just… just a moment…' Helligan said, closing his eyes, 'The room spins.'

Footsteps from beyond approached and Helligan opened his eyes to rest them upon another familiar human face. Sister Dora. He'd incinerated her initiate with his dragon-fire when

King Hansel had used the mind-control orb on him all those years ago. He'd never apologised, he realised, never made amends for that either. The anguish rocked him again, but Helligan repressed it, pushing it back within. In all the years he'd desperately wished to return, he'd never considered what it would be to do so, what devastation he'd left behind. His hand tightened on Niamh's and then he pulled it up, bringing it to his lips to kiss it. His sweet girl, his fair maid. Niamh moved to sit on the edge of his bed, facing him, and spoke to Dora across the bed.

'He's with us, but disorientated,' she said.

'To be expected. My Lord, Helligan, might I persuade you to drink some milk?'

Helligan looked at her again, his mind struggling to focus, to really bring him back. He nodded and managed another stuttered thank you.

'Here, I think you'd better take it for him,' Dora said, and handed Niamh the glass. With a tenderness which didn't feel deserved, she held the glass to his lips and allowed him to tilt it to drink. He took two sips of the ice-cold, thick creamy liquid and then pulled his head back. Niamh put the glass down on the side. She smiled over at Dora and nodded slightly, an indication that he'd drunk some, he guessed.

'My Lord,' Sister Dora said, coming to the edge of the bed, and fussing his pillow, 'I have done what I can to heal your malady, but the wounds themselves are invisible. Are they on your other form?'

All at once the agony returned, the terrible pain, heat, the stench of burning flesh. Helligan shuddered and Niamh's fingers tightened on his hand as he recoiled physically from the very thought of it.

'They… they are,' he managed. 'Ice-fire burns. I have had healing though. T-the healer said it might be weeks, or it might be months for the…' he paused to breathe, '…for the symptoms to recede.'

Niamh made a little murmur but said nothing. Sister Dora nodded though, more used to the ways of healing than Niamh. 'Good. Let's see how you go. I will bring a tonic for the pain and food, if you feel you can manage it?'

Helligan bowed his head. 'Your kindness is appreciated.'

Once Dora was gone, Niamh lifted the milk again to give him another swallow. He managed a longer sip and then pulled away again. His hand moved to touch Niamh's hair, and then to run his finger over her soft flesh over the hardness of her cheekbone. She tilted her head so that his hand cupped her face. Another tear formed and fell from her eye, rolling down to wet the palm of his hand.

'I thought you dead,' she finally whispered.

'I am sorry. I was prevented from coming earlier and I could not contact you. I tried, I asked for a message to be sent but my messenger did not dare.'

Niamh slid her hand to a necklace which fell between her breasts and pulled it up. His dragon-glass which held that tiny slither of his essence. It glowed blue with the mistiness of the vial about his own neck.

'It went black,' she said, 'for nearly thirteen years.'

'A spell. I was imprisoned in human form; my essence was put into a greddel.'

'A greddel?'

'A fae spell. Like a bubble in… in time so that a person might be imprisoned without the loss of years of their life … it is old magic.' Helligan closed his eyes again, he felt more tired than he could ever remember feeling, not just tired, but drained too. A tickle touched his skin, her hair, then a soft kiss to his cheek. Helligan slid an arm about Niamh and pulled her close to him, inhaling that sweetly familiar scent. His hands grasped for a moment as his own eyes filled with tears, but then he released her and sucked in a deep breath. 'I am so sorry,' he whispered. 'I…'

'We knew this might happen… I am just gladdened of heart to have you back now,' she said.

'I wish I could have got some message to you but…'

'Hush! We can discuss it later. For now, rest and recover. I like not to see you anguished thus.'

'My sweetling maid,' he murmured, then laid his head back down on the pillows. 'I do not deserve you.'

'Hush, sleep.'

And so he did, a less frenzied, more peaceful sleep.

The next time Helligan awoke he felt less raw, more himself. His gut grumbled for food and his pulse seemed normal. The room was darkened, early evening for the light coming in the windows. Helligan pushed himself to sit upright and was pleased to find that the room did not spin too badly, that his eyes did not blur. He glanced around himself, Niamh was gone – probably to eat, if his guess at the time was correct. He tested his arms, turning his shoulders in their joints to test flexibility, and then pulled aside the coverlet to rotate his ankles and wiggle his toes. Not bad, it all seemed to be working. He stood, testing his weight. Weak but not to the extent that he was in danger of falling down. Helligan flexed, stretched, and then shivered as a cool breeze came in through the window, caressing his naked form. Nakedness did not concern Helligan, nor did the cold but suddenly he needed to piss and that was something more of a matter of urgency. He knelt and found a chamber-pot under the bed, used it, and then carried it to the corner and covered it with the copper lid which was attached to it for the purpose. There was no water to wash his hands but Helligan broke the stem of a dusky spike flower and used the sap of that – common practice out in the forests where water was not abundant.

This done, Helligan moved back to the bed and sat down. A plate of cold cuts sat on the dresser beside the bed, along with a bottle of mead. Helligan uncapped the bottle and took a swig, enough to wet his whistle without being enough to render him intoxicated, and then lifted a chuck leg to his lips and bit into the flesh. It was an old bird, not a slaughtered youngling, the meat tougher and browner than with a younger creature. Helligan chewed thoughtfully and once the bone was clean, laid it down on the plate. He wasn't hungry, not really, but he took up the berries too and ate those. He might have to depend on his strength to recover over the next few days. That concern in Niamh's eyes had not just been for him, already he knew that! Once the berries were gone too, Helligan stood again and walked, still naked, to a clothes chest at the end of the bed. Inside were several pairs of men's trousers – just common cotton, nothing to loan any armour – and a tunic in black with a gold trim. Helligan tested the size, yes, they would do! Somebody had obviously placed them for him. He pulled on the clothing, the first he'd worn since the rags he'd finally discarded in his oubliette cell, and stretched his limbs. The pain is his back was definitely dulled, and even the itch felt less urgent. He stretched again, and then paused as a knock sounded at the door and Niamh entered without waiting for his response.

She looked tired indeed, dark circles under her eyes and lips which were dry from a lack of water. She smiled though, to see him up and dressed. 'Helligan,' she said, her voice very quiet, 'You are looking well.'

'I feel more myself. Thank you for your care of me when I… wasn't…'

Niamh's smile spread her lips but did not quite reach her eyes. Helligan watched her closely. This wasn't just tiredness, she looked fatigued and anxious. He hoped silently to the goddess that she was not anxious over his return.

'Niamh… is all… well?'

Niamh moved into the room and sat herself down on the edge of the bed. She sighed and looked down at her hands for a long moment, before looking up at him.

'The county is at war again,' she said. She sounded defeated. 'My brother's son, led by his grandmother, Magda… I presume you remember my father's second wife? She is leading the attack on the boy's behalf. They have invaded multiple times and every time we have driven them back. There are… they have a mage too – dark magics. The last time… the last time we nearly did not win. If not for… I… Helligan, your son is… our son, I mean…'

'What of him?' Helligan remembered the boy only as a babe but still something protective pulled from within.

'He is… is like you.'

'Draconis?'

'I… no… but his magic…'

Relief pooled, half-draconis children often showed signs of advanced magics. That was where the first mages had come from! Helligan moved to sit beside her. He considered taking her hand but thought better of it. Let her come back to him, if she wanted to, he would not push her, not after so many years apart.

'It is not unusual…' he began.

Niamh nodded before he had even finished speaking. 'I know it,' she cut in, 'but… but I have… I have gathered others – other mages – and they… they manage to contain and… and to control, with my tutorage but Alis… he just… just explodes with magicka, almost against his will. It… Helligan, it frightened me!'

Helligan sighed inwardly, he'd feared this might happen. Magic filtered through many generations was a weaker, more controllable form, straight from the source was not – and Niamh wasn't entirely human either, so they had her mother's chaotic magics to factor in too.

'What did he do?' Helligan asked, his mind racing.

'He… he brought down a rain of ice… of hailstones…'

'Hailstones?' that didn't sound too bad.

'Boulders of ice, not little pebbles, big enough to crush a man.'

'How did he do this? From whence did they come?'

'From thin air! He cupped the rain in his hands and then… then pulled down and the heavens opened!'

That caused Helligan to pause – that was magic as powerful as his own, if not more so! That was unexpected! His mind rushed. Could even he have brought a rain of ice boulders thus? He wasn't sure. Helligan began a reply but suddenly his ears brought him the sound of footsteps on the floor without. The knock on the door made Niamh jump slightly, her eyes flitting to the wooden aperture almost nervously, much as she had looked as a girl. Helligan put a hand over hers. 'It's just Dora,' he reassured her, 'I recognise her step.'

Niamh shook her head, frowned, 'No, something's wrong...' she murmured, ever that insight! It must be from her mother's blood. She stood and went to open the door, just as a second knock sounded. The door swung open at her touch and as Helligan had asserted, Sister Dora stood without. She looked harried though, worried.

'What, what is it?' Niamh asked, and Helligan could hear the panic starting in her tones. Perhaps his wife had begun to unlock her mother's gifts, he mused, she certainly seemed to have some foresight.

'My Queen, I hardly know...' Dora said, '... there's been another attack, not on Anglemarsh but on one of the settlements between there and the capitol.'

'How terrible is the news?'

'I can scarce believe it. There is talk of the dead rising up, walking again...'

Helligan raised an eyebrow but before he could interject, Niamh sighed heavily. 'Oh goddess! Not this again!' she sighed. Again? Helligan made a mental note of that.

'There's worse, oh my queen, it's your son...'

Helligan's blood ran cold.

'What... what of Alis?' Niamh's voice was frail, soft and broken in a way Helligan had hoped never to hear it again.'

'The messenger spoke of his bravery, of how he rode out to meet them in battle, Lord Shale at his side. In the heat of battle he used his magic and brought down the ice rain again.

Your son's magic saved the town but as he did so he was slashed with a sword about his mid-rift and…'

'Is he dead?' Helligan's voice was hollow. Could he really have come so close, only to lose his son before he even knew him?

'No, my Lord, not yet but gravely injured and his life is in danger. Lord Shale begs Queen Niamh to return, before it is too late… Prince Alistair is likely not long for this world.'

Eleven

Niamh's heart thudded wildly in her chest as she threw open the doors of Alistair's chamber and ran in. The room was very dim, all the drapes pulled to keep the sun out, much like for a lady in birthing. The furniture looked like silent statues, lost in shadow around the room, all except for the bed in the centre where her son lay. He was laid still on the bed, much as his father had been when she'd arrived at the temple. Jedda was in attendance, her sleeves removed and her dress plainer than her usual. She mopped the boy's head with a cloth and looked up helplessly as Niamh ran in.

'Sister,' she whispered, 'my husband tried to stop him but…'

Niamh shook her head, shushing her, and took her place next to the boy. Jedda laid a hand on her back as she sat, tearful, at his side. Helligan limped in behind her, he'd refused to stay behind as she'd prepared her horse to leave, and had climbed up behind her on the steed, dressed in the borrowed garb of the sisters: black tunic and cotton trousers with a gold-edged cape. Items which had been given to be passed out in charity, no doubt – more that she owed them in return. His presence was a comfort, even if she hadn't entirely settled her racing thoughts on his return. All the way, he'd whispered reassurances too, not imposing in her thoughts, but just gentle whispers to keep her going even though it felt as though her heart would explode with panic. His hands had been firm around her, his body something to lean back into.

As he entered the room behind her, Niamh glanced back to catch a sight of Helligan's face. Last he'd laid an eye on his son, the boy had been a babe in the cradle, now he was almost grown and perhaps about to leave the world entirely. How cruel if his father was present only to bring him into the world and to guide him back out! It was a crushing thought and she nearly bowed under it.

'Helligan…' she whispered.

Helligan limped to her side and put a hand on her shoulder. In the bed, the boy's eyes flicked open at her voice, moving to her face and then staring into the darkness beyond where his father stood. Niamh's heart sped up as she moved closer and took the chair beside him. Jedda kissed Niamh's head, 'I'll leave you in peace,' she said, 'call me should you need me!'

'O-of course, thank you darling,' Niamh murmured, then turned to her son, 'Alis…' she whispered, 'what *have* you done this time?' The words were no reprimand though, a gentle teasing from mother to son. Alistair found the edge of a smile, his hand came up to take his mother's and Niamh gripped it hard.

'Does it hurt?' she whispered.

'No,' his voice was dopey, sleepy, 'Freya gave me a drink and now there is no pain.'

'Good, good I am glad… I have somebody here who is eager to meet you…'

Alistair's eyes rolled over to Helligan, still dim and not quite comprehending. Helligan moved closer, still with a limp, but less so than before. Niamh wondered if he realised how quickly he was mending. As he moved into the dim candle-light, Alistair's eyes widened slightly, taking in blue-streaked hair and high cheekbones, so like his own. Helligan's identity could not be mistaken easily, even though the boy had never before laid eyes on him.

'F-father?' he whispered. 'What… Mother?'

Helligan inclined his head and moved closer still. With Niamh in the chair, he had nowhere to go but to the edge of the bed. Niamh's eyes followed carefully, her heart overflowing, as her husband sat himself down on the white coverlet with its yellow embroidery and laid a hand on their son's arm for the first time.

'Hello son. I hear you have been having adventures…' Helligan said softly.

'Father?' Alistair whispered again, his brow furrowing. 'But…'

'I am here. I am sorry it took me so long.'

'Are you a ghost? Am I dying?'

Niamh swallowed the lump in her throat. 'Your father is here in the flesh, Alis,' she said. 'I went to fetch him! That is where I have been whilst… w-what happened?'

'I am sorry, I…there was an attack and I decided to lead a group to repress it. L-Lord Shale said I should… should not but I didn't want… t-they would have sl-slaughtered them all. I'm sorry, I should have listened…'

'Hush, your concern for your people is admirable, if a little reckless,' Helligan said. 'You are young yet for command.'

Niamh felt the ghost of a smile, her eyes drinking in this first gentle interaction between father and son. Helligan and Alistair looked so very much alike too. She'd always known it, but to see them sat side by side enhanced the connection.

'Mother…' Alister whispered, 'I'm… I'm sorry! I thought…'

'Hush, I will hear no more about it! You were brave and just. Everything a prince should be. I…'

Niamh paused again as the door opened once more and another figure seemed to linger in the open aperture.

'The princess wanted to see Master Alis,' the woman's voice denoted the figure to be Prentice, Jessaline's nurse. Niamh looked to Helligan. She had other worries now, and she was not going to deprive her daughter of the chance to bid farewell to her brother, if he was moving across to the many-coloured land, even if it meant explanations later.

'Come forward, Jess,' she said, 'Prentice, you can go.'

Jessaline moved in quietly, and Niamh watched as Helligan examined the child wordlessly, his hand still holding that of his son. Jessaline looked more like Shale than anything else, dark hair, thick brows, somewhat pale of skin. She wasn't an unattractive child though, in her own way, but she'd never be a classic beauty. Niamh preferred it that way, anyhow. The child would grow more humble that way.

'Alis?' the girl asked quietly. At ten, she was grown for her age too, dressed well in fashions that a normal child of her years might not think of with her hair styled instead of the simple braids of children. Thus was the power of court life.

'Jess,' the boy croaked and Helligan shuffled slightly on the bed so that Jessaline could get to Alistair. The boy put up a hand painfully and tweaked her nose, something ever he'd done to irk the girl. Jess laughed but that laugh turned to fear again as Alistair shuffled with a groan, his hand going to his belly. Niamh put a hand to support the girl but she did not send her away. This was a lesson to learn, a life experience to temper the girl and to show her the true perils of war. Niamh controlled her own tears though. She would not weep whilst the boy lived, the goddess might save him yet! As Jess watched her brother with wet eyes, Helligan stood.

'I will leave you for now,' he said, 'I know this moment is sacred to you both and I need to go to the grove and speak with the goddess. Let us see if she will hear an absent father's pleas. I will return in an hour… unless…'

'I will call for you if I need to. Thank you,' Niamh whispered, grateful to him for that. Helligan leaned in and kissed his son's brow, then whispered a few words Niamh couldn't quite pick out into his ear. The boy's hand gripped his father's arm, but as Helligan stood, Niamh saw he was smiling a weak smile.

'Thank you, Father,' Alistair managed, 'I *will* see you in an hour!'

Helligan straightened and turned to Niamh. Any change, any whatsoever, have me sent for?' he asked again.

Niamh nodded. She half expected a brow kiss of her own but Helligan simply squeezed her shoulder gently and then left. The room seemed darker without him. Niamh lifted Jessaline onto her lap and squeezed the child gently. She'd not be a child much longer, Niamh realised, already she was showing her father's wearied look, his worldliness, if not his proficiency with a bow – Jessaline preferred her embroidery and dolls to any form of combat, despite how Niamh had tried to encourage her to learn a fighting skill too. Alistair coughed and then turned his head.

'He is very like me,' he said.

'You are very like him, in fact.'

'I… I am glad I got to meet him.'

'You will see him again, and often.'

'I fear my light dims, Mother.'

'Don't speak like that.'

Alistair put his hand out again. For a boy of but thirteen, suddenly he seemed the wise one, she the lost child. Alistair held her hand tightly, his was sweaty. He still wore his battle-garb too, minus the chunky armour. Niamh could see now that the bloodstains too still lay there. Why had nobody changed him? Given him clean clothes? The truth was most likely that he'd been in too much pain, but she could not even consider such a thing for her poor boy.

'Alis…' Jessaline said quietly,

'Yes…'

'Don't die!'

Niamh's eyes did fill with tears then and she had to hiccup them back. Goddess, how much easier it was to be young and to simply say what was on your mind.

'I will try…' Alistair chuckled, but then coughed again and the cough brought forth a groan of pain, both of his hands going to his guts.

'Alis!' Jessaline began to sob and that was enough for Niamh. She stood, lifting the ten-year-old as though she were still a toddler and moved to the door. Outside, as ever, were two guards. Niamh handed her sobbing daughter to them with one last hug.

'Take her back to her nurse,' she said, and then slumped against the closed door to try to regain control of herself before going back into the room where her son was slowly drifting off into a sleep he was unlikely to awaken from.

Twelve

Helligan left the stinking, infection-riddled chamber where his son lay dying without a backward glance, there was nothing he could do within, but plenty he could do without, in the grove when the goddess presence was stronger – if it still stood. Helligan presumed it did, Niamh loved the goddess more than most. He all-but ran down the echoey stone stairs, pain notwithstanding, and then out of the door at the side. There he paused. He needed to get to the grove, but a sight of Lord Shale practicing out in the courtyard stilled his feet. The day was grey and overcast, but no rain fell down on the rough stone courtyard. The wind was cool too and strong enough that a lesser archer might lose an arrow or two to it. Not Lord Shale though, Helligan noticed, watching as Niamh's best friend fired arrow after arrow into the middle of the target, never missing a single shot. Shale was in his fifties now, Goddess, these humans aged quickly! He was starting to grey at the temples but still as fit and lithe as he'd been when Helligan had seen him last. A good man, and a loyal subject to Niamh. Helligan turned his steps to join him in the courtyard.

'Your aim is still as true as ever, I see.'

Shale glanced over with a wary look in his eye. Helligan clocked it but shrugged it off – Shale and he were never the closest of companions.

'All the better to fight off these strange foes.'

'Dora spoke of necromancy…'

'It's just a rumour as yet. Welcome home, by the by.'

'Thank you. What do your scouts say?'

'Still nothing… the army appears to still be in retreat despite that Magda has slipped away from its head. We don't know who attacked the settlement, who this mysterious hooded figure is, anything.'

'If there is anything I can do…

'I will take your assistance and gladly, mage. Come to the next council meeting? Niamh will not argue, I am sure. How is the prince?'

'Not good.'

Shale seemed to sag. 'I am sorry for that. Alistair is a good boy, he was growing to be a good man, a good king.'

'He's not gone yet. I saw you on my way to the grove where I will say my own prayers to the goddess. He might still be saved if she shows mercy.'

'Good. She smiles upon your kind more than ours.'

'Not always,' Helligan muttered.

'No, I am sorry… and how do you fare? Are you well now?'

'I am well enough. Shale, I have a question for you…'

'Yes?' Lord Shale's voice turned wary again.

'Who… who is Princess Jessaline?' Helligan finally asked, unable to contain it any further. 'She's Niamh's daughter, is she not?'

Shale's demeaner did not change, his discomfort visible only in the wobble of his hand, in the arrow which sailed free being the first of the several Helligan had seen him fire which did not hit the centre of the target.

'Lord Shale?'

'Sire. Jessaline is… is Niamh's child, yes.'

'She has taken a lover in my absence? A new husband?'

'Not a new husband, my lord, but yes she has… has known another lover, several, I suppose.'

Helligan paused to analyse how he felt. Too many emotions to lay down. Calm, acceptance, the knowledge that he had been gone for so long, all those feelings combined with the twisting discomfort of jealousy and hurt. He sucked in a deep breath and mentally tried to practice the calming meditations he'd put into his mind during the years he'd spent below ground in his dungeon. He exhaled and pulled further on the calm, forcing a mental image of a soft blue light down through his body, into his fingers, down his legs, into his toes.

Helligan suddenly grew aware that Shale was watching him carefully, his eyes inquisitive. He pulled in a deep breath and then spoke again.

'Do… do you know who her father is?' he asked.

'Would that man be safe from harm and your retribution if I did know?'

Helligan gave the question serious thought as Shale raised his bow again and fired another arrow. It hit in the third ring, still an aberration for the kingdom's greatest archer. His shoulders were too tense, his hand shaky. His poor form and posture were more evidence than his confession would ever be.

'I think I need not ask again who that man is, do I?'

Shale sagged slightly, further confirming Helligan's suspicions. Another arrow flew, still not hitting target but closer again. Shale's hand reached for another arrow but found the quiver dry. He moved to the target to pull free the already used ones.

'Are you still…?' Helligan finally said. 'Your affair, is it over?'

'It was hardly that, Helligan. She was lonesome and lost. I was her closest friend, able to offer comfort… it was no affair, it was a series of ill-thought out nights which should never have happened. It stung sore when she said they must stop, but since then our friendship has been platonic. Niamh has taken others in, when the nights are coldest, but nobody she ever wanted to stay come morning. Even though we all thought you dead, she was still waiting for you to come home.'

'Thank you.'

'I love my daughter though. You know the pain of what I lost before; I would do anything to protect Jessaline now.'

Helligan inclined his head. Lord Shale's family had been massacred in the last war, the war to crown Niamh, massacred in retaliation for Lord Shale's defecting along with many other of the Goddess's patrons. Helligan looked over at where Josynne stood, bow in hand but facing him now, the arrows still in his quiver. Despite that he could easily fill Helligan with arrows in a blink, still it was he who looked wary.

'I… I thank you for your candour,' Helligan forced the words, 'I bear you no malice for your confessions…' and with that he turned and allowed his feet to take him away from the training yard.

Helligan said his prayers quickly at the grove just outside of the keep. He knew he'd been away longer than the hour he'd promised and something of an urgency was taking him. The goddess was still too, not even a glimmer of warmth to show she heard his pleas. After a few thankless moments, Helligan gave in to the urgency and turned back to the keep. He all but ran back, past the now empty courtyard and back up into the building where he'd left Niamh with Alistair.

Inside, Niamh was just coming down the back stairs. She looked tired indeed, her hair limp and her eyes drooping. Helligan paused.

'How fares the patient?' He asked her, blocking the path a little but declining from holding her, he knew not if she would favour his affects just yet.

'Worse,' her voice was dull, her eyes not meeting his. 'He seems not to rally and every moment he seems weaker.'

'Would you have me sit with him a while? You need to sleep, sweetling.'

'I… yes, b-but just for an hour, and only if he does not begin to … if he does not touch death yet' she whispered, 'I came out only for…for water but I am…' she sighed and looked to the floor, 'I am deathly tired.

'Go, I will look after our boy,' Helligan assured her, 'you don't have to bear these burdens alone anymore. I will send for you if it comes that… that you are needed.'

The look Niamh gave him was indecipherable but she nodded and then slipped past him. Again, Helligan resisted the urge to take her arm, to pull her to him; their broken relationship would wait awhile longer.

The stench of infection in Alistair's chamber was enough to make Helligan's stomach retch and roll. How could the rest not smell it? He moved in and touched his son's forehead. He was clammy and still. Worse Niamh had said, she had not exaggerated! Helligan steeled himself and then took a hold of the cloth of the coverlet. He pulled it away, slowly uncovering the wound so that the boy would not wake. His gut clenched again as he saw it. Thank the goddess Niamh was sleeping. Alistair's wound, two or three days old now by his reckoning, festered ill in yellow pus. The slash had opened him up from the top of his groin to his belly, and then across his hip. The herbs that Sister Freya had packed in were lilting, lost in the fetid decay of flesh. The whole area of his belly was red raw too, soft at the edges where the wound was wet. Lines of red moved up into clean flesh from the wound.

Helligan bit his lip and glanced to the door. Moving the boy was a risk indeed, but an idea was forming. Helligan was out of practice enough with magic, especially healing magic which had never been his skill – that was for the now rare White Draconis – but there was a sacred place where he'd once gone himself to cure wounds which were deemed incurable. The Glade of the Moon. The glade was about five miles back towards The Golden Keep. When Helligan had fallen in the battle for the keep, Niamh had taken him there and he'd survived. The goddess was kind and the Glade of the Moon was renowned for healing properties. Yes, it would be a risk to the boy to move him, but left here under human healing, he would definitely die. Helligan wrapped the stinking coverlet back over his son and laid a hand on Alistair's brow. He was burning up too, the fever most likely the reason for this prolonged sleep.

'Be brave,' Helligan muttered aloud, unsure if he spoke to himself or his son, 'Be strong now.'

He stood and moved to the closet at the far wall. Inside were Alistair's clothes. Helligan paused, taking a moment to glance over his son's simple tastes. It was much like his own closet had been, he realised, although without the leather and fur of a Wolder wardrobe. Helligan skimmed the clothes and settled on a black court robe and a fur-lined cape in wool. Those would be warm enough. The last thing he wanted was to lose Alistair to a chill. He moved back to the bed and pulled back the covers again, then sat the boy up, resting his body on himself to pull away the pus and blood-stained clothing he wore. Alistair groaned as he was moved and Helligan felt a bead of sweat drip down onto his back. He steeled himself again, trying to control his churning emotions.

'I'm sorry, I know that hurts,' Helligan whispered, 'I am going to lift you in a moment, and it'll hurt like the gaze of Ghara, but I have to take you out to heal you, you are festering here.'

The boy muttered again but Helligan doubted he was even able to understand much of what was going on about him, deep in the fever dream. Whispering apologies, *"sorry lad"* he pulled the clean clothing on to fevered sweaty flesh, adding a pair of woollen breeches under the garb to try to keep him warmer, and then wrapped the cloak about him. Helligan tested his own strength a moment, he was still not recovered and he could feel that keenly, but he thought he was strong enough at least to lift this waif of a boy that was his son.

Alistair weighed literally next to nothing. Helligan wondered, as he carried him to the door, if he'd been more rotund before the injury, or if the days abed not eating were paying their toll too. He semi-balanced Alister on his chest and hip to open the door, and then set out with him. As he approached the old wooden gate which led away from the great hall, and towards the kitchen entrance, Lord Shale appeared from the other direction. His eyes widened as he laid them on Helligan and Alistair.

'What…'

'I am taking my son to the moon glade, to try to heal him,' Helligan said.

'Without a word to any? Sneaking down the back stairs?'

'I did not think of human concerns. If I do not hurry, the boy is going to die. The wound is badly infected.'

Lord Shale balked at that and stepped closer, his hand going to Alistair's face. He seemed to inhale the air, sniffing for infection, and his lips curled. 'By the goddess, that is rank,' he murmured.

'Let me trade with the goddess for his life before it is too late.'

'And what shall I say to Niamh, when she awakes?'

'She knows I will not harm my boy.'

'And if he dies…'

'Then I will bring him home to be interred as you wish.'

Helligan shuffled from one foot to the other. Whilst his son was not heavy, the strain of standing holding him was not comfortable with his own injuries. Lord Shale watched a little longer, but then nodded.

'Come, take a horse-trap and cover him, we don't want the people to see what a load you carry!'

Grateful for the other man's assistance, Helligan acquiesced and allowed Shale to lead him not through the kitchen entrance, but through another door which led to the stables. A trap was already made up, as ever they were for the whim of the queen or her courtiers, and Shale helped Helligan to lay Alistair down and cover him.

'Go with the speed of the goddess,' Shale said, 'I'll wake Niamh and…'

'No, let her sleep, tell her when she awakes.'

'She'll be furious…'

'Let her expel that fury on me, if you do not wish to hold it yourself, but let her sleep. If the goddess is not kind, this might be the last sleep she gets for some time. As well as that, her mother's heart will lead her to follow me and she can't be there, for this. This is between Alistair and the goddess, with me as a conduit.'

Lord Shale nodded, somewhat stiffly, and then bent to kiss Alistair's head. He put a hand about the boy's face in a gentle gesture and then murmured, 'Come back to us if you can, my boy, and if not then go forth to the goddess in peace.'

Helligan's eyes took in how tender Shale was with Alistair, his ears taking in the endearment "*My boy*" and the anguish in his softly spoken words. Another bead of pain took his gut. This man had raised his son, he realised, and where gratitude was required, he felt more of jealousy. He cut that back at once, it was not a pretty trait to allow to fester! He nodded again to Shale and then climbed up into the driver's seat of the pony-cart.

'Good luck!' Shale said and Helligan managed a nod before geeing up the horses and setting off.

The Glade of the Moon was a small clearing in the wooded area just north of Anglemarsh. Helligan drove the little trap quickly and then, at the edge of the trees, lifted Alistair and pulled him back up into his arms. The boy was floppy, unresponsive, and Helligan felt a panic brewing. He refused to be too late! He refused to allow his son to die – not like this! Not as little more than a child!

'Come on Alis…' he murmured, using the pet name he'd heard Niamh use, '…just a little further.'

Alistair did not respond. Helligan carried him into the glade and lay him down in the soft Harrenmoss. The glade was shaded by the trees, and made moist by the little rivulet which ran through it. Various healing herbs grew throughout, as well as the odd clump of Oasha's Tears. There was a pool at the centre which soaked in the rays of the moonlight and which

gave the glade its name. Helligan, of course, had healed in his
dragon form when he'd come here but Alistair did not have
that choice so it was riskier. Alistair stirred again in the moss,
his fingers clenching, and for a moment Helligan was almost
bowed by love and grief. He laid a hand on his boy's brow
again, and then stroked his soft black curls. Niamh's hair, not
his, but for the colour; Helligan's hair was coarser and finer.

'Alis,' he said, still knelt at his side, 'Alis, I need you to wake
up now.'

Alistair groaned and one of his little white hands – Niamh's
hands too – went to his side, worrying the wound.

'Alis,' Helligan said again, cupping the boy's face, 'Come
on, wake up.'

At last, those pain-filled red eyes opened to look upon
Helligan's face.

'Hello son. Welcome back.'

'Father…'

'I need you to listen to me,' Helligan fought to keep his
voice steady, 'I need you to listen and then to obey.'

Alistair nodded.

'I have brought you to one of the sacred glades, that you
might begin to heal, but I cannot bring that healing upon you,
that is beyond my magics. I need you to… to connect to your
element, and to heal yourself. I will assist…'

Alistair's eyes were dropping again! Goddess! He wasn't
strong enough. Helligan moved to the moon pool and took up
some of the water in his hands. He used it not to wash the
wounds, but to splash water over Alistair's brow. At once, the
boy responded, opening up his eyes again.

'What is your favoured element?' Helligan asked, 'Is it
water? Your mother said about ice…'

'Water,' Alistair confirmed, through dry lips.

Helligan nodded, 'Put down your hands, here,' he lifted
Alistair's hands gently and placed them through the moss into
the mud beneath, 'there, see, so you are connected to the water

which runs free from the pools of this sacred place. Now close your eyes, but do not sleep.'

Alistair's eyes fluttered closed at once, but his shoulders showed that he was obeying and fighting the unconsciousness.

'Good, now begin to envision the magics, just as you do in battle. See them, visualise them. They might be a light, a current, a sludge, even, but for you they will be something different than to any other. Can you see them, in your mind's eye?'

'I am too tired…' came the voice of a child.

'I know, son, I know, but you can rest afterwards. Visualize them for me!'

Alistair's brow furrowed, his lips parting with strain, but then he nodded, 'It is water,' he said, 'water which courses through the earth, making a muddy… muddy river…'

Well, that made sense at least, Helligan mused, the coming together of water and earth, of his own water magic combined with Niamh's forest-fae heritage.

'Good,' he whispered, 'Now I want you to begin to pull it into yourself. Visualise it, a drip at a time, being pulled up into your form. I will begin to speak, to plead with the goddess, and you just concentrate on pulling the magical water inside you, spreading over your wound and knitting it back together…'

'I… I can't…'

'You must try! Think of your mother! Imagine her face when you return well again.'

Alistair's eyes opened briefly. He looked like he was about to weep, but Helligan could not soften; the boy's own life depended on his strength. He patted Alistair's arm and then stood. For a moment, he considered swapping form to try to enhance the magic, but he wasn't ready yet to test out his maimed and broken true form, so instead he moved to the pool in the centre of the glade.

'Hear me now, face of Herodite, the goddess face of mothers! I humble myself before you and I beg of you to return to me the life of this boy, my son. Feel his efforts Agamariss, feel how he battles against you! He is not ready yet!' Helligan glanced to Alistair and to his relief, a light was beginning to glow about his hands where they laid flat upon the earth. He was doing it!

'And to you, Ghara, goddess face of pain and perseverance, see how he struggles, how he fights even despite your gaze! Allow him his victory! Helston smile upon his battles. My son fights a personal war this day so give him your blessing! Leandra – face of materialism, even your gaze, I beseech, give him hope that he might come to have a house of his own, a family! Face of Zhara, guardian of wisdom, see how he is but a child! Allow him to grow to adulthood, in order to unleash your gifts amongst the others.'

Helligan paused to breathe. According to the stories, the goddess had blessed each draconic clan with a different face, back in the origins, and each clan then worshipped a different aspect of her. It was time to call of the deity of his own clan, and this was the most crucial, especially since his son was of the same blood, the same origin. Already the magika was swirling about them, Helligan could feel it's electricity, a warm tickle in the air. He took in a deep breath.

'Finally, our own aspect!' he called out, 'Kalihad, aspect of the magika! Bless my son's magics, benevolent lady! See how he uses your gifts to us, the blue draconis, in his valiant attempts to save himself from Agamariss! See how he gave up so much to use these magics for good! Bless him and reward his endeavours!'

Another glance, Alistair was tiring, but he was still fighting! Bless the lad! As Helligan paused, he felt a light shining onto his back, into his own flesh. He had the attention of the goddess now.

'All seven faces, I beseech you all, as one, as whole! My goddess! I beg of you to bless my son, and allow him to prevail now! Blessed be you, in your might! Praise to the goddess for your sweetness, your compassion!'

The light left him abruptly but Helligan was not concerned, as it travelled to his son, to Alistair. The light bathed the boy, blindingly so, and for just a moment, Helligan could almost make out her shape, almost. Then suddenly there was darkness again. Alistair let out a cry, his hands pulling free from the moss, and bent double into a ball. Helligan knew this step too though, as the infection literally and physically expelled from the wound. He ran to kneel beside Alistair, clutching the boy's shoulders in his hands to steady him. Alistair pulled up his tunic, his hands almost frantic, and there the wound was suddenly cleaner, less red and swollen. The pus and gore from within had pushed out to lay about the edges of the cut. Helligan's eyes took it all in, but he said nothing as his son sobbed in the agony of its expulsion. Instead, he stood again and brought more water from the pool, washing away the gore. When he was done, and Alistair laid back down on the moss, Helligan could see that the wound was knitting. Not closing fully, and ever would a scar sit where it had been, but the infection was gone at least. Alistair laid still and quiet for a long moment, not speaking, but then opened his eyes again.

'I can feel the magic working…' he whispered.

'Aye, not bad for a first attempt!' Helligan found a smile.

Alistair looked unsure for a moment, but then smiled too and put a hand on Helligan's arm. 'Are you really my father?' he asked.

'I am.'

Alistair's lips pressed and his brow furrowed again. Helligan's heart went out to him, at thirteen, this boy was more a man than most. He did not speak again though. Helligan stayed knelt by his side a moment longer, but then pulled Alistair's tunic back over the healing wound.

'Come, he said, 'we should really get you back to your mother now, before she banishes me from *her* kingdom too…'

Thirteen

'They need to be properly trained!' Helligan's voice rang out in the echoey council chamber. He sat opposite Niamh, next to Josynne and Lord Lorne. Niamh said nothing but repressed the urge to take Alistair's hand. This was his first council meeting, two days after his return, and he was all-but healed. Remarkably so. Alistair's eyes darted from one person to another, taking it all in as the men argued and squabbled around the old wooden table. The fate of the young mages was the topic for debate and it had taken exactly ten minutes to turn to an argument. Niamh hoped that Alistair was learning, as she wanted him to, of how petty and tiresome such meetings could be, and yet how necessary. No man – or woman – ruled entirely alone.

'But the mages are so crucial to our defences,' Lord Shelby said, he was still a young man, pockmarked and dark of hair. He had been one of the last to defect, after Niamh's father had massacred most of his family. He was yet to marry but had a reputation in the whorehouses between Anglemarsh and the capitol.

Her brother-by-law, Lord Lorne nodded his golden head. 'We could not have held out against the last two attacks if it were not for them!' his eyes were bright and his hand strayed to where he was beginning to grow facial hair. Niamh wasn't sure the new development suited him, really.

'Untrained mages fall dangerously close to warlocks,' Helligan said. 'A warlock is simply a mage who is unfettered by the code of conduct and rules of the Mage's council. They are wild, untamed, and risk doing more harm than good.'

'But the mage council is gone? Depleted?' Lord Lorne asked, casting bright blue eyes onto Helligan. Niamh was quietly pleased to have added him to her council, the man was never afraid to speak up despite his humble beginnings.

'They are not gone, not the old sages, but likely hidden away. I can find them – I know where their tower lies hidden,' Helligan said. 'Mages for eons have gone there to begin their journey and so should these.'

'Our queen is training them. *You* could train them!' That was the wiser and more experienced Lord Nightingale. He was older, not one of her father's court but a distinguished knight from those days. He'd come over with the masses, just before the end of the war. He was a quiet man, usually, thin of face and bearded. His prowess with money had given Niamh the confidence to name him treasurer.

'Neither our queen, nor I, are qualified to train mage initiates,' Helligan said. 'And to try to do so is dangerous. Not just for us but for them too.'

A silence fell.

'How long does such training take?' Niamh asked. 'Are we talking weeks? Months? Years?'

'Months, half a year perhaps, intensely, and then they can come back to their posts and begin to practice here, if you would not mind having a sage resident here for the time? The rest of the training could be months, could be years but after the initial six months they can work as apprentices.'

'Six months gone?' Niamh said, 'And… and Alis is to go too?'

Alistair looked up at his father, his eyes full of the nerves of shyness he'd inherited from his mother. Niamh hoped that was something he'd grow out of. Helligan looked back at his son, then to all of the gathered lords.

'I fear Alis needs to go more than any. He will be safe there, my lords, Niamh… My queen. The tower is well hidden and we can send guards if need be. It will be a learning experience for the boy too, and might well aid him in his journey towards kingship, to be away from here and learn independence for a time.'

The silence fell again. Nobody seemed to really want to argue with Helligan, but nobody seemed impressed with his words. Niamh glanced from one face to another, and then to her husband again. His eyes held hers and for a moment Niamh was flooded with the memory of their early acquaintance. If nothing else, Helligan knew how to rule, to lead; he just didn't want to. His advice was always worth heeding, she should not forget that.

'If you think it absolutely necessary… then they will go.' Her voice sounded like a dry whisper! Goddess, she'd got better at council meetings until this! Perhaps it was the emotive nature of what they discussed, or perhaps she was too tired. As weeks went, this one had been a real ride.

'Agreed, then?' Helligan asked and the council gave him the weakest of "Aye"s.

The group set off the very next day, with Helligan and Niamh both at the helm, and Josynne left in charge of the kingdom for a few days. It was risky to leave, especially in the current climate but Niamh was certain that the attack which Alistair had quashed had been a last-ditch attempt by some of the fleeing soldiers. Besides, her enemies had no use for her castle if she and her son were absent. She was tempted to take Jess with her but at the last minute decided to leave her with her father. She would be safe! They all would! Niamh would return once Alistair was settled and she was completely assured of his safety at the Mage Council. She could not leave him there if she wasn't completely assured of it and to do that, she had to see for herself. Helligan would escort her back, afterwards, and then there had been talk of his return to the mage council if needed, another blow for Niamh's already aching heart. At least that would give Helligan time to bond with his son though, she supposed. It was true though, that she felt suddenly like everything was slipping away. Niamh bit down on the growing panic, trusting in the goddess's plan. The goddess had saved Alis and so Niamh owed her a debt, if Helligan thought this was the repayment needed then this she would tolerate.

Helligan rode a little ahead, allowing Niamh and her mages to follow behind as they rode through the edges of the forests. Now that Niamh was tuning into it, she could feel the magics which hid the fey kingdom within, a gentle tingle, a movement at the corner of her eye. The spell was a befuddlement and transportation spell, where the rider would enter the woods, and then exit only a short while later, unaware that they had been moved miles to the other side of a forest that was on no maps, the home of the fae… and the dragonkind. Niamh was very quiet, just listening to their chatter and laughter of her mages. She was worried about Helligan, worried about her kingdom, the threat from the mystery necromancer, and most of all worried about her son who seemed suddenly so vulnerable and with a target upon him. Alistair rode at her side but he knew his mother well enough not to mind the quietness of her mood. His eyes rarely left his father and Niamh felt that as a worry too – for so long Helligan had been the hidden hero of her son, how was he coping now, with the man himself here before him? At least Helligan had taken on the role of father, she pondered, he could as well have not, after thirteen years away.

'We are almost there,' Helligan said from before them, 'just through this village and then to the coast.'

Niamh pulled forward a little further and found her horse stood on a cliff-edge above a tiny fishing village. She glanced about her, half-expecting to see some form of tower but the landscape was devoid of any such structure.

'Are you sure this is the place?' she asked Helligan, coming to his side. He glanced at her and his eyes twinkled with a half-smile. It was warming to see, a memory of the man for whom she'd risked her whole world.

'Aye, I'm sure…' he said. He touched the rein of his horse and led them down the winding cliff path to the village. The mages quieted now, their concentration on the crumbly path. Niamh glanced back, Alistair was behind her, followed by Nervoria, Elenni and the boys. Friggan, probably the strongest of them if he could put his vanity aside, came last, holding the rear and keeping a watch over his brothers and sister. Elenni came next, the eldest of them all, and his eyes were quick to seek out potential hazards. Niamh was pleased to see that he was taking on a more protective role, although she anticipated some hierarchy trouble with Nervoria as she came into her power.

As they approached the shore, some of the villagers came out of their houses, pausing to look upon the procession. Niamh found a smile and felt in her pockets for alms but she was beaten by her son, who somehow already had a coin to hand. Helligan paused, turning to watch as Alistair slid down from his horse to press coins into the hands of the villagers, rather than to just throw them down and potentially cause the chaos of squabbles over the little copper pieces.

'He has your royal grace, as well as my magics,' Helligan commented, quietly so that the boy would not hear.

'And your recklessness and my shyness,' she added, 'sometimes I despair, but I have high hopes for him. His heart is good.'

Helligan touched her arm, the first contact he'd initiated in days, and smiled again, causing Niamh's belly to hurt. 'It is. You have done well with him.'

Niamh put her fingers over Helligan's and he pressed them gently, before turning back to the little pack of mages.

'Just a mile further, so we are away from the village,' he said, and then moved the horse across the sand, leaving them to canter after him. The sand flicked up as the horse's hooves graced the ground, and Niamh felt the thrill of it, closing her eyes briefly to take in the sound of the gucs above, the spray of the sea and the scent of salt and rotting gillweed. For the first time in what felt like an eternity, her smile was genuine, bright. After an hour or so, Helligan stopped his horse again. The sea was low, and so there was plenty of beach to walk upon, the cliffs rising above them almost to the sky, dotted with little pink blooms and patches of grass and shrub which jutted here and there.

'Here, I think…' Helligan said, almost to himself, and then turned his horse, letting its hooves stir up more sand. 'Mages,' he said, 'We stand before what appears to be a blank seascape, and yet you must trust me when I say that it is not. Over yonder out to sea, lies an island on which there stands the tower of the mage council. Traditionally this council has been a brotherhood, a group of men who serve Kalihad, the goddess face of mysticism and magic.'

'Will they allow me to join?' Nervoria asked, her dark eyes concerned, 'If they are a *brotherhood?*'

'I will ensure it, and any other girls who wish to follow you. The old ways must be forgotten now, and a modern era entered.'

'Will they do as you ask?' Nervoria was not satisfied.

'They will. Remember who I am.'

Elenni moved forward a little to take Nervoria's side. 'If they will not take you, I will not join them either…' he declared and Niamh had to repress a smile as Alistair's eyes burned his back, then flicked to the pretty sixteen-year-old girl. Surely her son had something of a crush there… he was of an age for such, she supposed.

'They will take us all, or none,' Friggan spoke up, 'how do we enter, Lord Helligan?'

'Every mage who has come through, has had to learn their own way of penetrating the Wolder magics, and entering the tower of the ancient order of Magi, but with needs as they are, I will guide you in.'

Niamh watched as Helligan took in a deep breath and then exhaled and dismounted his horse. He handed the rein to her and walked to the edge of the waters. There he knelt, took two long, deep breaths, and then touched his hand to the edge of the water. At first, the swirling sea seemed to resist him but then the waters turned first to slush, and then to ice. Helligan grunted, his shoulders tensing, and then stood, sending a rush of ice forward, out to sea. The bridge formed almost instantaneously and as it moved forwards, the mists of magic seemed to flicker, and then to suddenly vanish, giving Niamh a view of a shore, not too far distant, on which stood a tower almost as tall as the temple of Herodite. Behind her, the two youngest of her brood, Maven and Genn began to murmur excitedly to each other, whilst even the older ones gasped and exclaimed in surprise. Niamh turned to see Alistair's eyes too were wide, but then Helligan caught her attention as he gasped and fell to one knee, his hand on his back and sweat pooling on his brow. Niamh dismounted at once and ran to his side, kneeling too.

'Are you well?' she asked.

'Yes, just about' he stood, somewhat painfully and allowed her to help hold his weight. He turned to the anxious faces watching, 'It would appear that I am not yet fully recovered from my illness. Magic can take it out of you, if you are not fully fit,' he explained.

'Come, let us cross…' Niamh said, leading Helligan back to his horse and helping him to mount, then taking the rein of her own. She wasn't entirely satisfied with his explanation, but it would not do to call him out before what were to be his new initiates… or his son!

The group moved to the edge of the ice bridge, but there Friggan paused. 'Is it slippery?' he asked. 'I am not the strongest rider…'

'It will be as stable and secure as a road,' Nervoria said, before Helligan could respond, then, 'I made one once, when I was younger, over the pond in my village…'

Helligan smirked, his discomfort from a moment earlier seemingly gone already, 'I see I have a rival for the role of tutor,' he chuckled. Niamh glanced to the girl. She was smiling too and Niamh saw a glimpse of ambition in her eye. It was no good aiming such at Helligan, though, he was hardly the type to be turned by a pretty face – Niamh herself knew that from experience, she'd had to pretty much lead him to her bed in the beginnings of their affair.

On the other side of the bridge, Helligan tapped the floor again and the bridge vanished, the shore on the other side remained visible though. The tower was tall and of stone, wide enough to encompass three or more rooms on each level, as far as Niamh could guess. Helligan rapped on the door and it was opened almost instantly by an old sage. The man must have been ninety if he was a day, bent, thin as a rake and with eyes that burned a striking purple, like lightening. He bowed before Helligan, his green robe hanging off him to an extent that his whole chest was visible when he bent. He stepped back and led them into a vast corridor with a black and white checkered floor and tall wooden beams. Another man came forward, more robust than his companion, with rosy cheeks and a robe of the same green.

'Lord Helligan, we have been expecting you,' he said, then to Niamh, 'and our good queen too.'

Niamh nodded and then indicated her mages, 'I have... I have brought those who s-s-seek training, ch-children I have gathered from the four corners...'

'Children, all, and yet none. All have already seen war.'

'They have,' did she imagine the reprimand in his voice? Perhaps.

The old man stood to one side. 'Either way, you are very welcome. Tomorrow, your children will show us their talents, and we will consider training. Tonight a good meal and a night's sleep, I think, are more in order.'

Niamh looked to Helligan, her eyes asking if this was normal, but Helligan just nodded gravely at the old sage.

'Thank you, Master Orien,' he said.

Niamh raised an eyebrow. Of course, Helligan had trained here, he knew these people well. She bit her lip but said nothing.

'You are welcome son, welcome home. Master Graves will take you to your chambers and provide food. I presume the boys can share a dormitory?'

Niamh looked over at her son. He'd never had to share anything in his life. It might be a good lesson in humble manners though. She nodded.

'The girl will have a different chamber and I will have guest rooms prepared for you both.

'Thank you,' Niamh managed, 'very kind.'

The night bore on but Niamh could not sleep. The weather around the tower remained dire, rolling growling thunder broken up by the pink and blue strikes of lightening which seemed never-ending about the tower. Her eyes were drawn to the window and, with sleep far distant, she stood and moved to it, looking out. The land was close and apparent from the tall tower, the cloaking magics obviously working only one way, and Niamh took some peace in watching the waves crash against the shore, calmer there than they were at the base of the tower where they whipped the rocks. It was difficult to tell in the dark, but the weather still seemed fairly localised to the tower. Niamh rested her elbows on the wide alcove by the window. She hoped all was well at home. Josynne would be just retiring, with little Jessaline already abed. Did he have a sweetheart now? She didn't know, he'd had a couple since their affair but never for long. She sighed, and her mind was just wondering again when she heard a knock on the door of her chamber.

'I... er... who is it?' she asked, her voice barely above a whisper. He heard her though, hadn't he always...

'It's me.' The door opened and Helligan entered, 'am I welcome?' he asked softly from behind her.

Niamh turned to look at him, 'always.'

He entered the room fully and closed the door. Niamh said nothing, but turned back to the window. 'It's a magical storm, isn't it?' she asked.

'Of a kind, yes. Raw magic spilling free from the core. Some say it was put here during the wars, a rupture in the fabric of reality.'

'It never ceases then?'

'No, and whilst it rages on, this tower will ever be populated by the mage council.'

'Are there just the two sages left?'

'There are four. All aged now. Normally members of the council step up to replace the sages but most of my brothers were murdered in your father's cull.'

Niamh still did not turn about but Helligan moved to stand right behind her, looking out at her view. 'The mages are the guardians of this magical place,' Helligan said, 'You have done this land the biggest service, bringing the children here. They will serve the rift, and the rift will serve them.'

'And our son?'

'Will learn some discipline and independence, which will do him no harm.'

Niamh sighed and allowed her eyes to drift back to the shore, watching the waves again. Her shoulders tightened slightly, 'and you?'

Helligan was quiet for a long moment. Then he spoke, 'Orien has asked me if I will stay and assist them just as I suspected he might. The council have offered me the role of Sage. I said I would ponder on it.'

'And will you?'

'That depends, sweetling…'

'On what?'

'On whether or not there is still a place for me at your side.'

At his words, something inside Niamh broke, she turned about to face him but the words just wouldn't come. She swallowed twice and then pulled in precious, sweet, oxygen. Her mind raced for the right words to begin this conversation.

'I will understand…' he continued in the wake of her silence, '…if the answer is no. I know that I hurt you badly when I left and that years – so many years – have passed since then. I understand that my life passes more slowly than yours, so that events to me which still seem close, like our marriage and our life together, are far in your past and lost.'

Niamh listened, mute, as he laid it all out, but her throat had closed, her heart rate overly accelerated. Yes, it has been years but hadn't she really been waiting for him? Her gentle rejection of Josynne, and the lack of allowing anyone in since. She knew, had known from the moment she'd seen him so still and ill in the bed at the temple, that things between Helligan and herself had not been finished but it was still awkward – how could it not be? In a normal state, with him, she might have been able to explain it all but with her emotions rising, the words refused to form, her anxieties causing an inability to even begin a sentence.

'I understand too,' Helligan continued after a pause, 'that love is not by nature endless and boundless to humans. Time causes it to fade and become washed white – a necessary decay which makes life liveable again when a loved one is lost. I realise that you might not still love me as once you did and I… I accept that. I don't expect anything of you, I am merely asking, I suppose, if you might consider me again, one day?'

Niamh closed her eyes. When the world seemed to rush past her, sometimes it took a moment of dark and quiet to recollect herself. Helligan's hand coming down to touch her shoulder made her jump slightly and open her eyes again though. His were kind, gentle.

'If it suits you to ponder this too then do so, ever I am your loyal servant, no matter the answer you give me now. Even if I come back to this place and serve out my years here, I am still yours to command. You do not lose me, if your heart is clouded now to what once we shared.'

'Helligan please just... just be quiet for one moment!' Niamh finally managed.

Helligan's eyebrow raised slightly, his eyes showing surprise and his top teeth biting his bottom lip but he said not another word. Niamh pulled in a deep breath and put up her hand to the back of his neck, under his hair. There she caressed the skin, forcing herself to hold his gaze. The moment seemed to snag and hang, but then she pushed herself up onto tiptoes and touched her lips to his, just a simple kiss, almost platonic but with so much held pressed beneath. He tasted like honey-wine, pommel berries and familiarity. Niamh's lips lingered just a moment and Helligan smiled under her kiss as she pulled away. He touched his forehead to hers in a gesture he'd used to use before, holding it there so that they shared breath. His hands came up to cup her face and slid into her hair. For a long moment they stood thus, bridging the years, and then Niamh finally spoke.

'So much time, so many years… and yet you make me a girl again, *Helligan the Mage*.'

'I…'

'No, shush. Let me speak.'

Helligan ceased his words at once. Niamh took in another long breath but did not pull away from the intimate space Helligan had created between them.

'I… I grieved for a man I b-believed to be dead and then – thirteen years later… that man came home to me. S-surely that can be ought but a blessing?'

'I am glad you find it so.'

'I did grieve but I n-never gave up hope either. M-my hope kept alive that love I held for you, even in the darkest hours… it exists still! But now we are like strangers, in some ways. I want to come to know you again, and I do not want you to go away. Apart we cannot… cannot come to know each other again.'

'Then I won't stay in this place. I will come home with you.'

'Thank you...' she paused but then her lips spoke again, almost without her permission. 'I crave intimacy with you again though, so badly that I feel a tremor whenever your hand brushes mine. Lie with me, my husband?'

At her words, Helligan's easy smile returned. He brushed his fingers through her hair again, seeming to test the thickness there. 'Who am I to disobey a direct order from my queen...' he said, teasing in his tone.

'That was not an...'

Helligan interrupted the sentence with a kiss, causing Niamh's heart to thud a little harder still. She ran her thumb over his cheekbone whilst her other hand slid to his waist, locking him in closer to her form. Helligan pushed the kiss deeper, no longer soft platonic kisses, but Niamh could feel his shoulder shaking slightly, his passion restrained but just barely. That same gentle touch as when he'd taken her first, when she was still a virgin maid. He still obviously felt he needed to treat her carefully and Niamh found that almost irksome. She was a million miles from that timid girl now. Rather than pull away though, she slid a hand up to grip his hair, deepening the kiss and parting her lips. Her spare hand she slid over the back of his trousers, gripping him and then guiding his body closer so that she could feel the hardness of him against her even through the skirts she wore. Helligan murmured but then pulled back, but his eyes shone and the slight panting of his breath showed her that her movement had had the desired effect. She took his hand and led him to the bed, then turned her back.

'Undo me?'

Helligan obeyed, as docile as one of her ladies as he pulled the material free of its little metal hooks. The brushes of his soft fingers on her skin made her want to turn back but she waited until the dress was loose, then slid it from her shoulders and wriggled it from her hips so that she stood only in her white cotton underdress. Helligan's lips came down on the skin of her shoulders from behind. Soft, trailing, gentle kisses. He slid his arms about her, his hardness against her buttocks, and moved his hands up over her belly to her breasts. Niamh put her head back on his chest, her eyes flickering closed as Helligan's fingers caressed her. She slid a hand down to unhook her cotton drawers from her hip and pull them away, allowing them to drop to the floor as Helligan pulled off his tunic behind her and fumbled the laces on his trousers. Niamh turned back to face him. Outside the thunder still crackled, the lightning still flashed, lighting up his lust-filled eyes. His hands gripped her underdress and pulled it free, then dispensed with the little tight lace chemise she wore around her breasts, leaving her stood naked before him. Niamh knew that her body was not as youthful and firm as once it had been – before two children had made it their home and then pulled free – but she knew also that Helligan didn't care. His eyes met hers, his lips pulled to a lust-fuelled smile.

'My beautiful wife,' he murmured.

Niamh allowed one more kiss but then pulled away suddenly and moved to the bed, leading him by the hand.

'Sit back,' she ordered, indicating the pillow-laden headboard and Helligan obeyed wordlessly, stripping away the last of his clothing as he did so. Niamh waited for him to move, and then sat astride his hips, taking him inside of her as she did so. She kissed him, her hips motionless to begin, and his hands cupped her face, holding her there to drink her in. Niamh smiled, then rocked her hips making Helligan moan against her, his hand slid down to grip her hip and push himself in even deeper whilst the other hand moved back to her breast and his lips, his teeth, moved to her collarbone, nibbling her as she rocked again and tightened her pelvic muscles, starting a rhythm and leading them both firmly towards oblivion.

And then it was done.

For a long moment they both lay still as their breathing returned to normal, Helligan put a hand up to cradle the back of her head whilst Niamh lay atop his body but then shuffled so that they were side to side instead. She held him, her stomach still contracting slightly and allowed her fingers to explore his back, his chest, his belly. Suddenly she felt tearful and overwhelmed.

'Niamh,' Helligan murmured

'Mmm?'

He paused, 'Are you all right?'

The words echoed without her response but Niamh was exhausted, too wrought and overwhelmed to respond straight away. Despite it all, despite the lost years and the suddenness of his reappearance, despite the pain and loss which had permeated her for so long, she knew the truth was still ever as it had been.

'I love you,' she finally whispered. 'I love you Helligan and I have missed you so much.'

Helligan pulled her in tightly to him, his arms holding her safe and secure in a promise that the lonely times were over.

'I love you too Niamh,' he whispered into her hair, 'I would not have survived what I have, if I had not had you to fight for.'

'I don't understand?'

'And for now you don't need to. Sleep, my love, let some of this tension on your back leave you now. We have a long day of it tomorrow.'

Fourteen

As the dawn broke, Helligan awoke from a fitful sleep and lay a moment listening to the chirping and song of a brave bird which had found the tower. The island was not entirely free of animal life, but it was rare enough that the birdsong was a somewhat unique treat to hear within the tower walls. Niamh was holding tightly to him in her sleep. He lay a moment revelling in that touch but then kissed her and removed himself carefully from her embrace. He paused a moment, stroking her hair as she slept, but then washed quickly in the cold water of the washbowl by the window and pulled on his trousers and tunic. The light was still dim and the echoes of the magic storm without were soothing. When Helligan had come first to this place, straight from Zaikanis, the sages had taken him in without question and so those echoes and crashes had been his introduction to a world outside of the draconis clutch. Helligan trusted these men with his life, just as he'd once trusted them with his secrets, a gamble which had paid off. When Niamh's father had turned on the mage council, back in the Wolder wars, forcing them to come to his side and serve his foul intentions, that was when Helligan had really realised what he needed to do to fulfil his mission. Cut the head off the beast – the golden king, rotten through and through. Helligan glanced at that man's daughter. He'd known almost instantly upon meeting her that she too was a key in that, many years before he'd come to realise she was half-fae. He'd known it even before he had loved her, when she'd been just another frightened child fleeing devastation. Helligan leaned in and kissed Niamh's forehead, his heart aching for her. He'd certainly never expected to fall in love with a human, that at least had been a shock to them both! Unlawful, as was Alistair's life, despite that no mention of any repercussions to the boy had been made at his trial. He was safer here, though, either way.

Helligan pulled on his tunic. It was silken, finer than the clothing he was used to. He'd been a Wolder Lord for so long that he'd become used to the coarser materials and fabrics they used to make clothing. He had sat at court before, but for less than an annum and even then, he'd not given into foppishness, despite the stereotypes about the Draconis love of wealth and luxury. Helligan did up the two buttons at the throat and then pulled the lace. He was in no position to be choosy! And what person complained of having luxury thrust upon them anyway? Mentally, he shook his head at himself and smiled.

Once dressed, Helligan knelt back on the bed and ran his fingers through Niamh's hair until her eyes opened sleepily.

'I will be downstairs,' he whispered, 'you get some more rest.'

Niamh nodded and put up her lips for a kiss. Helligan gave it and then departed the room.

Downstairs, the two sages that had been their hosts the night before sat at breakfast. Sages Horren and Tamm would likely not show their faces whilst there were guests. Years of magic use took their toll, and left physical signs too, especially when the person wielding them allowed the magika to prolong life where it should already have left the form. Tamm had half a face of stone now, with an eye which was blind, white and staring. Horren was bald, bent and gnarled like the trees from which he took power. The back of his body was like bark, rough and flaking. This was the penance for living years longer than a human should, and yet what choice did they have but to go on, when all their successors had been culled?

'Good morning, sages.' Helligan said, sitting. The room was a large one, on the ground floor of the tower. It was built with a higher ceiling than many of the rooms, and carried the theme of being lined with old books upon almost every free surface. The walls were stone, but covered here and there with wood which had been magically fused with the stone to offer not just extra warmth, but decoration too. The table in the middle was piled high with the morning feast, likely prepared by these two men themselves, as no servants worked in the tower, no one without at least some magical inclination could even enter the place. Back in Helligan's days as a member of the council, chores had been rota-scheduled daily duties. He supposed the new initiates might take on those roles now, for the time-being at least.

'Lord Helligan, it is good to see you back,' Graves said. His eyes had not been that shade of purple before, maybe another magika mutation in the making? Helligan hoped that the old man would be able to repress it better than Horren and Tamm.

'And to be so.'

'Did you sleep well?'

'I did.' Helligan said, then tore a hunk of bread to dip in the sweet nectarlaine syrup pot. The sages kept their own bumble-flies to create the syrup and to Helligan's mind nothing in the world quite rivalled the taste.

'Tell me about these children you have brought us?' Orien said, slicing into a tart fel-fruit, 'The queen gathered them herself?'

'I know little but that what she has told me of them. She is better to ask for details. All I know is that after her coronation, she made it her mission to rebuild the mage council herself. She had no idea, of course, that you were still alive and so she gathered them to her.'

'And each is tested?'

'They all have skill.'

'Hmmm,' Orien murmured, 'To accept a female mage…'

'… is to acknowledge all the untapped power that has been at your fingertips for a millennium. I know.' Helligan interrupted.

'There have always been witches, sorceresses…' Graves cut in. 'But never a mage…'

'All magicka is one and the same, you know that as well as I. You have few options, my friend.'

'Helligan is correct…' a voice came from the doorway, weak, with a croak which made it gravelly. Helligan looked up to see a figure in the doorway. The old man was bent almost double, and there was more of tree than there was of man. Helligan pressed his lips, Sage Tamm had been past 120 years old when he'd seen him last, but the past twenty or so years seemed to have aged him exponentially. He limped into the room, and Helligan stood to take his arm. The old man did not take his offered assistance though, merely walked at his side. Orien murmured an uncomfortable greeting and Graves continued with his thick stew. How a man could eat stew at 6am, Helligan did not know.

'We are an order depleted, on the edge of extinction, and you would turn away a candidate because she is a girl?' Tamm spoke to the other two. 'Are you madmen?'

'I merely said it has not been done before, not that we should not…' Orien murmured, not looking the deformed man in the eye. Helligan's spine bristled slightly but he said nothing. It was not his place to have a part in this argument.

'We are all knocking on the door of the goddess,' Tamm said. 'Admittedly, some of us more than others…' he let out a thin chuckle, 'Let us take them all. The girl too. It is only tradition which dictates a mage must be male. Let the girl show us what she is capable of.'

'She must match at least the weakest of the boys, if we are to keep her,' Graves said, 'that is final.'

'Agreed,' Helligan said. If what Niamh had said of the girl was true, she'd easily wipe the floor with all of them save the eldest – and Alistair… 'You will take my son too, keep him under your protection?'

'Of course, my lord, the prince shines with potential and already his deeds have come to our ears,' Orien said, 'on that we are already agreed!'

'And of you?' Orien asked, 'Will you accept our offer to become a sage and remain to teach your boy?'

Helligan parted his lips to speak but was interrupted by another chuckle from Sage Tamm, 'Lord Dericaflae did not sacrifice all that he has in order to take up the mantle of a scholar and live with a bunch of old men,' he wheezed, 'he has no place here and you know it as well as I do, Orien!'

'Whilst ever the council will have my love and protection,' Helligan said, 'my loyalty is to Queen Niamh and my place is at her side.'

'A shame,' Orien muttered, 'but as you will…'

Niamh arrived much at a time with her initiates, some two hours later. Sage Tamm had by then already departed and so it was just Helligan, Orien and Graves who still sat at the breakfast table as the rest of the party arrived. Niamh looked refreshed indeed. For the past few days she'd had the air of one run down and tired, but suddenly she shone again. Her hair was brushed and braided down her back, tied with four silver rings, and her gown, the same she'd travelled in, was worn over shoulders which stood firm rather than drooping. She smiled when Helligan caught her eye and he was sure he saw a blush in her cheeks. Goddess love the girl! The initiates too looked refreshed, if somewhat nervous, especially the younger two. Elenni seemed the calmest of them all. He was dressed in all black, much like the old standard tunics of the council and Helligan wondered if he had modelled his outfit thus purposely. Friggan was much more elaborate with a velvet, silver-threaded, fur-lined red jerkin and black hose. Hardly sensible wear for training but it was the new fashion. His long buckwheat hair was combed and tied back. His face showed the youth of his mere nineteen years, and his manner was one of privilege despite that Niamh had said they were all common born. He'd obviously taken to court life and as long as he kept his vanity in check, Helligan could see the potential for great magical prowess in his eyes. Of the two older boys, he was most likely to become a court mage, Elenni a sage.

Then came the girl. Goddess she was a pretty thing with her chocolate curls, styled much like Niamh's, and her sharp gaze. Despite that he had eyes for none but his wife, Helligan could see how the girl was causing a stir. Once she reached an age for such, she'd be an unstoppable force amongst the young men of the court! Nervoria was chewing her lip slightly, but she was also taking everything in. Good. She more than the others, would need to prove herself. Fast on Nervoria's heels was Alistair – Helligan mentally noted how often that was the case – obviously, his son was not unaffected by the girl's beauty despite that she must have been three or four years his senior.

Finally, the youngsters entered. Neither could have passed fourteen years of age yet and their demeanours were younger still. Helligan still did not yet know them apart. Not only were they similar in age, but of appearance too, both small and with non-descript dark hair. They weren't related, as far as Helligan was aware, but they could well have been.

Once all of the children had entered the room, Helligan ushered them to the table to eat. They would have a trial ahead of them in the following hours and Helligan wanted them fed and ready for it. Niamh took her seat at his side and Helligan touched her arm.

'Did you sleep well, my queen?' he asked, the hint of teasing intentional. She'd asked the same of him at a crowded breakfast table after the first night they'd spent together. Niamh chuckled and caught his eye quickly, but she did not reply, simply loaded her plate with food. For one so slender, Niamh had never skimped on breakfast.

The first trial for the initiates was the same as the first trial Helligan had undertaken before them. It was a simple test, to ensure that they were able to use the magicka within. In the basement of the tower was a training area. The location was essential for the lack of available space out of doors due to the mana-storm. At the bottom of the steps, the room was completely open, lit by torches all the way around the walls. The stonework was not covered below, and the room was chill despite the wooden-plank floor. Majoritively, the room was empty. There stood at the far wall a small fireplace, and above that a jar with a rose in it. Helligan supressed a smile. He remembered this challenge well – he had not excelled in it despite that he'd been fully grown and well used to magic use upon his arrival. It had been the task to remove his cockiness and to teach him the value of control over power.

'Now,' Master Orien spoke, 'This challenge at first might seem easy, but the second clause is harder and is as important as the first. You are, whilst standing at least a yard away from the fireplace, to light the fire in the grate. If you succeed, that will be one point in your favour. However to really excel at this task, you must not damage the rose in any way. Not by heat, by smashing of the jar, nor by boiling of the water. Do you all understand?'

All six students nodded.

'I do not expect any of you to master this first time,' Helligan murmured, remembering his own first attempt and how disastrous it had been.

Alistair swallowed, then wet his lips. 'But I have never used a fire magic,' he spoke up. 'My affinity is with water and ice?'

'As is mine, son, and yet ever I have fought with ice-fire… we are draconis blood, no matter our element, we can make fire.' Helligan pressed his lips, the memory of his own pain fleeting before his eyes.

'But I don't understand how water can become fire, I… I can only make hail?'

'That is for you to resolve.' Orien spoke firmly.

Alistair frowned slightly, but a brow bent in thought rather than petulance.

Orien clapped his hands together and a quiet fell. Nervoria stepped up first, taking the lead. This challenge was more difficult than first appeared for the lack of elemental base. All mages needed a connection to their element, in order to cast its image adequately. Nervoria first attempted to force free a flame bolt without a focus. Nothing happened but a faint crackle about her fingers. Helligan saw her sigh but inwardly he was impressed, magic without a base was hugely difficult! In human form, he could muster little more than she had of fire, especially without his focus – his dragon essence – close. He glanced to Orien, who caught his gaze and nodded, he was impressed too. Nervoria tried the same tactic twice, and then paused again. She looked down to the stone floor below and then at the fireplace. She put a hand down and touched the floor, causing two stones to rise closer to the fireplace. These she led into the grate and then began to move together. They created a spark, but little else.

'Close enough,' Master Graves spoke, but without the previous hostility he'd had when addressing the girl. 'Very good!'

Nervoria pulled back but her lips were set, her eyes dark. She still underestimated what she'd done. That would be a lesson for her, to be patient in her abilities.

The two younger ones came next, both together. The smaller of the two held out a hand and the other lay his flat against it. Interesting, but not unheard of for two to work together thus. The younger boy closed his eyes and pulled forth something of a bolt from the air.

'Good grief, he's using his brother as a focus!' Master Orien muttered.

'An unusual tactic,' Helligan agreed, but watched as the bolt fired. It was feeble and didn't quite last long enough to reach the kindling but still, it was a bolt! The other boy then used the same tactic. His bolt was stronger but rocked the fireplace causing the rose to fall.

'Still a very good effort,' Niamh said from behind Helligan.

'Indeed. Did you teach them this art, of tying together?' Orien asked.

'I suppose, yes, they were always stronger together.'

Graves stepped forwards to replace the rose and damp the fires whilst they spoke. His magic was quick and effective, despite that he carried no focus. Mostly the sages, especially the older ones, no longer needed them.

'Interesting. Now what of this young fop…' Helligan said, indicating Friggan. He was interested in how the youth would manage the feat. Friggan stepped forward and surveyed the task. His hands rubbed together but he did not attempt the spell, instead he turned back to the masters, Niamh, and Helligan. 'Is the challenge impossible?' he asked.

'Impossible?'

'Yes? A lesson in learning which battles to fight?'

'An interesting theory, but no.' Graves spoke.

'Hmm…' the boy said, then shrugged. 'Might I then ask for guidance?'

'Just get on with it, Frig!' Nervoria laughed, and the two younger ones joined her. Elenni, throughout was very quiet, as was Alistair. Helligan repressed a smile in watching Graves try not to roll his eyes. In Helligan's time at the council there had been an initiate similar – Jenson Hoist – he had been just the same, ever looking for the hidden meaning or shortcut. He'd become one of the best and had served at Court when Helligan had. He pushed down the thought. It was easier not to dwell on such, in the aftermath of what had happened to the poor court mages.

Friggan stood again in position before the fireplace. He inhaled and exhaled a few times, and then put out his hand and muttered a quiet incantation. The logs seemed to glow red but then spluttered out again. Helligan glanced to Niamh who smiled smugly. She obviously had expected this! Friggan turned back to them with a chuckle, 'got it to glow,' he said, unnecessarily.'

'Good, try again,' Orien said. His eyes glowing… and the old man *should* be impressed. It wasn't the solution to the test, nobody expected initiates to be able to cast just from within and so all of Niamh's mages were surpassing expectations so far! Friggan tried again, letting the magicka escape him with a roar. Even Helligan felt it. It rushed past and then for a split second, the logs ignited.

Niamh gasped, and Helligan too felt the shock. Thank the goddess he'd insisted on training, such power would be worse than dangerous, unchecked!

Friggan stepped back as the fire fizzled back out. 'Looks like that's me for now,' he said. 'That's all I had so I don't think I'm doing it right…'

'Doing it right?' Orien questioned.

'I mean, I don't think that is what I am *supposed* to do!'

'Are you sure?'

'Yes, for now. I will ponder it further and get it tomorrow,' the boy smiled, then winked at Nervoria who was making an effort to ignore him.

Helligan put a hand to his son's arm, 'Did you want to go next, son?'

Alistair pulled back. He looked nervous. 'Let Elenni go first…'

'There's no need to be shy, son,' Niamh murmured.

'I-I am… am not but I a-a-am not done thinking yet,' Alistair replied, his voice a whisper. Helligan caught Niamh's eyes and she nodded subtly; she'd heard the stutter too. It was painfully similar to her own. Elenni stepped up though. He, like the others, attempted first to make the flame without the focus, but he could not even produce what Nervoria had and so stopped and pondered.

Helligan watched him carefully. He had the boy pinned as a thinker and thus the most likely to ace this challenge.

'May I… may I look about the room?' Elenni finally asked.

'Of course,' Graves and Orien caught each other's eye. A smile began on Helligan's face. The boy was on the right track. Behind him, he could hear the others speaking, Friggan flirting outrageously with Nervoria, who was batting him down playfully whist the younger boys teased. Alistair stood at his side though, silently taking it all in.

Elenni skimmed the room quickly, and then bent to pick something up. Helligan watched him carefully as Niamh shushed the others who were becoming almost rowdy. They were still little more than children, after all. Elenni came back to the spot where the others had stood. Helligan saw that he had a small piece of straw in his hand. He pulled again on what was within, pressing together the fingers on his left hand. A tiny green spark flickered. At once the room fell silent. Elenni was too slow the first time, but after three attempts, he managed to ignite the straw. He stood still for a second or two, concentrating, and crushed the straw in his hand. for a moment, Helligan thought he was giving in, but then a rush of green slid from his fingers, not a bolt but a smoke. Ah! So he was guided by air then, forest-led, if the tint was anything to go by. An ancestor of the brother clan, the Emerald Draconis! The green sped up though, as it left Elenni's fingers, not entirely under control, and so although it lit the fire, the rose wobbled and then fell so that the glass shattered on the floor. Elenni still smiled though and turned back to them.

'The lesson was to look for a means of focus rather than to try without?' he asked.

'Very good,' Helligan said, 'and very close!'

Friggan came forward to grab Elenni and pull him back into the group whilst Nervoria congratulated him loudly. Helligan turned to his son whilst Graves moved back to clean up the mess again.

'And have you thought how you will proceed?' he asked.

'I have.'

'Good. You will do fine, son!'

Alistair looked up at him, eyes worried but filled with the same emotion that sometimes Niamh's held – unreadable. He waited patiently for Graves to move aside, and then stepped forward. Niamh stepped closer to Helligan and put her hand on his arm. He covered it with his own and turned to watch Alistair. The boy knelt at once, and put his palms onto the floor. The ground shuddered. Alistair stiffened, visibly, and then something began to happen, a glow about his form, pinks and purples, a flash of blue.

'What is it?' Nervoria asked, coming to join them whilst the boys squabbled behind, 'What is he doing?'

'He's channelling the lightning,' Helligan murmured, quiet as though not to disturb Alistair. The boy gasped suddenly, and then stood up and thrust two bolts of lightning at the fireplace. It ignited with a crash, hitting the mantelpiece, the rose and the wall. Another loud clash came to Helligan's ears as Friggan knocked over a scuttle in his panic to swing around and witness the explosion of dust and fire which suddenly seemed to engulf the entire back wall. Alistair gasped again and then turned about, looking almost panicked. Niamh moved to put a hand on his shoulder as Orien and Graves moved forward to put out the flames. The other mages moved in too, all patting Alistair's back, soothing him despite the devastation of his magic, whilst the air became momentarily choked with a thick sooty smog.

With the magic of Graves and Orien both, the fire was quickly contained and extinguished. Orien returned to the party and chuckled. 'Well, that certainly lit the fire…' he said, his eyes kind. Helligan inwardly thanked him for that.

Alistair just stared at him. His eyes were dry but his face was redder than beets.

'I… I'm sorry! I… I…'

'What you did… was exactly what your father did, on his first attempt…' Graves said with a wink and then smiled and indicated the door, 'I think that's enough practice, for now, don't you all?'

Fifteen

Niamh piled up vegetables and chuck meat onto a plate and then sat herself down at the edge of the long table in the mage-tower dining hall. She'd aided in the preparation of the meal, with both Elenni and Friggan as her aides. The chores were evenly split, they'd been told, and all would learn to master all of them as part of their training. Niamh had tried to imagine Helligan there slaving away over a hot stove and found the image lacking. Such contemplation of his past brought forth new questions, questions she'd once been too young and naïve to ponder. Draconis lived about seven or eight hundred years. At what end of the scale was Helligan? Was he young still? Or had he walked ten men's lives already? He obviously had family – a brother at least, but who else? Had he had a sweetheart there, before he'd been sent to perform his mission? How had he come to train as a mage? Had the sages known what he was? – she suspected that the latter answer was probably that yes, they had.

Niamh ate delicately. Her stomach was in knots, mainly from the events of the night before, as well as the knowledge that she was set to leave her son the following day in the care of the mages of the tower. Helligan sat across the table. He was deep in discussion with Elenni, a glass of honey-wine in his hand and his plate cleared already. His eyes moved to meet hers though and a small smile curled his lip. Niamh returned the smile, not her most confident but still a smile anyhow.

At the other end of the table, Nervoria and Friggan were chatting lightly and Niamh was pleased to see her son joining in, albeit shyly. The two youngsters sat in awed quiet, sharing a plate. They were ever going to be close, Niamh thought, you'd think they were twins, but she'd found them not only in separate towns, but with many miles between them. As she watched, the younger one, Maven, poured another glass of wine and put it to his lips. Niamh hoped that in the future the sages would keep more of an eye on that – it must have been his third glass and he was not far off childhood still.

'My Queen, might I tempt you with another drink?' Master Orien spoke from her side, making her jump slightly. 'You have barely touched anything.'

'I… just a little, thank you.'

He lifted the jug and poured her a glass of the tart wine. Honey-wine was often blended with berries and this one was such, with even a hint of fel-fruit in its thick sweetness. Niamh took a swig and then placed the goblet back down.

'Master Orien,' she spoke. As ever official business gave her more clarity of words and this was a conversation she had inwardly rehearsed. 'I wondered if you could teach me a little history? I hear you have rather an extensive library here?'

'Certainly! If I have the knowledge I will happily share and if not, I could look it up for you. What is it which you would like to know?'

'I am sure that you might have heard rumours of the attacks on my kingdom…'

Niamh caught a sight of Helligan's head turning as she spoke, his attention caught.

'Not much penetrates here now, my Queen. I am afraid I have not,' Orien said.

Master Graves too shook his head. 'I have had news of the wars and battles, of course, but no specific rumours,' the old man agreed.

Niamh sighed inwardly, this meant more speaking, more explanation! 'You know, then, that my nephew's cause is fought, by his grandmother, my late father's second wife?'

'Yes.'

'Good. Well on the eve of the last big battle at Anglemarsh, some of Magda's men defected. They, and one of my own commanders spoke of… of… men standing, once dead, and… and of them walking once again…'

'Necromancy?' Master Orien exclaimed, 'Surely not!'

'Apparently so. My… my man, Shale – one of my advisors – questioned the men extensively and… and it seems that… that it is a low-skilled necromancer. This individual, a hooded figure, can raise them but not for very long, and then they… they fall again but it is… is enough to cause their numbers to swell and we are… are struggling to ascertain who it is and why this person might be… be fighting against me.'

'This is grim news indeed,' Master Graves said.

Helligan leaned forward, pushing his plate aside. 'What of your tomes? Do you have any on this form of magic here? Not all of my brothers were massacred…'

'This is not the work of a human,' that was Orien, 'It's not possible…'

'Unlikely, or impossible?' Niamh asked.

'Impossible. When the rift was formed and our forefathers settled here in this tower, there were two types of magicka which none were able, nor ever have been able, to bend. That of druidic shape-changing, and necromancy.'

'And yet, shape-shifters exist.' Helligan said.

'Not of our kind, Dragon. Out in the forests there is talk… but they are Wolder at least, and certainly not common men. Whilst we are all Wolder at heart, very few come to us for training, preferring those such as your sorceress, Mother Morgana…'

'And yet, I came to you from a Wolder village – as far as you knew…' Helligan argued. 'There must have been others?'

'Do you really think, *Helligan the mage*, that there was a man here who did not know what you were, the minute you entered these halls?'

Helligan pressed his lips. His eyes flit to Niamh but she wasn't yet satisfied.

'So such tomes do exist?' she said at length, 'to have been studied and attempted?'

'Well… yes, I suppose.'

Niamh felt her heart skip a beat. It was possible then!

'Perhaps a knowledge stolen and misappropriated on one less than human,' Graves mused. 'That is possible.'

Niamh's eye glanced over the children. Nervoria was watching them, with Alistair obviously picking up on their conversation too. Niamh wet her lips. 'Shall we continue this later?' she asked.

Helligan followed her eye, 'Aye, I think that wise,' he murmured.

Later, the night had darkened as much as ever it did with the lightning without causing its constant flicker and glow. Niamh had become accustomed to that though, even in two short days. The adults of the party had moved up into one of the library rooms above. The whole tower seemed to be lined with books, but up here were tables too, and chairs comfortable enough to sit in for a time to study. Soon, her son would be one with these books! The thought dragged out feelings of pride from her very core. The room was a little dustier than those below, but Niamh did not mind that, other than the smell of dust, the place was almost as homey as her library back at home in Anglemarsh. Helligan sat on a chair across the room, he was slumped with his forearms on his thighs. He looked tired, Niamh realised, drained. That worried her too. In their previous acquaintance Helligan had always been the one to keep her going. Despite that she knew this was most likely the result of his recent illness, it was enough to set her worrying.

Master Orien entered with Graves behind him, both carrying books, and then, to Niamh's surprise, the more elusive two sages. Tamm, the tree-creature who had once been a man came first and sat himself down. The other, Horran was quite the sight to behold too. His face was almost rigid and grey like stone. One of his eyes was blind, white and staring and one of his shoulders seemed immobile too. Goddess! The man was turning to the very stone he wielded. Niamh's mind flit to the children – was this their future? Was it worth it?

Masters Orien and Graves put the books they carried down on the table and then sat themselves down. The two oldest sages sat wordlessly. Master Orien took the seat closest to Niamh.

'My queen,' he spoke, 'I have gathered these tomes and have spent the past two hours reading them. There is little we have not spoken of between their covers. No descriptions of how the magic is achieved, nor any notes where people have tried. Mostly they speak of the dark-elf, Oliah and his blood sacrifice…'

'The blood of his beloved,' Helligan said.

'Beloved? More his captive?' Sage Horren spoke for the first time, his voice slurred from the part of his mouth which no longer moved properly.

'That is how I read it, too,' Niamh agreed.

Helligan's eyes brushed over them both. 'Oliah and Oasha were, in my people's version of events at least, very much in love. That is why his sacrifice of her life was so potent. She was not his captive, she was his wife and he loved her. The focus would not have worked otherwise.'

Graves and Orien both nodded, it certainly made sense and, if true, it showed Oliah's desperation more so. To Niamh that was worse, somehow.

'Your tomes are probably better than ours,' Tamm spoke, 'everything we have is hearsay of a time nobody quite remembers.'

Helligan nodded.

'These books give no indication of how to practice such magics,' Graves spoke, 'but they give hints and with enough experimentation… not human though, I repeat, no blood magic is usable by humans… you know this, Lord Helligan!'

'No,' he mused, 'human blood itself usually does not contain enough magicka. What of my brother mages? Do we have a definitive list of who was killed and who fled?'

Orien produced a piece of parchment with lush thick handwriting on it. 'Here, to the best of my knowledge.'

Helligan took the parchment and ran his eyes over it. His lips were very tight. Niamh's heart went out to him, once those had been his friends, close enough to be called "Brother".

'Brothers' Jennings, Corl, Nirroas and Griffen executed by beheading or quartering,' Helligan read aloud. 'And Harrison… goddess! He was just a child!'

'He was fifteen – old enough, by the old King's reckoning. He was hung drawn and quartered on the great lawn beside his mentor, Griffen, the rest were beheaded.'

'How did one so young come to be thus… thus sentenced?' Niamh asked, trying not to shudder at the image of a fifteen-year-old boy – just like her boys who lay sleeping below – half-dead from hanging, being sliced from throat to groin. The victim was often still alive throughout the ordeal and so watching as his innards were pulled free of his body and burned whilst still attached to him. In her mind's eye, Niamh saw Friggan laid thus on the board before her father's court, or even little Alis, and found a shudder. Had her father's people cheered? Had they roared and laughed at the agony of that child's horrific death? Niamh had once walked the traitor's walk herself. Her father had ordered and almost been granted, her death by execution but even in the fear and horror of such, at least she'd walked with anticipation of a quick and easy death. How must it have felt to walk on, knowing that there would be no dignity, no release until the very end?

'It was done for cruelty, nothing more, to send a message out to the others. Griffen was the most respected of them all barr Helligan, and his charge beloved by all. Their deaths were a message to all. Once served, it gave the others a cleaner death too.'

'Why was the boy even at court?' Niamh asked, still aching within for this unknown boy who in her mind now wore the face of each of her child-mages.

'He was our apprentice,' Helligan said, then sighed. 'He was so eager to be a court-mage, so disciplined and studious.'

'Goddess bless him – all of them,' Niamh whispered, 'I… I am glad that we…' she could not finish the sentence; it was too painful and her emotions set her mind reeling again. Helligan's eyes ran over her and she saw he mirrored the emotion.

'The goddess takes the dead to her bosom, even the tortured,' Tamm spoke. His gravelly voice set a shiver into Niamh's spine but she was careful not to show it. 'It is the living we must concern ourselves with.'

'Agreed,' Helligan said, then looked back to the scroll. 'Dannis, Killen and Forne are all dead since? You have tracked them down?'

'Yes.'

'So that leaves… Loris Pregater, Portian White and Janel Hores, to my mind. Those are the only three we are sure are not dead, at least?'

'Yes.'

'But nobody knows where they are now?'

'No, nor even if they still live now.'

'When they fled, why did they not come here?' Niamh asked.

'The risk of infiltration and discovery was too great directly after the executions. We…' Orien sighed, then took her eyes. 'I know it was cruel, my queen, but security of our location was paramount. We took down the magics which allowed the council members to cross. Nobody could get in or out. It has been thus since and it was only when we sensed Lord Helligan close by two days since that we allowed the gate to reopen.'

'So we have three powerful mages, all gone into obscurity, all of whom are likely angry to have had the doors of the tower closed on them?' Niamh asked. 'All of whom have had access to these books?'

'In a nutshell, yes.' Helligan said.

Niamh pulled her reins and allowed the wind to whip her hair about her. She was mounted on her usual horse, a white palfrey she called Asha, atop the cliffs which led up from the beach where Helligan had sealed off the mage tower once more. Whilst it was bliss to be free of the constant rumbles of thunder and flashes of lightning, the wind was more bitter up on the clifftops despite the glorious sunshine which beamed down on them. Niamh pulled her cape tighter around her against the wind. She still wore the same clothes she had been wearing for the past three days – she'd not thought to pack another set – and the scent of her body was starting to rise. She'd doused herself, armpits of the dress and all, in rose-water but still she was looking forward to a long bath before the fire in her chamber at Anglemarsh, and a clean gown. She paused her mare and waited as Helligan ascended the cliffs. Once again, his using magic in their exit of the tower had flared up something in his wounds, rendering him a little slower than before. Niamh was determined to have Sister Freya have another look at him when they got back.

Helligan's horse finally appeared at the top of the slope and his eyes found hers with a small smile. If it weren't for the slowness of his horse, the occasional wince and hand to his back, she'd never have known anything was wrong. Niamh smiled back. Helligan had come to her chamber the night before yet again, but had fallen asleep almost instantly after making love, exhausted and beaten. Much like he'd done with her the night before, she'd simply held him as he slept, her own sleep pulling her away more slowly and not allowing for restfulness. She had slept enough though, not to be too exhausted for the trip back.

On the way to the tower, Helligan, Niamh and the children had taken the road, but the way back, however with just the two of them, they turned the horses towards the more densely overgrown forest.

'We're fairly close to Havensguard, are we not?' Niamh asked.

'It is about a half day's journey south,' Helligan agreed.

'If I were not so eager to get home I would suggest a visit. You seem troubled still.'

'I am. I'll come back to see Morgana once you are safely home. I have matters to discuss with her.'

Niamh nodded and then stretched her shoulders. 'I need to rest soon.'

'I too. If I recall, there is a glade close by with a pool which stays warm until dusk on a day like today. I'd like to bathe the dust out of my skin, if you will indulge me?.'

Niamh nodded and allowed Helligan to take up the lead. The trees grew denser for a mile or so, but then suddenly they opened up, the glade one of lush green and abundant growth. Helligan dismounted and led his horse in, then turned to Niamh. She sat, still mounted, awestruck at the beauty before her. The grass was soft and lush, past her ankles and in it, dotted here and there were little flowers of red, white, yellow, pink and so on. At the centre was a dip, and in the dip, surrounded by tall reeds was a pond. The land moved up, behind, so as to form something of a cliff-face, giving the impression of privacy and from here fell a trickling white waterfall. The entire glade was a welcome sight for tired eyes and Niamh got the impression that should they have been a wholly human party, this might have seemed not to exist at all. She dismounted and tied her horse, and then moved to Helligan's side.

'It's… breath-taking…' she murmured.

'It is. Will you come into the waters with me?'

Niamh nodded.

Helligan stripped off his tunic and put his hand to his leather trousers but Niamh's eyes widened as she looked over his back. Deep in the skin, under it even, were a series of thick black bruise-like lines. Not straight but curved and breaking into rivulets like veins. Black, fading to purple, they led from each shoulder-blade, out into the soft tissues of his shoulders, down into the middle of his back.

'Helligan... what...' she gasped, and stood to pull his hair away from the white skin of his back for a better look. Helligan froze as her hand brushed them, and she felt the shudder of him repressing a wince.

'Helligan, what is... what are... these?' she whispered.

'What is it?' he asked, his voice was dull and quiet over the swishing water of the waterfall. 'What do you see?'

'Here,' she whispered, 'some sort of... I don't know, infection? The skin is pure and unraised, but there are odd bruise-like lines... under the skin...'

Helligan seemed to tense, but then turned to face her. His eyes showed that tiredness she'd seen in them several times, and his lips pressed tightly. He put a hand up to her cheek but dropped it before it touched her skin.

'Helligan?' she whispered.

'I didn't... I don't... want to burden you with this,' Helligan said.

'With what? Oh goddess – what are you still hiding from me?'

'Niamh...' Helligan paused again, then, 'Niamh, you have accepted my absence in the manner that only a heart as big and sweet as yours can, and you have not asked me why I was away for so long, and how I came back.' he said.

'I... I have pondered it...'

Helligan tugged her so that she sat down on the wet and muddy riverbank with him, swimming forgotten. He wet his lips again, and then spoke, his tone was very grave. 'When first

I returned home, I was tried and imprisoned by my people for my crimes.'

'But you did only what they told you to do! You recovered the sphere! You came across the barrier in the first place only on their say-so!'

'Not… not entirely so, but enough that it would be arguable. That was not my crime though. My crime was to show form – I alone allowed humanity the understanding that my kind still exist. More so, I broke a fundamental rule, I fell in love with a human, married her, and had a son…'

'Me…'

'Yes, you, my love. And I knew it when I married you, I knew that I risked it all.'

'Yet you did it anyway?'

'And I would again,' he said, looking at her with eyes that burned. '…I was sentenced to die.'

'Goddess!'

'My mother's pleas for my life, when they came, were expected though, and so I suspect that the death sentence was never intended to be carried out,' he plucked a piece of grass and played with it in his fingers, 'I think it was all planned. My father… my father is… was… a man of great status amongst our kind – he was due to rule our people for this century and so… so I don't suppose that I was ever at risk, really.'

'A cruel lesson though,' Niamh managed, her belly hurting with the memory of her own near execution, and that whilst heavily pregnant. Her own father would not have made pains to give her mercy, though, he'd wanted her blood.

'I was pardoned, but my indiscretion was still an embarrassment. It was my father who suggested that I be imprisoned for a hundred years. That way I was punished and you would be dead by the time I was released. My dragon essence was preserved, so that only my human body aged, and I was left to rot. I should have remained so, if it was not for my brother who took me out on the death of my father. He offered me a bargain. To abdicate the position I inherited on Father's death and allow him to take up the mantle of head of our clan. In return I could take banishment instead of imprisonment and come home.'

'And you took this bargain?'

'Yes.'

'You gave up leadership of your clan, to come home to me?'

'Yes,' he said, 'An easy decision!'

'And the marks on your back?'

Helligan paused and took up her hand, he kissed it and then sighed, 'Zaikanis – that is, our kingdom – is a network of platformed fortresses placed up the tallest mountain in the forest to the southeast of Anglemarsh. It is inaccessible to any who cannot fly. When… when a draconis is banished from Zaikanis certain measures are… are put into place to see that they do not return… that they *cannot* return.'

Niamh did not understand for a moment, but then realisation set in. 'Oh… oh goddess! Not your wings?'

Helligan nodded, 'yes, my wings. They are gone… what you see on my back is the wound to my core, burning into this form where it sits on my dragon-form. The trauma of the loss, of the injury is burning its way through my human skin too.'

Niamh clutched his hand, horror coming over her in waves, along with guilt at what he had endured in order to come home to her. Helligan held tightly to her hand for a moment, but then released it.

'I will recover,' he said, 'I have had healing magics administered by my brother's elven healers but it will just take time. Come, bathe with me?'

Niamh allowed him to take her hand, but inside, her blood was boiling. She paused still and he turned back to her, his eyes soft.

'I just want my life back,' he said simply, 'I want normality now.'

Niamh pushed the emotions down within, and wet her lips, forcing her anger away. 'Come then, let us bathe,' she whispered, her fingers pulling at the laces which held her gown closed, 'and… and if you wish…'

Helligan smiled, hooking an arm around her waist, and pulling her in so that they were nose to nose, 'If my queen will allow a common draconis serf to pleasure her too, I am yours to command,' he said, then claimed her lips. Niamh allowed his kisses to chase away the mixed emotions but deep in her belly, she could feel the thorn of anger still at his people.

Sixteen

The smoke was visible from miles away. Twisting, weaving plumes of grey and black which reached up their grasping fingers into the skies. Even a flame shooting up here and there – magical flame, for none could ever rise so high and nor could they flash with the crispness of the purple flame. Helligan's mouth was dry, his chest heavy. He glanced over to Niamh. Her grip on her reins were white, her face a panicked grimace. He knew already, and so did she. Her reasoning about the safety of leaving had been flawed, and her castle had fallen. All about, houses stood empty and abandoned, even so many miles away. Doors stood open and belongings strewn. Helligan couldn't tell if the occupants had fled, or been taken. His eyes moved back to Niamh. He was worried about her more than anything; her daughter had been in the keep. He spoke not though, no words he had could soothe her now, not until they knew what they were dealing with.

The ride was slow and arduous, Niamh's horse was tiring from the speed at which they rode and so she was forced to slow the beast. Helligan was half -tempted to lift her onto his, but that would mean leaving her mount and he knew she was attached to it. As darkness began to fall about them, the lights from the magical flame grew brighter. Helligan spurred his horse a little harder as something caught his eye. This left Niamh a little behind but for now that was fine, his eyesight was better than hers anyhow. He rode for ten minutes or so at speed, until the keep was clear before him, but then paused and waited for Niamh to catch him up. The flames seemed to be concentrated on the gatehouse, on the entrance to the keep. Strange. He glanced back as Niamh arrived at his rear. She turned the horse to meet him, her eyes mad with worry.

'They have taken Anglemarsh in the *three days* we've been absent?' she asked, her voice held the same shock he felt. What army could lay siege to a keep so quickly and then apparently vanish into the ether?

'I… it would seem…' he began but she wasn't really listening anyway so he allowed the words to trail off. He'd not patronize her by telling her what she could already see for herself.

'I have to…' she murmured, and then despite the fear in her eye, the tiredness of her mount, she spurred the horse into a sudden gallop towards the keep. Helligan called her name but she was headstrong and panicked. His eyes ran over the strange wall of flame, examining it. Something didn't sit right at all, that was some sort of barrier, a mirage! Once he realised it, Helligan could make out the blurriness of the magic as it flickered and swirled over something else, something deeper. But why, why place such a powerful spell over the pillaged and ruined keep thus, if there was nothing to hide? Helligan squinted, his horse still at a standstill as his instincts pulled him back from the gate and his eyes began to see the swirl of purple flames behind the mirage.

Goddess! It was a trap!

Niamh didn't seem to notice the danger though, spurring on her horse even faster in her desperation to get to the entrance – likely spurred by thoughts of her daughter and her friends. Helligan had no such concerns and so his mind was clearer.

'Niamh,' he called after her, 'Niamh wait!'

She didn't listen though, headstrong in her panic.

'Niamh!' Helligan shouted again. He spurred his own horse on but she had too much of a head start – he'd never catch her, not unless… Helligan threw up his arm and muttered an incantation, holding his horse with his thighs only as his fingers moved to the essence about his neck. Pain shot through his back, but he ignored it, and then twisted his hand. A wall of wind formed suddenly ahead of Niamh, blue tinged as all his magic was, but unpassable. Niamh pulled her rein, her horse skidding to a stop before it. The horse reared and for a moment Helligan feared that it might throw her but somehow she kept her grip, holding the beast with her own knees. He relaxed, and then called her name again. Niamh spun about and the look on her face was one Helligan had hoped never to see there. Sheer unadulterated grief and pain. She dismounted, leaving the horse where it was, and ran back to him. Helligan dismounted too, but then grunted as she struck his arm with her fist. Not a hard blow, but unexpected.

'Take it down!' she demanded.

Helligan shook his head, 'Niamh you don't…'

'I said take it down!' she almost shrieked, tears exploding from her eyes. 'My… daughter! I need to… she was…'

'It's a trap!' Helligan gripped her flailing hand as she tried to swipe him again. Her face was a sea of tears and snot, her lips pressed and her eyes flaring. 'Calm down! A minute or two to gather our wits will not be the difference now!'

Niamh broke into sobs, finally allowing herself the weakness. Helligan pulled her in and cupped a hand around the back of her head. As he did so, the spell he'd cast beyond vanished, leaving the entrance once again free. Helligan held Niamh for a long moment, his heart aching for her and his lips caressing her hair in a manner he hoped was soothing. He knew and understood her pain, but it served no purpose but to make her reckless. Once the water at his throat had begun to dry and the hiccups in her shoulders calmed, he pulled away gently.

'Up, where that gate looks clear and enterable, there is a magical illusion of some kind,' Helligan said.

Niamh turned back to it, drying her eyes, 'What?' she murmured.

'I can't quite see, but there is a magical flame behind, and the… the gate is covered by an illusion. Had you just ridden in, you were… it is a trap, my love.'

Niamh's eyes widened, her breath shuddering free. 'Goddess,' she murmured, and then looked back to him, 'If Jessaline and Jos… Shale are within…'

'Then they are already captives.'

Niamh's body juddered again as the panic tried to retake her but to Helligan's relief, she controlled it, her face smoothing.

'And so… what?' she said, 'We have to get inside…'

Helligan kissed her, slipping an arm around her shoulders. 'I am going to…' he paused, 'have your bow at hand…'

Niamh nodded and moved back to her horse where the weapon and arrows that fuelled it still hung. Helligan pulled in a deep breath. He had a suspicion that it was using his dragon essence as a focus which was causing the pain, but he had little other choice, if what he suspected was correct. Niamh armed herself and threw her arrows onto her back. Helligan took the rein of her horse as well as his own and tied them to a nearby tree. He then approached the gates to Anglemarsh, slowly and with caution.

'Stay behind me,' he said, as Niamh's steps took her back ahead of him again. The spell he was about to throw was a powerful one and he had no idea what would happen if she stood between him and his target.

'I can fight at your side, Helligan!'

'I know it well, but I'm more afraid that you will get yourself caught in my magic. I don't want to injure you.'

Niamh nodded and moved so that she was stood just behind his shoulder.

'Good,' Helligan murmured, 'Good. Now steady yourself!'

It took a full lungful of breath, heavy concentration, to begin the spell. Helligan was adept at water magics, but what he was about to do used a different force. He resisted the urge to clutch for his focus though, and instead pulled the magika up from below, from the earth. At once he felt it encompass him, a long-lost embrace which blessedly did not hurt. In his years of solitude, Helligan had almost forgotten the feeling of building magika up in his veins, almost forgotten how it felt to be the weapon of the goddess, his own agent, but in her hands. He gasped twice and then fell to one knee, his fist striking the ground as he did so. Niamh gasped, he heard her, and it was that which told him that his spell was working, before he even had a chance to look up and see the damage.

The ground had split slightly, not his intention but good enough, and the little river of torn earth moved like a snake forward towards the gate of Anglemarsh. As it reached it, the illusion shattered, showing Helligan what he had suspected. In truth, behind the illusion, the gate was there but open. There had been no siege then, no battering rams. The gates simply stood open and unharmed. A strange purple fire burned endlessly in the open space between the gateposts, magical fire in a wall – and put there by somebody experienced at such! Behind that, Helligan caught sight of the spine-crawling image of something, somebody, moving.

Helligan's eyes skimmed the figures, it was hard to see how many there were through the flames, but he got the impression that they were hemmed inside, captive rather than waiting to ambush.

'Wh-what is it?' Niamh asked, her hand coming down on his shoulder. Helligan put his own hand up to gently press her fingers, but then stood.

'I fear it is… the worst case scenario,' he said, watching the shadows shuffle and lurch about. Not true men, not anymore.

'The worst case?' she asked.

'Yes. Is there, in this world, anything I can say to convince you to leave here, to leave this as it is now? To go for aid of the Wolder before we storm open gates?'

'None!'

'Fine, then stand back and get ready to defend yourself.'

Niamh raised her bow and Helligan did her the service of not seeing the fear in her eyes, the slight wobble of her hands. He paused a moment, unsure of himself too – not a feeling Helligan relished! – if he were to smash the gates open, he'd want his full strength for what would flood out but that came from using his essence, which aggravated his wounds. He pulled in a deep breath, he had no idea how he'd even combat the flame otherwise though, he just wasn't adept enough with earth-magic. He exhaled slowly, his eyes darting about, but then clenched his jaw and put a hand to his focus. As long as it was done quickly…

'Get the stragglers,' he said to Niamh, and then pulled the sweet blue magika into his body. At once the pain started up again. Helligan grunted but held it. The pain danced down his spine, dull and aching within his flesh, moving like a snake, or more correctly, like a mass of snakes, across his back. He held back the roar of pain though, pushing through with teeth grit so hard that his jaw too started to ache. With a moan, he pushed the magika free, a wave of ice water, blue like the summer's sky but heavy, lethal. The same magic which had shorn his wings free… no! He could not think of that!

At once the purple fire froze, and then smashed. Helligan felt a trickle of water stain his forehead but he could not cease, could not give in to the pain, as an army of what must have been a hundred or more animated bodies spilled free. Soldiers, commoners… and courtiers! Lord Nightingale amongst them! Niamh's own people – her friends! He recognised some of the bodies, some of the women and even children who stumbled free, and so he was sure she would too. He could not break his concentration though, not even to check on her. At once, his magika turned to hot blue fire, bathing their bodies so that they took up with azure flames. They were eerily silent, not screaming or crying, just shuffling on, some still aflame.

'Goddess!' he managed to growl, dropping his hands. He took two long and sweet lungfuls of air, bending so that his hands clasped about his knees just for a moment, but then stood again despite how his brain ordered him to shut down. From behind, three arrows whizzed in quick succession, taking out the closest two men. Good girl – she wasn't giving in to the horror either! Helligan pulled rich, sweet, soothing oxygen into his lungs, he had to go bigger, hotter. He gasped and then put his hand to his focus again. The dragon essence pulsed under his fingers. Helligan closed his eyes, let the magika fill him, and then once again expelled it, but instead of blue flame, he let loose a wave of air so violent it was almost sonic. The wave left his fingers and spilled out in an arc, and – thank the goddess – it worked, rushing forward to knock the figures backwards, scattering and shattering undead bodies. Helligan braced himself, waiting for the next assault, but none came. Silence fell, and the gate remained clear.

'Is that it?' Niamh whispered from behind.

Helligan could not reply, the pain was re-entering his consciousness where the panic of battle was receding. He fell to his knees with a moan, putting his hands into the dusty ground beneath him. Goddess! It felt as though he were being cleaved in twain. His hand tried to move to his back but any movement was enough to render him in agony. His eyes took Niamh's again, a plea, and then he fell facedown into the dusty dry mud.

Seventeen

Niamh spun about as Helligan fell. Her breath left her body in one big exhale as the last of the necromancer's animated bodies fell. Those she could not even look at yet, could not bear to count the dead, to look upon the familiar faces. She rolled Helligan over, checking for a pulse and finding one, and then almost instantaneously being rewarded with the opening of his eyes and a groan of pain. Everything suddenly seemed to be too bright, every sound even the rustling of the trees beyond too loud. Niamh's chest hurt from repressed emotion but she fought everything back and ran her fingers over Helligan's hair. A feeling of warmth began up in her belly, spreading through her. Niamh allowed it to build – a similar thing had happened before, when Jess was a young child and had broken her arm falling from her horse during a lesson. A soft yellow magicka which came from the reflections of light in the beams of the sun as it burned down. Niamh forced the feeling into her fingers and allowed it to spill over Helligan's brow. She was no mage, no sorceress, but if the goddess chose to work through her on occasion, she would not rail against it. Helligan's eyes moved to hers, his lips parting. Niamh moved so that his head was in her lap, protective and mothering.

'What happened?' he murmured, still confused.

The light burning within Niamh faded somewhat, but left enough of the glow to leave her feeling calmer to face the horrors which lay behind her.

'You lost consciousness,' she said in a gentle tone.

'Oh.'

'It's when you use your magic, isn't it?'

'I think so,' Helligan whispered.

'Then you need to stop. I have already seen you almost dead twice, and then lost you for so many years. I don't think my heart able to take very much more of this.'

Helligan nodded, 'I'll have more of a care,' he said.

Niamh kissed his lips and then helped him to sitting. He seemed weak and pale, but at least he was upright and speaking again.

'I have to...' she indicated the keep. 'The bodies... I still don't know if... if my family were... were in there...'

'Shale would not have allowed himself and Jess to be captured, and I'll wager he's taken your sister and your council somewhere safe too.'

'Unless they were taken unawares. Last time I was away Alis nearly died, and now Jess...'

'And both times at my behest.'

'No! Both times my choice. At least Alis is safe now. That is a salve, but I need to find my daughter. If she is alive she will be so frightened and if not then...' she broke off and wet her lips. It still didn't truly seem a possibility.

'Come then,' Helligan struggled to his feet. He was still unsteady, his boots not firm on the worn-down grass on which he stood. Niamh stood too, a hand on his arm.

'I can do this alone if you need more time to recover?' she whispered.

'I can't allow you to do that.'

'And I can't recommend ye to go in there at all...' a voice spoke from behind. Niamh jumped but already she knew that voice. She spun about to see Kilm walking up the path behind them. He was battle-worn, still in torn leather armour with hair which made him look as much the wild man as he was. Mud encrusted his face and there was dried blood from a wound to his brow. Niamh choked back a cry of both surprise and joy, and moved to embrace the old man. He kissed her cheek and then put her aside.

'Yer daughter and Shale are at the Golden Keep along wi what's left of yer court.'

'Oh thank the goddess,' the news hit Niamh so hard that she actually staggered and it was Helligan's turn to support her.

'And my sister? Her little babies?'

'All safe too, long wi most of the childer and bairns.'

Niamh took in a long deep breath and allowed the wind to whip over her, soothing her.

'What happened?' Helligan asked, his arm not leaving her back.

'Not sure I quite know, te be honest with ya. There was no army approach, no nothing, just silence. Then there was an almighty bloody roar, and then the keep was chaos. Shale got as many out as he could, through the tunnels, but we lost people – so many – as ye can see.'

'I don't understand, how could there have been no approach?'

'I can hazard a guess,' Helligan said, 'There's a burial ground within the walls, is there not?'

'Of course, at the back by the chapel.'

Helligan caught Kilm's eye and for a moment a look passed between the two, but then it began to dawn on Niamh what they were implying.

'Oh goddess… you don't think?'

'I think their necromancer simply walked in and made himself an army from your dead,' Helligan said. 'Yes, exactly that, I'd wager.'

'Oh goddess,' Niamh managed again. She felt dizzy and sick. 'How… how do we fight? How can we defeat such an enemy?'

'Reckon that we can't, reckon we have to pull back for now. Every man we lose is another for their ranks as 'tis. Let us pull back and consult our elders as to how to fight such a foe!'

'Agreed,' Helligan said. 'Let us ride first to the keep though, Niamh needs to see her daughter.'

The Golden Keep was a place Niamh had hoped never to set foot into again. Her father's castle and the place of her childhood, it was filled to the very brim with unhappy memories. Set on the very top edge of capital city, the keep was bright and bold in the silhouette of blue skies in the late afternoon sunshine, still majestic despite that it had not been used by ought than servants in so many years. The gates to the capital stood open still. That would have to change, Niamh decided as they rode by. No open gate was safe until this sorcerer was apprehended and killed! Niamh and her men took the path not through the city, with its hustle and bustle of curious faces, and the stink of an overloaded system of people animals and units of business, but around the back, along the cliffside walk to the far gate of the keep. Although Niamh doubted their presence would be unheard, at least there was less commotion that way. Her heart thudded; her vision clouded with memories. The sea air was refreshing though, that same salt and seaweed scent that had permeated the Mage Tower. Niamh breathed it in. She'd not spoken a word since they had left the smouldering ruin of Anglemarsh, and neither had Helligan or Kilm pushed her to. Helligan seemed to be nursing his back again too as he rode, she'd have a sister sent for – maybe Dora – as there was definitely something not right there. Then what? Niamh didn't know. Armies she could fight, normal hot-blooded men, sword to sword and bow to bow, that was easy! But a man who could sneak in and raise the very corpses from the burial grounds, raze her keeps with her own dead… that was something too much to even comprehend, to even bear.

The gates of The Golden Keep were firmly closed as the party arrived but upon a glimpse of her, the portcullis was opened at once and the group were given entry. Niamh sucked in another deep breath, and then exhaled, before turning her horse to the gate and starting the trek inside of a home she'd rather forget she ever had.

Inside the walls of the castle part of the keep, Niamh had to take in several deep breaths to calm herself. She hated this place, hated all it stood for, and yet once again her goddess had brought her home. The old ceilings held cobwebs and even a quick glance showed her that some of the old carvings and the like had been looted at some point previous to their return. Helligan was behind her, and Kilm too. Niamh took strength from them without even having to turn. As she entered, a cry went up and then little Jessaline was throwing herself into her arms, sobbing. Niamh felt her own eyes leak as she held her little girl and then looked up at Josynne, just entering from the hall beyond, a sea of faces behind him.

'Thank the goddess,' he spoke softly, love in his tone and the worry not yet gone from his face.

'And thank you, Jos,' she whispered, 'Kilm has told us of how your quick actions saved so many…'

'Lord Shale saved us,' that was Jedda's voice and Niamh spun about to embrace her sister too, where she'd come up from behind. Jedda's hands clutched her arm.

'Jedda, thank the goddess! And your husband?'

'My husband and many others went out to fight but I am lucky, for when he saw it was hopeless, he fled the battle and found his way back to us! Lord Shale led us out and brought us here. He is a hero!'

Josynne bowed his head, not humble enough to deny it, but not brass enough to claim it either. Niamh stood, one arm still about her daughter, the other hand on her sister's sleeve, and looked to where people were beginning to mill by the entrance of the great hall. She supposed she'd have to address them.

'M-my good people, how thankful I am to have… to have found you all alive and well and how my heart bl-bleeds for your losses. I… I am wearied indeed, as is Lord Helligan, but I will… I will take court tonight, here in this hall… have you…' she turned to Josynne, 'has everyone a chamber and food to eat?'

'Already assigned, my lady. The kitchen is understaffed but some girls from the city have been brought in.'

Niamh nodded again and swallowed. She looked back to the people. 'I… fear not, there will… I will find…' she paused and wet her lips again, Jedda squeezed her arm gently in support, 'I know all seems dire,' she managed, 'but I will make this right! I will make you safe again!'

'Here, here,' Shale said, 'now, go and rest my queen, you and your husband both look fit to drop. Your old chamber has been made up for you.'

Niamh nodded again and then bent to kiss Jessaline's forehead. 'Mama is very tired,' she said, 'but I will speak with you later too my love.'

Jessaline hugged her tightly but went back to her father without a protest. Jedda nodded too and indicated the stairs, 'go,' she murmured.

'May I suggest a council meeting?' Helligan suggested, 'later today?'

'Good shout,' Kilm agreed and even Josynne nodded.

Niamh took in another deep breath and turned back to Josynne, 'can you arrange it? Give me two or three turns to sleep, and then I shall join you.'

'Of course,' he said, 'go.'

Niamh took Helligan's hand and began to lead him away from the group. It was surreal indeed to be walking those old halls again and more so to guide her husband with her. Past her father's old war room, out into the great hall and then up the stairs, past the entrance to the tunnels where she'd met him for the very first time, and then into her old chamber. Helligan was quiet, even still not quite at full health. At the door of her old chamber, Niamh paused. She'd been a child in that room, and then for a short spell as Anglemarsh was restored, a nursing mother, but never had she been a wife. Helligan seemed not to feel the wonder of the situation though, and crept in behind her, pulled off his boots and lay himself down on her childhood bed. He'd lived here too, as a younger man, part of the mage council in the old sage's library. Niamh wondered if those old books still drew him in now. Her room was unchanged, her old wooden wardrobe still standing and her bed just the same. A desk by the window, and a shelf of old dusty knickknacks which had escaped the looters during the wars. Niamh suspected that her discarded clothing would still be in the wardrobe too and her mind's eye put the old bow on the wall – the one she had lost, burned up with the body of her brother.

Helligan was almost asleep by the time Niamh took herself to bed. She wanted a bath really, to be clean again but she was too tired for thus. She lay down on the bed and took Helligan's hand in hers. He opened heavy eyes to look onto her face.

'You should undress,' she murmured 'You cannot be comfortable in your clothing thus.'

Helligan murmured but obeyed, peeling off the linen from his legs, and the old tunic he wore over his bare chest. As he stripped off, Niamh's eyes ran over those odd black lines. They covered his back, now, and were curling about his sides. She pressed her lips but spoke not as he curled back up on the bed. They were spreading, and that was a conversation which needed to be had, but sleep was more important to begin. She slid her fingers into his and allowed consciousness to escape at last.

The council meeting was held in the old war room that Niamh's father had used. Even as she entered, Niamh was flooded with memories, more specifically of that first night of her new life, when she'd heard her father's terrible commands and had fled to join Helligan and his men. How difficult and frightening that had all seemed, and how petty compared to what they faced now.

The room was not a large one, but was an anti-chamber to the great hall. It was no longer lined with carvings and adornments, and the stained glass of the windows was still pretty, with enough light of the day left to cast the colours onto the walls and table before her. Of her old council, the survivors were low. Kilm, Helligan, Josynne of course, and then an empty place where Lords Carver and Lord Glenn would once have sat. Lord Shelby, the young man who had joined her at the end of her war for rule still sat, pale in a seat his father had once taken at the side of hers. Opposite him was Lord Lorne – Niamh was grateful for his presence. Nightingale was missing though, and there was of course no representative for her mages, all locked away in the tower which she had to hope was impenetrable. Niamh cast a long eye over them all, and then took her seat at the edge of the table.

'My Lords…' her voice sounded quiet in the echoey chamber.

'It is good to see you well,' Lord Lorne said, 'my wife was pale with worry for you.'

'I saw her briefly earlier. How is she holding up?'

'Well enough, she has seen much struggle in her short years in this life, but she is resilient. If I am correct, we are soon to be making yet another announcement of a new arrival!'

Niamh repressed a smile. By her reckoning, this would be the couple's sixth child – quite a brood now, especially for a girl several years her junior.

'Joyous news, in spite of the circumstances we are surrounded with,' she managed, with a small smile.

Helligan cleared his throat and looked over her remaining lords. He linked his fingers with hers. It was Josynne who spoke first though, of the men.

'I see the sad evidence of missing faces,' he said, 'I am sorry to see it, for we have lost good men here. Kilm assures me though, that none walk without their minds.'

'Aye, Lord Helligan and our Queen took down the stiffs,' Kilm nodded. The old man looked tired too, Niamh's heart thudded miserably.

'We did,' she said, 'but with them were most of my guard, most of the army. We are sitting ducks here.'

'We are completely without defences,' Josynne agreed.

A short silence fell, unusual in any council meeting. At last, the youthful Lord Selby spoke, 'would it aid us to try again to discover the identity of our hooded assailant?' he asked. 'If we knew who had joined them, who was on their side…'

'There's merit to that,' Helligan agreed, 'Although, so far as I know, there has never been a human necromancer…'

'By our books, there has only ever been one necromancer,' Niamh interjected.

Helligan tapped his fingers on the table, 'and officially that is true,' he agreed, 'one who mastered it… but a few have dabbled. Never human though…'

'Could it be a dragon?' Lord Lorne suggested, his voice calm despite the tension of his words.

Helligan shook his head, 'my kind are reared to fear and despise such magics,' he said. 'They go against our goddess and are an abomination to us.'

'Not even a youngling?' that was Josynne.

'I am a youngling,' Helligan laughed, 'There is but one younger than me, who is mature and grown, and that is my brother. I assure you Argosus is not responsible for this.'

'Might a human ever master the art?' Lord Shelby asked, his hair was a little longer, shaggy, and Niamh thought again about perhaps offering him a wife – the lad needed somebody to have a care for him.

Helligan sighed, 'I would never have believed it but mayhap? Under the right circumstances.'

'Such as?' Niamh was interested, this was the first inkling they'd had that Helligan was changing his mind on this.

'If a person was twisted enough with hate, and perhaps one who had looked upon the face of death. If… I mean… a human cannot possibly hold such magicka and so if it is such they must be using a focus. It would have to be strong, though. Oliah sacrificed his greatest love, if you believe our version of the tale, in order to create a focus powerful enough and he was fae…'

'What of the boy?' Niamh asked, 'my nephew? He and Alistair are of an age now, and Alis shows great promise…'

'Alis is half dragon,' Helligan reminded her, 'your brother was fully human, as is his wife. I doubt a boy could do this.'

'What of the mother then?' Josynne asked, 'Lady Kyran has not been present at any battle this past year and you did roast her husband before her eyes whilst she was heavy with child.'

Helligan's face paled, but he did not cast off the rebuke. It was true. He had. Laurin had been trying to kill Niamh, had already betrayed them, but his death had been hideous!

'She is a possibility,' Niamh murmured, her voice quiet and low.

'Perhaps,' Helligan agreed. 'We know it is not Magda herself, as she stands beside the figure on the battlefields…'

'There are others too, are there not? still connected to Magda…' Lord Shelby spoke. 'Your wife, Lorne, Lady Jedda…'

'How dare you, sir?' Lord Lorne's temper flashed, 'We have been nothing but loyal since our marriage – a marriage we would never have been permitted, if it were not for our fair queen!'

'Sit down, Justin,' Niamh said, 'Nobody is accusing you or my sister!'

Until this point, Kilm had been uncharacteristically quiet, but then he spoke up, his low tone catching Niamh's attention for its grit. 'I don' much care who it is, really. That figure is our only target. Magda's army is defeated just as ours is, she has the upper hand only because o that necro. Helligan, can ye not do something? No mage is as powerful as a dragon. Burn the fucker just like your old clanswoman did to Oliah all them years ago.'

Helligan closed his eyes, the long lashes falling on his cheeks. Niamh wanted to pull him away, upstairs, and wrap him up in the blankets of their bed so that he could not be more hurt. He looked to her though and thank the goddess, he heeded her words.

'Not this time,' he said softly, 'I am… somewhat out of action I am afraid.'

At once Lords Shelby and Lorne both began to ask questions but Niamh lifted a hand to shush them.

'I do have something of a plan though,' Helligan spoke again, shocking her.

'You do?'

'Yes. I *might* have friends still, amongst my kind. If I could get a message to them… they might loan us aid.'

'That's a lot of *"might"* for my liking,' Lord Lorne said and Shelby nodded along.

'I thought it was forbidden for your kind to leave your haven?' Niamh asked, ignoring her advisors for the moment.

'It is, but there is one clan who just might... and their leader owes me a boon.'

'So send word…' Josynne spoke, 'A dragon or two could really turn the tide for us!'

'I don't know if they will come,' Helligan warned, 'and… and I will have to use… to use magicka to summon them…' he looked to Niamh, 'It will be but a beacon, my love, it will not harm me too much further…'

Niamh weighed up the options, but she trusted Helligan not to lie to her about his limitations. 'Do it then,' she spoke but her voice wobbled.

'And if the army gathers in the meanwhile?' That was Lord Shelby.

'There is a spell which might help, one of the ancient rites. It would involve more than one man though and I could not partake… It is a boundary spell, to ward against any undead passing through our gates.'

'That seems useful…' Josynne said, '… or would be if you could actually cast it!'

'I cannot perform it, but the mages could, just about, I think.'

'It would take days for a message to go out to them,' Lord Lorne said. He sat back in his chair and Niamh prepared herself to scold him in case of his dusty boots going up on the table as he'd done in session before. He didn't though, he learned his lessons.

'I might be able to contact them, from afar, and they have magics to bring them here to us, should they agree to help us.'

'Will they?' Niamh asked, 'Will they help us? They don't usually hold much sway with royalty, and after my father…'

'I think they will, for you and for our son. I have a plan to contact them… I cannot use my innate magics, but I could utilise the magic of humans. You have a good library still here, I presume? There must be at least some books on wizarding and their spells?'

Niamh nodded. It was true, the wizards, less powerful by far than mages, more like magicians really, did have some hold of magicka and there were surely books of their secrets up in the library – she'd not have had them brought to her in Anglemarsh, what use would she have had for them?

'And you think this will work?' Josynne asked

'I think it has to,' Niamh answered, then looked around the faces of her men, she would not lose any more of them, she couldn't!

'Helligan, send out your signal,' Niamh said, 'As for the rest, we are safe enough for tonight, I think, there is no hint of any mischief at all abound and I could do with food and more sleep – as I am sure could the rest of you?'

Josynne nodded and then stood, 'Come then, let us prepare on the morrow. For tonight we close the gates and hope to high hell that our dead lay still until tomorrow at least!'

Eighteen

Helligan's eyes followed Niamh carefully as she moved to sit in the oversized throne at the head of the great hall. The seat was up on a dais, with another, slightly smaller seat at its side, that traditionally the demi-throne of the consort. His signal was sent, an ancient Draconis rite which allowed a little of his essence to rush free of his vial, exploding into the night like a distress flare. He'd dared just the one in his current condition, but if Korbyn had seen it he would come, or at least Helligan hoped he would.

Whilst he had been out at the shrine, Niamh had bathed and changed into a gown which was pretty in its yellow fabric with gold trim but a little worn and faded too, likely scavenged from the previously deserted keep. She looked majestic and queenly as she sat herself down, just as he had known she would when he had crowned her in the first place. Helligan wished he'd not been too tired to taste her flesh before the evening's affair as something within him stirred. So very beautiful, but then she always had been. Niamh wore no crown, but her golden hair was set through a circlet which crossed her forehead with a green gem as its centrepiece. The light of the afternoon sun came in through the skylights to bathe her in a golden glow, an effect which the architects had purposely achieved with the strange design of the room. Niamh didn't look comfortable though. Her eyes were wider than usual, her chest showing that her breathing was not easy. She looked to him, sitting at an old wooden table across the room, and the smile she gave was definitely forced. Helligan smiled back, full of pride for his wife, but also for the first time beginning to ponder her as the queen. A gift he had given her, but had it been an edged bequeath? She'd always been shy but he'd presumed that a part of the repression of her father's court. He'd always assumed that given time she'd grow into the potential that he saw when doors were closed. The realisation that she hadn't ever really grown into the role of queen was startling suddenly. After ten years of rule, the girl on the throne looked as nervous as she had the day she'd snuck to the door of Kilm's house with her father's battleplans in her little white hands. Guilt washed over Helligan suddenly. He'd taken over her life with little thought to the consequences of that. In that respect, his actions had been as bad as her father's had been! Thoughtless and careless in his own mission as to the needs of those around him.

As Niamh made herself comfortable, what was left of her court came to mill about her. This seemed to be something normal, in the most abnormal of circumstances. All seemed subdued though, and the worry in Niamh's eye was reflected in some of the nameless men who gathered about her. The finely garbed women who fluttered about looked much the same, although you would not have believed from the fine dresses and perfectly coiffed hair, that just days before they had been fleeing for their lives! Helligan could not even begin to imagine how new dresses had been acquired so quickly, let alone hair pins and the rose and briar scented perfumes which ever seemed to drift from these peacocks of court.

Niamh looked out over them all with eyes as compassionate and yet as wide and nervous as a child's. Helligan wondered if ever she had been thus when in session. Another wave of guilt rolled over him.

'M-my lords and ladies,' she finally spoke, 'H-how fine... how fine you all look considering... considering what you h-have been through this past day.'

She'd noticed it too then, the thought put a slight smile to Helligan's features.

'I... I can only offer you m-my condolences for...for lost ones and...' she took a deep breath, '...and my apologies for... for not being there to lead and guide you when... when it happened. I can only imagine the terror you must have felt. I... I thank Lord Shale for his quick thinking and... and firm actions in removing you all as he did from harm's way.'

Helligan glanced to Shale who was at the back of the small assembled crowd leaning on one of the marble pillars with a felfruit in his hand. In some ways the man was ever his rival but Helligan bore him no ill will for that, nor for the smiles of the people, whereas they regarded his own form with a level of curiosity and fear. He could understand this. It wasn't every day a dragon walked amongst them and Lord Shale was the hero of the hour. Helligan pondered Niamh's attachment to that man too, maybe the people secretly wished she'd married him. Perhaps she would have been happier thus. Helligan shook the thought aside, if nothing else, he knew his wife's love was as infinite as his own and such musings dishonoured them both!

Niamh seemed to take a moment to think, then continued. 'I hope that we can be assured of – of safety here,' she continued, 'the council have met and we have agreed that for now the gates will... will remain closed. Nobody in, nobody out. This is for...for our own safety until we have a way to defend ourselves. I... I will not protect you from the worrisome truth of it though. We have no army. We have few provisions for battle. The city below is a target which I do not doubt that Mag... that Queen Magda will attack. T-the council have discussed our options and... and we might have a way to contact our allies the mage council where... where our own glorious prince, Alistair, is a... is now an initiate. Helligan...

Lord Helligan that is, has too sent for help and we can but hope that they will come through for us in time.'

Helligan's heart swelled. They would, they had to! It seemed an age already that they had stood in the protection of the mage's tower and yet it had been mere days. At least, if nothing else, their son was safe there. Niamh spoke again though, diverting his attention from his own thoughts.

'For now, be as at peace as it is possible,' she said. 'I have... there are musicians here, and food and drink enough for now. Please... make as merry as you wish, and take comfort that my men and I are doing all... all we can to keep you safe.'

'What if Queen Magda attacks here?' A voice from one of the men gathered, not a lord of the council but a man finely dressed either way – one of the courtiers who milled about but seemed to play no role. 'Before your mages arrive, my queen?'

'Then we are not... not defenceless. The walls will hold and... and their necromancer cannot enter as he did b-before, due to the lockdown of our gates.'

'And is there escape, if by chance they do breech? Or are we all to be slaughtered?' a woman's voice, high-pitched.

'We have ways of escape via the tunnels. As a last resort, we can go to the temple sisters and claim sanctuary.'

A good answer, Helligan thought... and a good solution.

There seemed to be no more questions. Niamh stood a moment longer, but then sat back down. Helligan waited for her to settle, then moved through the courtiers to the foot of the platform.

'My queen,' he said quietly, his heart brimming for her.

'Join me up here?'

Helligan cast an eye over the empty throne at Niamh's side, the one he had sworn off forever. It was easy to have such morals without her doe-eyes upon him, her screamed plea in a whispered invitation. He would never be king, there would be something fundamentally wrong with the balance of things, for one of his kind to take the human throne but could he compromise? Could he be consort to the queen? Suddenly it felt as though all eyes were upon him, and likely they were. His actions now would concrete a pattern. They would put the pieces into place. As Niamh's husband, he was entitled to that uncomfortable seat, the same he'd thrust upon her, and now which she offered in a manner difficult to refuse – just as he had done to her. Helligan bowed low, probably too much so for human conventions, and then glanced at the throne.

'My queen – Niamh – do you know what you ask of me?' he whispered.

'I do.'

Of course she did, Niamh was no idiot, she'd proven such time and again. A hush fell and Helligan could feel the whispers which were waiting to form. He straightened his back and then turned to glimpse the faces of Niamh's people. He expected hostility, annoyance, but instead was purely curiosity and anticipation. He pulled in a slow inhale, his mind taking him back to his leadership of the marsh clans. Was this really any different? Really? Above and before it all too, was the almost hidden gleam of pleading in Niamh 's eye. She did not need him to rule, she'd proven that, but she wanted him at her side, and that too stood for something.

The three steps up to the golden throne felt mountainous. The act of sitting he did with his eyes closed, feeling the hardness of the metal, the slippery coolness which embraced his body in a manner to bring both comfort and coldness. Then he opened his eyes.

The three lords at the foot of the steps bowed, taking their ladies to curtsy with them. Helligan's gut coiled tighter. The pattern was like a wave, moving across the crowd as nobleman after nobleman bent knee to him, lady after lady bobbed. For some reason, his eye was drawn to the face of his rival, Josynne Shale. He should be in this place; he had proven himself a leader of these men time and time over. Shale held his gaze for a long moment, his eyes burning but unreadable, but then he put up his fist to his chest and bowed his head. Not subservience, in many ways he and Shale shared a rank, but still a sign of acceptance, of friendship. Helligan nodded to him, and then laid his hand over Niamh's fingers on the armrest of the throne. The minute stretched, long and painful, but then almost as though time snapped into place, the people stood again, and normality returned.

Niamh glanced over. 'Thank you,' she whispered.

'For you, anything.'

Night drew in in an embrace of purple and navy-blue hues through the tall windows which lined the royal chamber. In the grate, a fire crackled and gave the room a hazy smoky hue, from chimneys which had not been properly swept in decades. Helligan buried his face in Niamh's skin. Her hair was so long and fine, when free to fall about her form once she had removed all of the decorations from it, a mane of gold which whispered in long fragile strands around her lithe form. Helligan slid a hand up her naked back, allowing her hair to caress his fingers. The curve of her body was irresistible, her smooth, white form a distraction of intoxication. He ran his fingers over the skin again, and then pulled her body closer still to his own, the heat of skin on skin, a wet sweatiness even, where they'd already spent passions upon the slightly dusky and damp bedsheets. She moved against him without protestation, her lips at his throat in gentle caresses, her hands on his chest, in his own hair. She smelled of honey and fresh lavender and all the whimsy of summer; overpowering, overwhelming. Helligan moaned quietly against her and allowed his hand to grip her buttocks whilst the other held her across the shoulders. He'd already given her his seed, spilling into her in a climax of sheer abandon, but the touch of her skin, her soft smoothness, that was something he could never get enough of, a craving with no release. Niamh kissed him again on his collarbone, and then pulled his face up to meet hers. He laid his forehead down on her smooth skin, feeling where the hairlines touched. She opened her brilliant blue eyes and looked into the depths of him.

The silence deepened, not an uncomfortable one, but one of heavy atmosphere. Niamh put up a hand to brush his hair out of his eyes and then smiled.

'You look sleepy,' she murmured.

'It's been a long few days.'

'It has. How do you feel now?'

'I can feel the corruption in my skin, but at least it is dormant.'

'It's all over your back now,' she said, 'curling around almost to your belly button and the front of your shoulders. Are you sure it is healing?'

'That is what my brother's healer said. It might take weeks, but it will heal.'

'Does it hurt?'

'Only when I aggravate it.'

He pulled away, in truth, he was more worried than he was letting on and he didn't want her to read that in his eyes. As a distraction, his hand moved to the water jug but there found it empty. The mead bottle was no better.

'Are you thirsty?' he asked Niamh, 'I can go and refill the water…'

'It's fine.' Helligan sat up and swung his legs out of bed, 'I will go anyway. I am restless.'

He glanced back to see concern on Niamh's face but she said nothing, just watched him with eyes turning wary as he pulled on his clothing. He hated that look when it came to her, wished he could chase it from her forever but already he knew that the years they'd spent apart had robbed him of the gift, at least for now. In an effort to still her worries though, Helligan knelt back on the bed and slid a hand over each side of her face, up into her hair and then brought her face up to his to kiss her soft lips. 'Don't fret,' he whispered.

Niamh nodded, the ghost of her smile retuning.

Helligan kissed Niamh one last time, and then lifted the water jug and slipped out of the room. The keep at night was almost eerie in its silence. There was a guard at the door where

Niamh and himself slept, and another at the end of the corridor, but both were silent, merely nodding as he passed. At the foot of the steps, the soft body of a little kretch rubbed against his ankles. Helligan paused to rub its head, half-wondering if it had been a servant's pet already there or if somebody had rescued it from Anglemarsh as it fell. Its fur was velvet soft and soothing. The little beast purred and arched its back to him, and then scurried off into the darkness leaving him alone once more. Helligan had brought just a single candle and the temptation flared to use his magic to push the flame brighter. He didn't dare though, if his magic was flaring up his wounds somehow, he did not want to fall here alone in the dark.

The kitchens of the Golden Keep were vast and still a slight glow emanated from then. It must be midnight, but likely there would still be servants bustling about who could tell him where to fill his jug. Before he could enter though, he caught sight of a figure seated in a chair by the fire. The light glowed over his old features, illuminating his beard and his aged and wise old eyes.

'Is that you, Kilm?'

Kilm had once been one of his own generals, and, way back, had once almost killed him too. The older man still looked like a Wolder lord, the only real one in Niamh's court now. There had been four of them originally in Helligan's council. Alfric had turned on them though, and Jalsen had been killed in their first battle for the crown. Morkyl had retired to the village of Havensguard where old mother Morgana kept her court as the unofficial and unnamed Queen of the Wolder.

Kilm glanced up and then his grizzled old face fell into a smile. 'Helligan the Mage,' he said, an old title, then lifted a mead jug, 'canne sleep either?'

Helligan shook his head, 'No, I am troubled tonight. Let me find a goblet…'

Once the mead was poured, Helligan found a seat closer to the fireplace. He'd been feeling cold all day, likely another symptom of his wounds festering, or whatever illness it was which had him in its grip. The smoky glow of the fire was soothing though, its reflection on the stonework which surrounded it giving little dancing figures of light. Helligan allowed his eyes to follow them as his fingers wrapped around the hard, cold, steel of his goblet. He moved his eyes back to his friend.

'And so it comes to this again,' he said. 'ever you humans are fond of battles!'

'Aye, I think we are.'

'It feels less hopeful than before.'

'Your queen is tired.'

'She is,' Helligan agreed, his response almost a whisper.

'And yet more alive since your return…'

'I am glad to hear it.'

Kilm took a swig of his mead. 'It seems a lifetime ago that I stood on the battlefield out yonder, trying to work a way to scale these walls.'

'Which time?' Helligan chuckled, making the old man laugh with him.

'Aye, a fair point. The time I nearly took you out, now how many years ago was that?'

'I suppose it must be nearly twenty. That was the night I first met Niamh...'

Kilm nodded and then took a deep drink of his mead. 'These walls echo,' he said, 'men like us don't belong in castles like this.'

'I suppose not. I'll stay wherever she is, though.'

'Aye, I dare say you will, dragon.'

'The lifespans you humans have seem so very short to me. Already I have lived more than one of them and I am still young. It is no hardship to stay here awhile to be close to her – too soon she will be gone, you all will.'

'And you live on.'

Helligan sighed and drank more mead. Generally speaking, he was not given for maudlin musings but the night seemed thick and dark suddenly.

'I think our lady will be with you longer than you think,' Kilm said, though, interrupting his thoughts.

'Hmm?'

'Ye said yerself, the girl's half-fae. I counsel you to look closely at her, when you go back upstairs, and ask yerself, does Niamh look like a woman approaching her fourth decade?'

'You don't think she's aging?'

'Aye, she's aging for sure, but slower than we mere mortals. She reminds me a bit of Morgana: ageless, and the rumours do say the old lady has a bit o elf blood in her too. If Niamh is half fae, could be the same sort o thing. Either that or she merely looks after herself well. Who knows…'?

'Who indeed,' Helligan said, lifting the goblet to his lips again in craving of another of those sweet bursts the honey-wine brought to his lips. He was more thoughtful though. Another gulp and the goblet was empty, he moved to put it aside but his friend tipped the jug again. Well, one more would not hurt and Niamh wouldn't mind. He nodded a thanks.

'Reckon the mages really will be able to help us until your folk come – if'n they come?' Kilm asked, suddenly changing the subject. 'We spent longer discussing how te contact them, than the possibility that they mightn't be able to actually do anything, if they do come, or what to do if yer kin stay silent.'

'The mages will be able to help guard us for a time at least,' Helligan said. 'The spell I have in mind is not overly complicated, I just can't do it. And my kin – or at least a man amongst my kind – will come too, I am owed a boon!'

'Can ye not just burn the lot o them wi' yer fire, when they come? Or wi' yer magic?'

Helligan shook his head. 'Sadly, no.'

'And why is that, why can ye not use yer magic?'

Helligan stood and lifted his tunic, showing Kilm the corruption spreading over the skin of his belly by the light of the fire, then turned so that the mottled grey of his back was visible in the meagre candlelight.

'Goddess...' Kilm breathed.

Helligan let the silky material fall back over his skin and sat back down. 'I think it's a curse,' finally he said the words aloud. 'By the rite of banishment, I gave up my wings. My brother sent a healer to tend me, but I think she duped him and cursed me. It flares whenever I use my magic, burning, and then spreads a little further each time.'

'You be needing the counsel of the mother, I think.'

'Perhaps, but my problems can wait. Let us hold the keep, win this battle, for now. Later I can go to Morgana, once I know it is safe to leave again.'

'Hell of a risk. Ye could be dead by then.'

'Not if I am careful,' Helligan said, 'and I will be... but I'm not going to allow this keep to fall. It's the least I can do after being gone for so long.'

Kilm finished his own drink and put the silver tumbler down on the table, he glanced to Helligan, 'least ye can do? Aye, maybe. Best thing ye could do for her though is to take her away from here and give her a life she'll actually enjoy.'

Helligan nodded, wordless.

'Mind you sleep tonight, Helligan, we've a day of it tomorrow.'

Niamh was dozing when Helligan slipped back into her chamber. The room was very dim, all of the candles out but for his own, and yet the moonlight that bathed the room in its soft glow picked up the gold in her hair, the curve of her skin atop the coverlet. He put the jug down quietly on the side and then moved to sit on the edge of the bed. Niamh rolled over groggily.

'Stay asleep, sweetling,' he murmured, 'Don't let me wake you.'

Too late though, already her eyes were open, her expression moving from serenity to concern quicker than he'd hoped. 'Helligan?'

He sighed, 'my love.'

'You are ill at ease tonight? Restless still?'

Aye, that he was! 'Nothing to trouble yourself with,' he demurred though, wishing for a moment to ponder. Niamh sat up though. Her long hair fell to flow around her form, over her shoulders, between her breasts. Helligan resisted the urge to silence her with kisses. He took her hand and nuzzled it, but then dropped it and stood to look out of the window at the city below. He stilled his thoughts, and then turned back to her.

'I never actually asked you, did I?' he said, choosing his words carefully.

'Asked me?

'If you *wanted* to be queen. I never asked you…'

'You did, in your own way…'

'After I had already declared it to a room full of men,' he said, 'Kilm asked me if I was going to put the crown on my own head and I said no, that I was going to put it on yours… and then I turned to you and I asked if you were willing. Do you remember? I asked you only as an afterthought.'

'Helligan I would never have declined! I would have done anything you asked of me.'

'And yet, that makes it worse, not better.'

'My love, it was the Goddess's plan for me, my fate. Don't chastise yourself over what is gone – *that* is a human trait.'

'Perhaps I am more human than I care to admit,' he sighed, moving closer and trailing his fingers into her silky hair.

'Mayhap,' she replied, 'but this is not something to hold onto. I bear you no ill-will for it, for any of it.'

'And if this kingdom falls and we have to flee again?'

'Then that is what the goddess wills. As long as you and I and our dear ones find safety, then what will be will be. I love my people, Helligan, but I will not keep myself awake at night crying if I am dethroned.'

Helligan opened his lips to speak again but Niamh covered them with her own, shutting off the thought, the kiss was soft and gentle, and then she pulled away.

'Come, get some sleep, brooding one,' she murmured. 'It'll be a long day tomorrow.'

Nineteen

The day dawned brighter than Niamh could have imagined at such a time. A gloriously warm and vibrant morning, with the sun high in the sky, and the early Karrahs and Sigs singing in the day with a sweetly high-pitched melody. Niamh sat in the dining chamber of the Golden Keep with a plate laden with eggs and silvers – the little whitefish that were found just off the shore beyond. Plain fare but then the servants had not been expecting such an influx and so the food must be sourced from local means. Her men were gathered but Helligan was absent, had been when she'd awoken. He'd ever been an early riser. She managed anther mouthful and pushed the plate away.

'My Lords,' she murmured and then stood. There was work to be done and it would not be done by dawdling over breakfast. At once everyone at the table stood too, a habit which ever had irked Niamh but which she'd not been able to train them out of. She merely nodded though, and then made her way out of the side door which led to the gardens, glorying in the warm sun on her pale skin. If Niamh knew Helligan well enough, he'd be outside somewhere – likely at the shrine to the goddess, blighted as it now was as the site of a massacre where her father had laid dead the humble priestesses who had once served him in these halls. Her father had done a lot of wrong in his time, she had to remember that – it helped.

Outside of the keep, the grounds were richly green, peppered with rose gardens, statues and hedges of tall green. All was a little dilapidated, but already she could see work had begun to make it beautiful once again. How quickly things fell into a pattern! Of her men, only the Lords had broken their fast with her, them and a handful of courtiers. Kilm was absent, maybe with Helligan for ever they had been close, but Josynne came to her side as she walked, his own breakfast abandoned. His hand took Niamh's arm, causing her to pause at the edge of the steps she'd been about to descend.

'Are you well, sweetheart?' Josynne asked her softly.

'As well as can be expected, Jos. And you?'

'The same,' he agreed. 'Jess wants to see you, Niamh – don't forget you have a daughter too, in all this chaos. All this change, as well as the attack on the keep, has rendered her timid and afraid. She asked me twice this morning before breakfast, when Mama would come.'

'I am sorry, I have neglected her. I shall see her as soon as I have spoken to Helligan.'

'He's not right, is he?'

'He ails – of spirit as well as of body, I think.'

Josynne said nothing more, but then suddenly he turned her to face him, pulling her arm gently. 'I don't suppose I shall ever grow used to having him with us,' he said, 'but then so much has changed these past days – I know not if I am coming or going. I am glad for your sake though, that he is alive. I see the joy in your eyes even through all the trials we suffer and I know that he is the one who put it there, more so than I … or any man… could. I am trying to… to…'

'I know,' she interrupted. 'I need to find him now though.'

'He's in the library tower.'

'He is?'

'Yes, I passed him on the stairs. He's gone to find that spell of which he spoke, to open up communication with the mages.'

Without even breakfast? Niamh did not approve and was determined that he'd eat before he tried any form of magicka.

She glanced up at Josynne though, her daughter still her immediate concern.

'Go and tell Jess Mama will see her in an hour,' she said, 'and then… then ready her for removal, should it be required.'

'What do you mean?'

Niamh pressed her lips, 'I mean, show her a means of escape, like once you did for me, so that if we are taken, she can survive.'

Josynne nodded curtly, and then dropped his grip on her arm, 'Of course, sweetheart,' he murmured and then was gone.

The old tower where the library was held was one of those which seemed to go on forever, a spiral of old grey stone steps which did not cease and made the back of the calves scream before a person was even halfway up. Niamh knew it well, she'd spent much of her girlhood in this singular tower. She ran up half of the stairs, and then slowed to a quick walk. Goddess, hadn't she once been fitter than this? Luxury and comfort had lost her a little of her fitness and it was not an easy realisation.

Finally, though, Niamh reached the splintery old wooden door, complete with its black iron plated hinge and circular iron handle. She turned it and slipped inside. Even on the brightest day, this tower was dim – a poor trait for a library! Helligan was seated at a table which once she'd favoured, closest to the window – that aperture which sat open allowing in a little of the daylight at least. Helligan glanced up as she entered. He looked tired still.

'H… how goes the reading?' she whispered.

'I have the spell I need. I think. A simple wizard's spell.'

'Should you be doing magic?'

'Wizard magic is not like ours,' he said softly, 'It uses outward energy, not inward. I will be fine, if I am learned enough to cast this properly.'

'And are you?'

Helligan glanced up at her again, and Niamh suddenly wanted to run to him and hold him, he looked afraid., never in her years of knowing him, had Niamh ever seen fear in those eyes, not even as they had faced execution together.

'I suppose we will find out,' he murmured.

'Breakfast first, perhaps?'

'There is no time. I know not how long we can hold out if your nephew's forces attack with no army to protect us and no mages either.'

'You... you seem fit to drop though?'

'I am fevered. The sooner this is done with, the sooner I can rest and seek aid for my own ailment!'

Niamh pressed her lips tightly closed, so much so that her jaw ached. Helligan stood and moved to collect a quill and ink, a pad of parchment and another old book. Even his movements were slow, tired. Niamh moved to put a hand on his arm as he sat back down. His skin felt hot, clammy.

'Helligan, I'm afraid,' she murmured.

'This will work, I promise!'

'I'm afraid for you...'

His eyes, when he looked up at her, were dark and veiled, full of pain. The look reminded her of how he'd looked at her before he'd stepped back into the mists, before.

'Niamh...'

'No, I know... you are stubborn and wilful and you will do this even at your own expense, but you cannot stop my concern, my worry that I am going to... to lose you again!'

Helligan took her hand in his, turned it over and kissed her wrist where her pulse ran too fast. His touch was gentle, soft.

'I will go to Morgana after the battle,' he said. 'If we manage to hold the keep or no, it will be our next move. I promise you! I am careless in your eyes, but not enough to risk my life for a human cause.'

'It's not the cause though, is it? ...but to protect us...'

'I'm not going to die,' he whispered again, 'now will you help me with this spell? It's unfamiliar magic.'

The spell, despite being unfamiliar to Helligan, seemed somewhat straightforward, as far as Niamh could tell. The mere writing of words on a page, and then simply blowing them over a candle-flame, after carving the shaft of the same candle with what looked like runes. Niamh did the carving, and Helligan the writing, and then both took turns at the blowing.

'There, do you think that could have worked?' Niamh murmured, snuffing the candle and filling the room with the scent of newly snuffed wick.

'I suppose we have to hope it did,' Helligan said. Niamh moved to sit beside him, he had turned very pale.

'And… and if it does not?'

'Then we prepare to escape these walls, much as we did in your youth.'

Niamh sighed and then suddenly she felt overwhelmed again. Not wanting to show her anguish, she sat herself down on Helligan's lap and buried her face in his chest and shoulder. His arms came down around her, and his long hair tickled. For a few moments, she breathed in the scent of his soap and the orange spice he'd used on his skin that morning. Whilst his scent was the same as ever it was, his soft tunic was an oddness, especially on the eve of battle where usually he'd be clad in leather. He didn't even have any armour now, she realised, he had but the clothes he stood in, and the ones gifted by the sisters. She'd make that right, she thought, before the battle was underway – well, as much of a battle there could be with no army to defend but for Kilm and his handful of Wolder, and the archers who ever shadowed Josynne. Another wave of panic threatened and this time it did pull free tears from her eyes. At the wetness, Helligan pulled away and examined her face.

'Tears?' he murmured.

Niamh wiped her face with the ball of her hand. 'just overburdened,' she whispered.

'Would you like to come with me, to the shrine? 'he asked, 'It will be cooler outside and we can send someone else up to guard this room lest the mages find some way to respond.'

'Half of me fears leaving in case we miss something,' Niamh murmured.

'We won't, come… you are wearied and it's no good preparing for a battle when your spirits are so low!'

Outside, the air was crisp, the later afternoon starting to creep in, stealing away the hottest of the sun's rays, with no sight still of an invading army's approach. Niamh tried to let the soft wind with its scent of the city below soothe her, the sound of the little birds singing out the day. Helligan led her by the hand down the steps where once she'd been led in the chains of the accused, past the archery butts where she'd spent so many a day watching Josynne practice when she'd been but a girl and he still a young man. Niamh held back tears, this place was not helping, all the memories stirred by the old walls she'd hoped never to have to hide behind again. Helligan's hand was gentle on hers though, his fingers smooth where they held hers. At the edge of the archery range was a small gate which led past the east side of the keep, past the overgrown gardens where she'd played as a girl, and down the little path which led to the shrine. Still within the walls, but at the edge of the grounds, there were a few trees dotted about, and then in the centre the old, bowed tree which cast its boughs out over the three standing stones which still remained. Once, long ago, there would have been one of every goddess face but now this was all that remained.

Niamh viewed the stones with mixed emotions. Her father had razed the temple in the city below and had dragged the sisters and their patrons here to be executed. To Niamh still the old stones held the echo of those screams, still the panic of that evil deed lived on. She knew too though, that those echoes could not be allowed to entirely wipe away the sacred feel of the glade, the soft and sweet presence of the goddess. At the edge of the three stones were two more, both fallen, and then in the middle was a rock pool which was filled with rainwater that was clear as the day. Before this pool were a handful of crystals, empty plates, and pieces of jewellery – tribute and gifts to the goddess, often in exchange for some request or boon back. Helligan knelt before the pool and closed his eyes, Niamh's hand still clutched in his own. As he bowed his head, she saw that the strange lines of his injury had moved up onto his neck. They'd be visible soon to all even despite his clothing. She inhaled again and dried her eyes, then knelt beside Helligan. He glanced over and a small tired smile dressed his lips. With a shaking hand, he scooped up some of the water from the pool and held his hand out to her, 'drink,' he murmured.

Niamh hesitated, she'd never known this tradition before, but she did as he bade, supping the water from his palm. It was like sugar water, fragrant and with a hint of something earthy and raw in its sweetness. Helligan smiled again, 'let her strength fill you up, and trickle through, from your fingertips to your toes,' he murmured. Niamh held his eye, and then dipped her own hand to offer his the same. Helligan took it, and then hooked an arm about her waist, pulling her to him. He touched her lips with his, and then rested his brow on hers.

'Nothing is going to beat us,' he said, 'we've suffered enough already, the goddess does not make our paths easy but her rewards will be worth the fight we have had to give to earn them. My people *will* come through for us, and we *will* be victorious! This latest threat will be gone and we can retreat to watch from the side-lines as Alis finds his feet and takes his place as the king of Rostalis.'

Niamh nodded, her heart swelling at how earnest he was. This was a side of Helligan she'd forgotten, one she welcomed back. With his words too came a strange fullness, a warming of hope. Surely this must be their time now? Surely the goddess could have no more trials for them?

Twenty

As the sun began to dip over the stones, bathing them both in a soft yellow light, Helligan shuffled back from his knees where still he sat in reverence of the goddess. At his side, Niamh did the same, putting up a hand to shield her eyes from the brightness as the sun hit the point in the sky which was blinding. Helligan sat for a long moment, bathing in the sweetness of that golden glow, and then turned to kiss Niamh's brow again, his hands sliding into her hair to do so, feeling the weight of the soft strands in his fingers. She seemed in better spirits now, more alive again. He was gladdened greatly of that at least. Niamh carried her burdens on her features, and her worries heavy in her heart. If nothing else, Helligan was determined that he would ease both.

'It will be well, I promise,' he said again, with more conviction than he felt.

'It will, I should go in and spend some time with my daughter before we have to prepare.'

'You should.'

'Will you come inside too?' her eyes were soft but he saw her steel beneath. She didn't need him, just for now and he had a goddess to beseech.

'Give me an hour more, I want to pray a little longer alone,' he spoke softly.

Niamh nodded and kissed him again, and then she was gone. Helligan put his hand down on the shrine and allowed just a smidgeon of his magicka to surface, not enough to hurt, just enough to allow him to connect with the great mother. He inhaled and exhaled, but then paused at a sense behind, a tingle.

There was another non-human in the glade.

Helligan put his hand to the sword on his belt. He barely knew how to use it, but it was better than no defence. 'Who is it? Who is there?' he demanded, spinning about.

For a moment there was nothing, but then another rush of soft white magicka, and the figure of an old man moved into view from the edge of the trees. He was dressed only in a white robe, with his long grey hair falling about his shoulders to his waist in a wave of fine silk. He had a beard too, and was bent slightly as he walked. The walk of a man with nearly a thousand years behind him. Helligan's breath left in him one sharp exhale, and he put his fist to his chest in a salute of respect.

'Well met, Helligan Dericaflae,' the old man said.

'Korbyn of the white.'

'How fare you, banished one?'

Helligan bowed his head, then let out a sigh, 'not the best I have ever been, in truth.'

Korbyn walked closer and took Helligan's face in his old soft hands. He was close enough that Helligan could pick up the scent of cinnamon, spice and honey on the other man's breath as he looked into his eyes.

'I see it. That is a vicious curse indeed,' he said. 'I don't think even I can…' he closed his eyes and inhaled. A white light built up around Helligan. It was comforting, soft like the blankets of his bed in the Golden Keep bed and scented with the sweet scent of vanilla tart and cinnamon buns. Korbyn inhaled again, and then stopped and shook his head. The light retreated at once, returning Helligan to the slightly fuzzy-headed, painful curse of his form.

'No, whatever it is, it is rooted deep within you, son.'

'I know it, elven magics.'

Korbyn's slate eyes examined him. They were ringed with red, about the iris, but no longer the bright crimson of albino that was his legacy. 'Perhaps,' he murmured.

'Thank you for coming, Korbyn,' Helligan stepped aside and sat himself down on the stone by the edge of the shrine, 'I am aware that you are breaking every law we have…'

'Just as you did, on my command. You broke the laws for me… well, the crossing at least.'

Helligan smiled, 'Indeed, the rest was my own foolishness!'

'Is love ever such?'

'Always,' Helligan said not losing the smile.

The old man shuffled to the shrine and laid a wrinkled hand upon it, then sat himself down opposite Helligan. His eyes were conflicted but bright. He swallowed and then spoke again, 'I have told my daughters to prepare to slip away unseen, and to ready themselves for a battle,' he said. 'I presume such is needed?'

Helligan nodded.

'Good, and then we are square.'

'We are, I thank you, old man.'

'It is what it is. I do wish you had not given up the clans though. You have the potential to have been one of the greatest leaders we have known.'

'What choice did I have?'

'You had every choice! You could have fought for your place. Do you really think they would have kept you bound thus once you were the leader of the Draconis? And even if so, you could have taken your punishment and come through to rule for the rest of your term.'

'I could not have gone back into that hole and as I recall, nobody was fighting my corner…'

Korbyn paused at that, and then sighed, 'You know as well as I that one voice in your corner would have done no good.'

'I suppose,' Helligan dropped his gaze.

'Better to be smart than send myself and my daughters after you. You knew the risks when you stepped through the mists. I would not have let you go naïve! I had no idea though, what you would give up to get back here, to humanity, in the aftermath.'

'I never was fated to lead our people.'

'So you say, and yet you could have been great, Helligan. Our people need your wisdom and just heart! You should have been the greatest leader yet, of the clans.'

'And yet I would have been miserable without my wife, without my son.'

'As much as I am sure that in your youth you will rally against this, in truth one human girl was not worth the loss of everything we were fighting for.'

Helligan cast his mind back to the last conversation he and Korbyn had had, back before it all started. The old man had come to him in the purple light of a dying day, just after the ceremony of the wheel turning. The gifted baton from white to blue. Korbyn's reign was coming to an end and Helligan was sad of it. He wanted not for his more volatile house to rule, and wanted too for Korbyn to stay – Korbyn was wiser and fairer by far than his father had been – not that he'd have dared say that to any though. The old man had sat himself down after shooing Helligan's mother and brother from the room and had looked Helligan in the eye, "*I have one last decree, as elder*" he'd said, "*and with it a boon to ask of you.*"

And with that boon, the simple words that Helligan was to leave Zaikanis and travel through to the human lands, where he would begin to make subtle changes, to end the rift betwixt Wolder and humans. It was the first step, Korbyn had explained, in building a future where the Draconis and the other fae could return to Rostalis – in peace. In the end, Helligan had not really had a choice; no Draconis would ever disobey their leader, even if it did mean breaking the laws of old. Besides, the cause had felt worth fighting!

Helligan snapped back to the present, with the touch of Korbyn's hand on his own. 'Did I lose you there, for a moment?' the old man asked.

'I was just remembering.'

Korbyn nodded. He seemed very old, very pale. Helligan tried to recall if he'd always seemed so frail, so defeated.

'I never could understand, before, why it was you came to me,' Helligan said, 'But I think I have come to understand, in my time here. We need to reunite this fractured civilisation. We are not destined to remain in hiding forever but neither should there be war between us and them!'

'I am glad you have learned something.' Korbyn smiled a wry smile, 'I am one of the few who remembers the end of the war, and this hatred of humankind that the draconis carry is one born in the bellies of those who did not live through what we did. Nobody remembers, on either side, that the stalemate we claim is a falsehood. Humankind could not better us – even with the fae-magic artefacts they created. We could have wiped them all out but we chose not to! It was kindness which led Zenna to take charge, and it was kindness which led us away, not to hiding for fear of them, but so that we did not do the unthinkable and wage full-scale war on them. We left so as to be kind. It was not supposed to be forever, and nor was it supposed to incite the hatred it has. I made it my life's work, to undo this great wrong that occurred when the rise of hatred took up in our ranks.'

Helligan nodded, it all made sense to him, but for one thing, 'and why me?' he asked.

'I came to you because you were one I trusted. One I knew would follow the right path. I came to you because I knew that your mother would have… have raised you right! I came to you… son… because you are the only male remaining who directly carries my blood.'

Helligan closed his eyes for a long moment, but then opened them again, 'you claim to be kin?'

'I claim to be your father, Helligan.'

Helligan looked down at his hands, examining his dirty fingernails. Whilst it was true that he did too have the healing energies, but his scales were all blue, his eyes not albino.'

'How? How can it be that I carry no physical trace of you, if that is the case?'

'Mainly you have a look of your mother about you anyhow. When you were born, your skin was white, your eyes were brightest red… but your mother sent for a spell to change them to what they are now. Nobody but she and the midwife who tended her, saw your true appearance.'

'This cannot be the truth?'

'But it is. You were never supposed to know, nobody was. It was no brief fling, I love your mother even still and ever I have but she was sworn, upon the death of Kalysis, her first husband, to marry your father. Had I been another blue, then perhaps I might have been given permission to wed her, but I was from the wrong clan. Your mother and I shared a brief spring of three years, but then she did her duty and married him, with you already in her belly.'

Helligan said nothing for a long moment, digesting. 'I always knew my father liked me less than my brother,' he said softly, 'I never supposed that there was a true reason for that. He knew, I presume?'

'He at least suspected, and I fear now that you should have a care. The curse you wear feels like one of kinship and I assure you it is not from me or my daughters.'

'Argosus would never harm me.'

'Would he not? Are you sure of that?'

'Why would he? What reason does he have? Father is dead and we were ever brought up to be brothers.'

'Your father – or at least the man you call father – was murdered, Helligan. Things are not right in Zaikanis. I am afraid for my own life, and should this secret come out, I am afraid for yours. I have, since the very beginning, been the most staunch in a return to the old ways of peaceful coexistence. Your father was my biggest adversary. With you at the head of the clan, I had a comfort but your brother is much like your father in that respect. I fear to utter this to you, but already he has decreed that should your son ever try to come to us, he will be killed.'

Helligan was alert at once, 'What? But none threaten to come for him? He is not in danger here?'

'Not yet, as far as I understand it.'

'This is all too much,' Helligan finally said. 'I have to go and prepare for a battle I seek to win without an army, with a curse upon me, a target on my son, and the hordes of the bloody undead rising to fight for my opponent!'

'What?' Korbyn if it was possible, paled even more so than usual.

'You had not heard? We have a necromancer amongst us.'

'That is a grave tiding indeed. Have a care and remember that in such abomination, the goddess will fight at your side! I will warn my daughters and then send them to you.'

'Thank you. What of you, what will you do now? Is your absence known?'

'Likely, I intend to make my home on this side of the mist for my final days. I have not many left, I suspect.'

'Will you come inside then, and… and meet my wife, your grandson?'

The old man smiled, 'I think not,' he said, 'These old bones are done for wars, I am afraid. I will make my way to The Whites, to our ancestral home. It will be good to rest these old bones in the same place that they came into the world. Goodbye son.'

'Goodbye… father…'

Helligan made his way swiftly back up to the keep, his stride as big as he could manage in his addled state. He needed to find Niamh, needed to hold her and his son, but he knew already that the conversation he'd just had with Korbyn could wait until after the battle, aside from the assertion that help was coming. His heart was heavy though, and his lips pressed. Everything that Korbyn had said, he could believe, but for the idea that his own brother, young and gentle Argosus, could have wrought this curse upon him. Inside, he was met at the door by Lord Lorne. The man was smiling, his eyes bright with relief.

'What? What is it man?' Helligan asked.

'It worked! My lord, a portal opened in the rooms above nearly an hour since! Your mages are here!'

Helligan sighed a sigh which opened up his whole chest, sharing in that relief. Thank the goddess, perhaps things would go their way after all.

The little library room, upstairs, was packed with bodies, or so it seemed to Helligan as he puffed his way up to the top of the narrow staircase. Niamh was sat at the table they had been at before, with her daughter on her lap and his son at her side. Nervoria and Elenni were both sat on the actual table, and the sages Orien, Graves and even old Tamm sat in a circle about the table behind, with Friggan apparently regaling them with a tale. Only the stone-sage, and the youngest two boys were absent. The whole atmosphere in the room was light, a feeling of jollity about the youth who piled into the room. It had only been a matter of days, and yet with the events of those days it felt like years since he'd seen any of them.

'Helligan!' Niamh beamed, depositing the little girl onto the floor to stand and take his hand, 'Look! It worked!'

'Sage Orien allowed me to help with the portal!' Friggan boasted.

'Indeed, but it was I who saw Helligan's note and took it to Orin,' Nervoria added, 'And Alis helped with the portal too! Only he made it all icy!'

'I didn't!' Alistair defended, 'Orien said my magics will always have a hint of blue but it wasn't icy!'

Elenni was quiet as the others all chimed in, but then put up his fist to his chest and bowed to Helligan. Helligan felt his eyes crinkle, Elenni would go far with the sages.

At length, Sage Orien clapped his hands and the children were quiet. Niamh was laughing still though, and his son was beaming him a smile as he teased his sister. Helligan grinned and resisted hugging the boy in front of all of his friends. If what he'd been told about Argosus's rulings were true, the boy was better off hidden but Helligan could not help rejoice in his return too.

'So,' Orien said, 'What is it you need of us?'

'The necromancer's army moves closer and we are defenceless. We have…' Helligan glanced at Niamh he'd rather have told her the news in private but there was no time for dallying, 'We have the support of Korbyn, the white draconis clan leader, in the form of his two daughters, but they must escape our city unnoticed or be banished forever just as I am. Until they are here, we need to keep the undead out of our city.'

'We have them?' Niamh asked, 'You are sure?'

'I have just spoken to Korbyn himself.'

Niamh sucked in a mouthful of air and Helligan could see a million questions on her features. She shook her head though, and then turned back to Orien. 'Helligan has a spell – a ritual in fact – which might work to keep them out, but he needs your help, if you will offer it?'

'Indeed…' Helligan moved to the table and sat himself beside his son. He paused a moment, but then lifted a piece of paper and began to write. 'This is the basics of it,' he said, 'I'm not sure of the rest though…'

'Orien took the paper and viewed it, then pushed Elenni aside to sit down opposite Helligan. In the background, Nervoria began to tease Friggan again and then there was the laughter as Elenni joined in, moving to the other side of the room. Helligan glanced at Alistair, the boy seemed content to sit away from the other youngsters, more interested in the spell than the frivolity. Helligan hoped that he at least joined in sometimes – it was good to be studious, but there had to be a balance. As Helligan became lost in thought again, Niamh leaned back in her chair, she seemed content now that the children were home and Helligan pondered their part in her life – more than just mentees, he gathered. As all this occurred,

Orien had dipped the quill and was making a few amendments to the paper Helligan had given him

'It's possible this would work,' he said, placing it back before Helligan, 'Better suited to the removal of ghostly spirits – but the adaption works, I think?'

Helligan glanced over the paper,' then nodded, 'Agreed. Do you think the children can manage it? Structured spellcasting is more difficult than elemental casting!'

'I'm willing to try!' Friggan said.

'And I!' Nervoria of course would not be outdone.

Helligan looked to Niamh, still silent but shining with joy, she looked down to their son, 'And you, Alis?' she asked.

'I will do what is needed, for the kingdom,' had his voice ever seemed so youthful? Childish? Helligan resisted the urge to bundle him up and send him right back through the portal to safety. If the boy was to be king, he needed to do his part but it wasn't easy to allow it to happen thus. Helligan pressed his lips and tried to force a light heart.

'Fine then Orien best start to teach it then…' he said, then, 'I'm in need of food, I shall return in an hour or so…'

'I'll come with you,' Niamh said, standing, 'and give the mages some room to study! Jess come with me to find your father! Frigg, mind you concentrate - this is no game! ...and Vorrie, don't you be teasing him now!'

Nervoria laughed but nodded as the children began to cluster around Orien. Helligan took Niamh's hand in his, and suddenly the world did seem a little lighter, despite it all. That lightness though, was not to last. Niamh and Helligan had literally just sat down in the hall with their repast, when Lord Lorne ran into the room, pale and with fear on his handsome features, even before he spoke, Niamh heard the sound of Kilm's war-horn.

'Laurin's Army? They're here?' she asked.

Lorne nodded, 'The enemy has been spotted!' he confirmed.

Twenty-One

Niamh stood on the battlements with Alistair at one side and Helligan on the other. Kilm and Josynne stood just below her, as her main commanders. Together they looked out over the battlements as the whole of the undead army shuffled closer and closer still. There were hordes of them and Niamh could not bear to think where the necromancer could have gathered so many corpses in such a short time. Some of the men, from what she could see, were tumbling and rotted, but others were fresh, almost like the men they'd once been. The tide had swung too, in the proportion of the army which was animated in this way. There were few, if any, of Magda's original army left, not living men. Magda herself rode at the edge of the army letting the hooded figure lead; sat tall on his or her horse, with the army marching along at their side. The invaders were in no hurry. The hooded figure rode at a trot, undead lords, as much they were, riding alongside. The figure paused, about half a mile from the keep, and there held up its hands, indicating that the army should go ahead, making an arc about the gate so that no man could flee, but so that a great semi-circle of green grass stood clear.

'So many…' Niamh whispered to Helligan.

'Yes, and not one that can enter these walls, now. Magda has put the death knoll on her own army, by using so many of the dead as her troops. Our mages will keep them out.

Josynne looked over his shoulder, 'And my archers can take them off at our leisure,' he added. 'we might not have much of an army, but with an enemy force unable to gain entry to the grounds, it might be enough to keep them at bay.'

'We will hold the spell for as long as we are standing,' Alis added, 'Sage Orien has taught us it all well.'

'So long as you hold your temper, Alis,' Josynne murmured. 'You cannot break free to bring down your rains of ice – you have to stay at your position.'

Alistair flushed and looked at the floor. Niamh wished Josynne could have chosen his words better than the chastisement but she said nothing. Helligan put his hand in hers.

'Alis will do us proud, I am sure,' Helligan said. 'Have we sisters at hand, for healing?'

'All in place,' Niamh agreed.

'And food and drink aplenty for when the men parch?' Kilm added, 'Many disregard the need for food and water in a battle.'

'Is it as you requested, all set up below,' Niamh said, then drew in a deep inhale. 'We can do this, men. Have faith.'

Below, the army finalised its pattern of surrounding the gates. Niamh's gut was aflame, panic trying to tell her that the spell would fail, and that these hordes would soon be upon them, the commoners of the city first, joining that army, and then those she loved, one by one. She wet her lips again.

'Is Jess safe, Jos?' She asked.

'I placed her behind a locked door by the west gate,' he said, 'she knows where to go, should she need to, where the tunnel entrance is.'

'And so history repeats,' Niamh murmured but not loud enough that any might have heard her. Once she too, had been placed by that same man in a position to flee – only then she'd been the child and he a young knight with his heart in his hands, whereas now the child he served was their own daughter, their beautiful little girl who was so much at risk. In her father's world, a guard might have been put upon the child too, in order to slit her throat should the invaders break in. That was how the rest of her siblings had died, in her own childhood.

Niamh pulled herself free of tumultuous reminiscence and with a final squeeze, she dropped Helligan's hand and stepped forward so that she could be seen from the battlements by those below. The figure looked up, close enough that the form could be seen but far enough to exclude any features. They rode forward so that their horse was below the keep, an arrow shot from Niamh. She did not finger her bow, though, no man would attack thus, lest he be a true coward. A battle could so easily be won in a moment of parley, but honour dictated that they not strike. Niamh was sure too, that such a powerful mage did not stand so vulnerable as he looked, without protection.

'Queen Niamh…' his voice carried on the wind, distant and quiet, but audible enough now that he was closer. Definitely not Kyran, definitely male.

'Who are you, and why do you march against me?' she called back.

'Have the decency to come down, and perhaps you might learn of it.'

Niamh looked back at her men.

'No, stay up here where you are safe!' Josynne said at once, 'it's not worth the risk!'

'I agree, Niamh,' Kilm said and even Helligan was nodding.

'I can't, that is not how civilised battles are fought!'

'You call this civilised, with the bloody army of the dead at our gates?' Kilm exploded, 'You'm out of yer mind, my queen.'

'I can't protect you,' Helligan said, 'If you go down, I don't have it in me to cast that level of spell…'

'But I can,' Alistair spoke, 'or the other mages,' he gestured behind, where his brotherhood were gathered, heads together in deep conversation, likely a final rehearsal for the epic spell they were about to cast.

'They need their energy for the shield, as do you!' Helligan interjected.

'I will be safe, there is such dishonour in an attack during a parley and I will stay close enough to the gate that I might retreat if I need.'

'It's too risky,' Josynne said again, stubborn.

Niamh cast her eyes over the mage council, her last defence, 'get to your places and begin the spell as I go down,' she said, 'If the gate is to open, I want us protected. She put a hand on her son's arm but she could not find the words. Alistair leaned in and kissed her brow – how long had he been tall enough for thus? It did not seem real!

'It will be well, mother, the spell will be in place before you reach the gates.'

Niamh went back to the edge. 'I am coming down,' she called.

The figure nodded.

Niamh sucked in a deep breath and moved to the stairs Helligan and Josynne both followed, neither content to leave her to her fate alone. Alistair had joined his friends and Niamh watched as they sat in a circle, hands linking. She hoped the magic of those children would be strong enough to save them again, they were literally her last defence. Niamh's legs shook as she walked, and she hoped that they didn't see her fear. She put a hand on the cold, rough stone of the wall as she used steps which once she'd walked down before in a similar state – the day of her failed execution. That had been the day she'd learned Helligan's true form, how ironic now that he who had once been her saviour was rendered all but powerless.

At the gate she paused and turned back to the men. Suddenly it seemed very important to her to say her goodbyes, in case this time she really did walk to her death.

'You have both been so very much to me,' she said, 'know that I love you both, and if I don't return, look after our children…'

Helligan gripped her hand, 'if you in any way believe that you will come to harm, I beg of you don't go out there!'

'If I can defuse this without bloodshed, surely that is better? This is what my role dictates, Helligan.'

He shook his head but then stepped forward to kiss her again, 'go then,' he whispered, 'I understand honour, if nothing else.'

Josynne stepped forward then and put a hand on her arm. 'I will allow no harm to come to your loved ones,' he said, 'do not go too far out and should you feel afraid put up your hand and my archers will fire.'

Niamh nodded again and then swallowed. A groom bought out her white destrier as tradition demanded, and so she mounted with shaking hands, hindered a little by her leather armour. It could have been worse; she could have been pregnant – she thought to herself – like last time! She pushed the thought aside and straightened her back, her gloved hands taking the reins.

This was it.

A loud creak sounded as the gate began to move, the portcullis lifting first, and then the old wooden gate, fifty foot of ancient wood, crept open. Niamh's gut ached, and the need to urinate began to pull again. She bit it back though and moved to stand in the shadow of the gate. The sun beyond was hot indeed and the army stunk to high heaven. Niamh hadn't noticed it above, but on the ground level it was fetid, ripe and cloying. She gagged.

The hooded figure rode closer, his horse coming to meet her in the field as Niamh rode out tentatively. She'd never done anything like this before and her heart was hammering. The army was all around, and terror tried to take her. Niamh repressed it though, her belly hurting but her lips firm, her eyes like slate. She pulled rein and stopped before the figure right out in the middle of the field. He did not speak at first, his hood down over his face, but then put up two gloved hands and pulled the cowl down so that it fell onto his shoulders.

Niamh gasped, her hand tightening their grip on her horse. At first, she didn't quite understand what she was looking at, some sort of deformed gargoyle. He had no hair, no lips and only the stumps of his ears. His nose was flat and his skin leathery, like parchment.

The man watched her reaction, emotionless. His eyes burned though, bright crystal blue. Just like their father's had been…

'Hideous, isn't it?' he said, 'see what your dragon did to me, sister.'

Niamh's eye drank him in, the burned face, the blue eyes. Goddess, could it be? 'Laurin?' she whispered. Her fingers clung to the reins of her horse whilst her heart hammered in her chest as she began to understand. A human twisted with hate, one whom had seen death and stood in its shadow. She could well imagine too, what fate had befallen his beloved Lady Kyran: the vial of blood lying on top of his cape, about his chest, the power needed to make such a focus. The sacrifice of that which one loves most. Tears threatened. Her brother was unrecognisable, other than those eyes and yet, Niamh would have known them anywhere.

'Ah, so you do recognise me then?' Laurin pulled what Niamh supposed was supposed to be something of a smile on his twisted features. The black hooded cape draped about him covered most of his body, so Niamh was unable to see the full extent of the scarring to him, other than his face. Not Laurin. Not him, surely? Laurin had always been the sweet one, the kind one. He'd been the only one of her siblings to care, the only one to acknowledge "The King's Idiot" as a sister of his own. Her eyes skimmed his face… and she'd betrayed him, she realised. She was the usurper, and this scarred hulk before her was the true heir to the throne.

'Go ahead, take it all in. Grim, isn't it?' Laurin said, watching her with those perfect blue eyes.

'But… but you are dead!'

'Am I? that would explain a thing or two…' his chuckle was a dry rattle in his throat. He shook his head though, 'No, they saved me, they hid me and they have kept me hidden all these years… recovery from this,' he indicated his face, 'is a long road, sister, and at times I thought that never again would these eyes be recovered enough to see the day, never again would I ride a horse without absolute agony at every bump in the path.

'Laurin… I…'

'Hold anything you are going to say, none of it matters.'

'I loved you Laurin, of them all, I loved you! I never meant for…'

'For what? For my roasting alive? For my years of agony, hmm? For the betrayal of your family? You were so wrapped up in dethroning our father that you just happened to… what… forget about me?'

'You were never supposed to be hurt, brother.'

'Was I not?'

'No, you fired upon us… you tried to kill me, with my own bow!'

'I did, I fired upon the girl trying to steal my throne, my father's life – a man who had gifted you that very bow, if you recall?'

'It wasn't…' Niamh's emotion threatened to overwhelm her. 'It was not supposed to be this way,' she whispered.

'No? So, had I survived intact, then what? Execution like our father? Banishment like the rest of our family? You murdered our father, stole the kingdom. You had your dragon roast me alive, and forced my wife and my son into sanctuary, to obscurity. You took everything you could from whomever you could and cared not about who you hurt to do so! So very noble, my *Queen*. So let me ask you again… what if I had survived, intact? Would you still have stolen everything from me?'

'I… Laurin…'

'Say that name one more time, *my queen*, and I will have your tongue, parley or no! Your brother is dead. I stand in his place, in his form, but I am not he.'

'What are you then? Who are you, if not my brother?'

'When first your dragon struck me down, then I was nothing. I became a husk, pitiful and broken. The agony was so great that I spent every waking moment trying to scream in agony though a throat which barely moved. Our stepmother nursed me, along with her daughter, my wife.'

He fingered the vial of blood about his neck as he spoke the words, and Niamh's gut twisted again. Just as Oliah had sacrificed Oasha, to use her blood as a focus. Poor Kyran, what gratitude for her love, for her care – or had she offered herself up?

'It was Magda who put the book into my hands, when once again they had skin to cover them, a book of children's stories to soothe a tortured heart… and there I read that great prophesy. Even as Oliah died, the book said, so he whispered one last spell into the ground. One day, another soul crisped and burned in dragonfire would rise again and continue his work. This became my obsession, and so I had purpose once again, despite how every inch of my body is shrivelled and twisted from that fire, and despite how every step I took was agony. Despite that my son screamed when he saw my features, and my wife sobbed quietly in corners at the very thought of me. Still I pushed on with my recovery. I made it my very mission to stand again, to delve into these old rituals and revive myself.'

'But… but how… the mages tell me that… that no human man can… can harness such magicka as… as you do?'

'Not quite so. It can be done, despite that it takes a little of a person's soul,' his voice became more brittle, 'A deal wrought with a demon…' he lifted the vial from his neck, 'her blood, and my soul. I severed it with my own knife, I gave it over to the darkness. My love's blood is my magicka, but it is powered by the destruction of my own soul.'

'And so, you have come for your revenge?'

Laurin indicated the keep beyond. 'I have come for my birth-right, for my son's status and name,' he said. 'We can still end this without bloodshed, sister of mine. Abdicate now. Surrender yourself and put my son on the throne.'

'And then there will be peace?' the very idea of it was almost tempting. 'If I abdicate and allow Laurie to be king, my family go in peace?'

'Then there will be peace, yes. You, my wife's sister and her children, your daughter, all of the womenfolk you harbour there…you will be spared. You might join the sister order and live out your life therein as one of them. It's where you should have gone to begin with anyhow.'

'And my son?'

'Your son is forfeit his life, as is the rest of your council. I will make an example of those who have walked in treason all these years. As for your husband, I will have his dragon head speared on the gates as a warning to all that I will tolerate no aberrations in my kingdom.'

'You must… must realise that I… I would never agree to such terms?'

Laurin smiled again, that awful twisted grimace of pleasure, 'Oh… I know,' he said.

Niamh sat up a little straighter on her horse, her lips pressed. 'Then I believe this parley to be exhausted,' she whispered. 'I trust there is enough honour in you to allow me to return to my men.'

Laurin inclined his head. 'Fare-thee-well sister, and I wish a noble death to you. Cleaner than the one you tried to give me, at least.'

Helligan's face peered anxiously though the portcullis as Niamh turned her horse back towards her home. She rode hard, half-convinced that one of those terrible ghouls would rise up, tear her from her horse and devour her. They didn't though, Laurin was, as good as his word, allowing her to leave unscathed. The ride, just a mere few minutes in truth, dragged on exponentially but finally she was back behind the gate, and Helligan was pulling her from her horse.

'Niamh?' he whispered. In the background she could see Kilm lining the walls with tar-barrels. Josynne was in deep discussion with his archers just beyond. Nobody was under any illusions that the parley would work in their favour – did they ever really solve anything at all?

'It…' Niamh's voice clogged and suddenly she was rushed with tears. Helligan's arms held her tight for a long moment, but she pulled back and looked up onto his face with wet eyes. 'It's… it's Laurin…' she managed.

'Laurin? Your brother?'

Niamh nodded.

'But he… didn't I?'

'He wasn't dead,' she explained, 'he's come… come for the kingdom. He says… that… that if I surrender, Jess and I and the other women will go to safety… he wants me to crown his son.'

'And you declined?'

'He said… said that you and… and Alis would be… be my sacrifice. All of my council would die and I…' she shook her head. Helligan pressed her to him again and kissed her brow.

'He must have known you'd never give up your son!'

'I'd not give up any of you, my love.'

Helligan kissed her hair one last time, giving her his strength, and then pulled away and looked down onto her face. His countenance was very dark, his eyes grave. 'I wish I did not have to say these words,' he said, 'but our hand is forced. Let us prepare for battle.'

Twenty-Two

The murmur of the young mages' still high-pitched voices seemed to envelop Helligan entirely. He closed his tired eyes and let the chant soothe his aching mind, bathing in the hum of magika. It had been hours already and they were unrelenting, put into something of a trance by the old sages in order to aid them in their all-encompassing mission. Still, though, they were but children and Helligan feared that their vigil could not last more than a night or so. And what then? Still they had no word of Korbyn's daughters! No flap of wings in the sky to save them! In the first minutes of the battle, Laurin had sent his army at them, but they, unable to enter, had piled at the gates and so the mangled prince had pulled back, and thus the waiting game began! Without Korbyn's daughters, who were still yet to appear, there was little to stop Laurin from storming the gates when the children fell to exhaustion. Laurin knew that too, his jeers, shouted up at the keep, had been enough to tell them that!

Beyond them, on the next section of wall, Josynne Shale stood with his archers. He'd managed to muster about twenty, all garbed in chain and wearing those odd metal helms of the old king's guard – likely pilfered from the armoury of the Golden Keep. Already they were firing on the horde below, but the simple shafts had little impact on those already dead. The vats were lit too, at Kilm's command as ever, since he was the battle master of Niamh's army. A Wolder was an unusual choice for such but Helligan understood it well. For years the Wolder had been feared by the common man, why not put that to use? Kilm still had his men too, waiting below for an order to fight. At last count, Helligan had counted about a hundred Wolder who had made their homes in the wild lands between Anglemarsh and The Golden Keep – the crowd below in the courtyard showed that many, if not all, of those had gathered. Not much of a resistance against an undead horde of thousands though. Of other actual fighting men, most of the lords and courtiers had gone to ground, hiding away inside the keep. Niamh's sister Jedda had the charge of the children, ready to lead them out, and her husband had stayed to guard them. And then that left the mages. Helligan glanced at them, sat upon the circular platform which was hidden behind the east wall turret. Niamh had wanted them to stay inside but that would never have worked. They needed to be able to touch the wall they used as a boundary for the spell, and this wall curved not just about the keep, but about the city below too. Their efforts made the air crisp with magika, and Helligan enjoyed the buzz of it on his skin, despite that it added to the temptation to tune in himself.

The army below was silent. That was enough to send the chills down any man's back. A silent army made no sense at all, usually chanting, shouting and the clink of metal would drift up, not this nothingness. Queen Magda had joined Laurin at the head of the army, riding in on a black horse which was a rival even to her son-in-law's but even she sat quiet on her war-beast, proud, just waiting. If Niamh was correct in what Laurin used as a focus, that meant that the old lady below had allowed him to murder her own daughter for their cause. Helligan glanced back at his son who was whispering the words of protection with the others. He'd give his own life to protect that boy, and so the idea that somebody could callously send their offspring to be murdered in the name of power was abhorrent. Helligan's eyes ran over them again half-wondering where the boy for whom they both fought was – likely hidden away in some safe place until after the battle, he supposed.

'Niamh!' her brother's voice, calling again. Helligan put a hand on Niamh's shoulder to gently restrain her. He'd not have her make herself her brothers beck and call girl. Niamh put her hand over his, she was trembling but her shoulders were very firm and tight. Her face looked very strained though and Helligan wondered if she too realised the potential disaster if Korbyn's daughters did not come through: Laurin's army needed not to eat or to sleep. They could wait out any siege without even a flicker of worry. The same could not be said for their mages. If the children tired, lost concentration, then all was lost. Helligan glanced to Shale and his archers. Over and over they fired on an impenetrable foe. Wasting arrows. Niamh's eyes darted to the front as her brother shouted for her again.

'Don't,' Helligan said. 'I barely trusted him at parlay but now he realises he can't get in, then I trust him less! All it would take is one well-fired arrow…'

'I won't,' Niamh nodded, 'you speak sense, my love.' She shuffled a little and played with her hair. The wind up in the rooftops had pulled a braid free from the lace which held it and her hand worried the strand relentlessly. Helligan wanted to move forward and tuck it in but he knew such overprotectiveness was not needed. Niamh was stronger than almost anyone he knew, under the thin layer of anxiety which dallied on the surface. She looked much the battle queen in garb too, hair braided, leather armour and even the lines of the Wolder painted across her nose. Her freckles were showing for the warm day, but her skin was still creamy and pale. Niamh twiddled with her hair again, the movements betraying her nerves, and Helligan gave in to the urge, stepped forward and tucked the braid back into her headwrap. She smiled a wry smile as she realised she'd been fidgeting and pulled the hair wrap a little tighter. Helligan was overwhelmed suddenly with a rush of love for her. He wanted to grab her and pull her away downstairs to where no eyes were upon them and… but no, that could wait!

Niamh seemed not to sense his thoughts. She glanced over to Shale and his arrows again, then back to Helligan.

'We can't win this,' she said, 'if your dragons don't arrive soon… if only we'd considered keeping even one of the mages with us! Even just Alis, we could have at least begun to dent this army!'

'Our son could not win this battle alone,' Helligan replied, 'Or even the mages as a unit… there are too many below and our mages too few. Besides, they need them there, my love. They need all the power they can get and our son has magical ability in abundance! I doubt this shield would work as well without him.'

'Orien and Graves could surely…'

'They cast the spell but they need the trickle of magika the children give to keep them going. A spell like this would drain even the sages in an hour. It's the circle which keeps them going and Alis is a big part of that. His dragon essence is almost as strong as mine, he will be able to give to Orien and Graves, even when the others are drained.'

'You knew that, when you wrote the spell?'

'I did!'

'And the children won't be hurt?'

'Of course not! Tired, drained for a few days, but they have each accepted their role in this.'

Niamh stood up on tiptoe to look at the army spread out behind the old great slate and stone walls. Helligan watched her eyes take it all in.

'How long?' she asked.

'Until?'

'Until the siege breaks?'

'Until the mages tire,' there was no point in sugar-coating it so he didn't.

'And then?'

'And then I suppose we fight or flee if – as it appears – the help promised is not coming.'

There was quiet for a long moment, but then Niamh stood up on tiptoes to look over the wall. 'Magda's gone again,' she observed.

'Has she? What is she up to?'

Niamh shook her head and shrugged, 'You don't like me on the forefront of a battle either,' she said.

Helligan nodded, that much was the truth.

The thack of another load of arrows sounded. Helligan watched as Shale and his men reloaded. Kilm had already given up and had vanished off somewhere, probably below to prime his warriors. The undead weren't close enough to the walls for the oil vats to be of any use and so the commander had likely re-joined his men as they waited below for the real battle to begin. The Wolder were always hungry for battle if it came their way. Helligan eyed the fire beneath the vats though. Now, there was a weapon they had that might work!

'Shale!' he shouted, then ran along the walkway, the stone floors were slowly becoming hazardous but he was fairly sure of foot.

Lord Shale glanced up; his long hair tied away in a tail behind him but it whipped around as his head turned to Helligan. He looked panicked. 'What?'

'Use the fire! Light the bastards up!' he shouted. Shale's brow creased, but then his eyes brightened.

'Good thinking! Men, light your arrows at the vats, he called and fire on my command!'

Helligan watched as the group – some twenty men at Shale's command, dipped the arrows into the fire, and then Shale gave the shout to hock, aim and fire. A sea of flame flew out over the open air and then onto that eerily silent army below. The ones which were hit stood as still as the rest with their bodies burning. As the flames took hold though, they did seem to crumble. Much to Helligan's satisfaction, though, Laurin pulled back – a slight retreat taking him out of arrow range despite the magics he used to shield himself. Helligan, unlike Niamh, didn't have to guess at their use, he could see the purple magika surrounding Laurin.

And thus it remained. A stalemate for the meanwhile at least. The siege was a long one, a quiet one with the night broken up only with the sound of the mages chanting. Helligan watched as Niamh's eyes strayed to their son, the boy must be exhausted and yet there he sat, as staunch as the rest. Helligan was immeasurably proud.

Then suddenly a scream permeated the night.

Niamh jumped, her whole body moving with the shock. Another scream came, and then a yell. 'Jess,' Niamh murmured, her voice showing her panic.

'It wasn't from within the keep! She's safe! Jedda will lead her to safety if need be and they have Lord Lorne for protection!'

Niamh's whole face showed a panic so raw that Helligan just wanted to crush her to him but then, as ever she could, she rebuilt her calm façade over the top and sucked in a deep breath.

'We need to find out what the screaming is though,' Helligan added, as more of that sound echoed. It sounded as though it were coming from behind the keep, towards the shrine where he'd met his father just hours earlier. Niamh nodded and then ran to the wall where the army idled. She looked over and then turned back to Helligan. 'Laurin is doing something…' she whispered.

Helligan glanced a look too and saw that the figure of her brother had dismounted his horse and stood amidst his undead horde with his arms raised up. The purple creeping mists were all around him, and seemed to be travelling down under the very gates.

'What…' he murmured.

'It's the ones inside!' Kilm's voice as that man suddenly appeared again at the door which led to the main bailey, he looked frenzied, 'he's raising the bloody burial ground!'

Helligan whipped around, his eyes mad with panic. 'He shouldn't be able to!'

'Well he is! Your spell is failing!'

Still the mages looked serene, still the magicka hummed, it wasn't that then! Helligan's gut tightened, had he really miscalculated so badly? Could it be that the spell would keep the undead out, but not the necromancer's magics?

'Kilm, call up everyone from the courtyard and have them barricade indoors,' he said, then spun about at the sound of a cry just behind them.

And then there was chaos.

The scream was Alistair's, and with it came the cessation of the hum of magicka. Niamh was spinning around too, her own bow in hand and an arrow already hocked. Alistair was held fast in the grip of an old woman. Helligan didn't know her at first, but then realisation dawned as Niamh moaned out the name, "*Magda!*" Helligan didn't even stop to pause and think of how the old woman had managed to get up onto the roof. She'd lived in this keep for several years and both Helligan and Niamh knew well that there were hundreds of ways in, you just had to know them. The rest of the children were scattering, and below, Helligan could hear the unnerving shuffle of Laurin's undead army moving, mobilising now that the keep was undefended. Panic threatened. At his side, Niamh fired, her aim as sure as ever but the arrow clattered to the ground before Magda. Obviously the old witch was protected by her son-in-law's magics.

'Give it up, or I will end the boy's life,' Magda said, an ornate dagger held tight in her hand. the weapon had a bejewelled handle and a blade which looked as though it was edged in gold. Surely something Magda must have stolen from Niamh's father, back when she'd fled.

'Magda… please…' Niamh murmured at his side, her bow arm hanging at her side and panic in her eyes again.

'Your gates are breached, your mages depleted and your son in my control. You have lost! Surrender, Niamh, and allow the rightful line of succession to revert!'

'Only if you will release us all, unharmed…'

Helligan felt the magicka building within as the sight of the blade to his son's throat. The other mages were scattered, the sounds from below were chaos, and the night was darkening. Despite the pain, despite it all, Helligan allowed the magic to begin to burn. He put a hand up to his vial, blanking out Niamh's cry to cease, blanking out it all. He harnessed the sweet blue light within, and then turned to Niamh. 'Fire,' he whispered, his guts clenching as the pain shot through him.

She, despite her wet face, did not argue, and as Helligan shot out a flame from his hand, she fired her arrow through it. As Helligan had suspected, the blue ice flame cracked the flimsy magicka shield about Magda, and before she could react, Niamh's arrow pierced her throat. Alistair fell to the ground with another cry, as Magda sagged and then stumbled. Her hand went to her throat as through she could dislodge the arrow but it was stuck too fast there. She gurgled blood, gave Niamh one more shocked look, and then fell. The magicka left him suddenly, and the agony which shot through was second only to a sudden feeling of dizziness and confusion. Niamh ran for their son, as Helligan stumbled, his hands going to his head.

From behind, Shale seemed to shout something, but Helligan could not hear through the ringing in his ears. He dimly watched as Niamh bundled their son to her, but then it was blotting, pulling away. He put a hand over his ears, trying to stop the ringing, and fell to his knees. Niamh was screaming again though, and then he felt the presence of kin. With a real effort, Helligan managed to stagger back to his feet, Niamh's hands dragging him about to see the sheet of white flame coming down upon the undead army as they flooded the gates. Half of the gatehouse was falling too, but it mattered not, so long as the people inside were saved. Helligan forced himself back to clarity, finding a smile even through the pain and the dizziness. They were here! they had come just as Korbyn had promised! His son moved to his side and Helligan clapped a hand on his shoulder, watching the boy's eyes take in the sheer destruction of their kind. Shale moved away from the archers too, joining them.

'Seems your kin came through,' he said.

'A…aye…'

'Are you all right, there?'

'Just… just a little woozy.'

Helligan moved to the edge of the keep wall, not just for a glimpse of the battle below, but also for the chance to hold himself steady. He felt sick and the essence about his neck pulsed and burned, almost willing him to pull the cork, to submit to his dragon form. It was not like before though, not when Niamh's father had had the orb which had controlled him, more a craving than an impulse. The ground all about was red and white with the flames of the White-scale draconis fire. Laurin had fallen already. His death certain this time, as still his body smouldered. No great exit for him, not a martyr's death – they'd not even witnessed his fall.

'I'll go and find Jess,' Shale spoke, 'And spread the good news! We are saved!'

Helligan's eyes began to droop again, victory was theirs and so now he could sleep, go to Morgana for her healing – if even she could lift the curse upon him now. He allowed his eyes to begin to close, but then something, some other instinct made him open his eyes again, heavy and painful lids which just barely lifted at his command.

'Look! Helligan! It's one of yours, too!' Niamh's voice, joyful!

Helligan forced his eyes to the sky. His head was spinning to the point that for the first moment it looked as though there were a whole flight of blue dragons. He shook his head, then tried to murmur that this was not right! His own clan were not their friends. His lips were too dry though, his body too far gone. Even as Argosus seemed to hone in on them, and turned in flight to sweep over the keep, Helligan had not the strength to warn them of the danger, not the words to send them to hide. Instead he was rendered mute as his brother swooped down and plucked his son right from the rooftops in his claws.

Then there was more screaming, Niamh's voice. Helligan could hold human form no longer. His hand flipped the stopper on the vial, and he allowed the blue mists to envelop him.

Twenty-Three

Niamh heard her own screams of frenzied terror break free as the blue dragon carried her son over the parapet, then dropped him down onto the roof across the way. How far had that drop been? Three foot? Four? Or was it more? Did her baby now lie broken on the hard stone? She did not know and her eyes, no matter how they strained, could not see that far. The blue mists of Helligan's submission cleared though and Niamh felt her guts clench to see how the dragon which held the true form of her husband was maimed. Infection had spread into the wounds, leaving them to fester and pus. The stumps of his wings were black, and an odd mist oozed and wafted about him. He stumbled up to his feet, the vial which had held his essence falling with a clink across the old stone and down over the edge of the battlements. Niamh barely took it in, her eyes glued to Helligan's wounds, to his obvious pain!

Helligan, in form, staggered fully to his feet, and then with a pulse of muscular movements, he leapt from the roof. Niamh screamed again, fearing he was trying to fly, but he must have already known he could not. Instead he found purchase on the side of the old keep. The whole building shuddered under his weight as he landed. His claws dug into hard stone, making it crumble as he leapt, and then again, throwing himself around the turret and going after his kinsman – and his son. Within a moment or two, he was clambering up onto the roof, his body moving with jerky, swaying movements. As he climbed, a chunk of stone pulled free and fell, clattering, onto the ground below. All around Niamh, the heat of the dragon-fire which flooded the fields below where she stood was stifling. She was covered in sweat. Still the two white dragons circled, killing off the last of the invaders. If she had been able to tear her eyes from her husband and son, Niamh would have just about been able to pick out her brother's prone smouldering form. How horrific and yet how just, for him to be taken again by that which had claimed him the first time.

Niamh's heart thudded as Helligan slipped again. The black crust of those wing stumps was heart-breaking as, despite that the wings were gone, still the stumps moved back and forth as though he were trying to flap them. A hand going around her waist made Niamh jump violently, but it was just Nervoria, sliding in to hug her side. The girl was crying, as was Friggan behind her. Despite their maturity, they were just children after all. Niamh clutched at Nervoria's shoulder, sharing strength and solidarity with the girl. Beyond, Helligan had made it to the top of the turret, just about. Niamh put up a hand to shield her eyes and there suddenly was Alistair's dark head popping up into view!

'He's alive!' she murmured.

'What's Helligan going to do?'

Niamh's hand tightened as she recognised the building of flame in Helligan's gut. She closed her eyes, unable to watch.

'It's the rose and the mantle,' Elenni spoke from behind.

'What?'

'To… to light the fire without destroying the rose…'

Niamh's brain was too addled for the analogy but she nodded anyway, her heart in her chest as Helligan belched flame at the other blue. She had never felt so helpless, not since those early days of the first attack where she'd had to stand by and watch Helligan fight for them both. Then suddenly it hit her. She wasn't helpless, far from it! And she wasn't alone either! She sucked in a deep breath, and then grabbed for Elenni's hand.

'Come,' she urged, 'All of you, link up with me! Use me as a focus! I have the power of my fae mother in me! Use it!'

Three confused pairs of eyes stared at her. Niamh spun about to Seer Orien, still dozy from where the circle had been broken. He'd be no use then! The other two sages were still unconscious from where they'd been deep within the grasp of magicka when the spell had imploded, but the children, combined, would be power enough! She put out her other hand to Nervoria, who took it and then beckoned for Friggan. He moved in too, closing the circle.

'Now, close your eyes,' Niamh said, 'and imagine a shield around your brother!'

At once the three child-mages seemed to catch on. Niamh felt the power as her energy began to drain, to be the focus of all three was a hard task, but for her son, she'd let them drain her until she fell. Her eyes moved back to the turret. Yes! Something was happening! A light of blue green and red formed like a shell around her son, just as Helligan's kin-dragon let out its own bellow of flame. Niamh's heart was in her throat but the flame passed harmlessly over the shield and the boy within seemed still intact. Niamh gasped again, her knees feeling weak.

'Keep at it,' she murmured to the three, 'you have just saved Alistair's life!'

Nervoria's eyes sprung open at her words and Niamh felt the magika waver.

'No! Concentrate!' she hissed but it was too late as the other blue breathed again and Helligan seemed to waver. The blast passed over what remained of the shell, but the force of it knocked Alistair from his feet. Niamh moaned, dropping the hands of the two young mages she held, as her baby flailed and then stumbled over the edge. Helligan went after him but it was too late, the boy was falling.

'Quick!' Niamh all but screamed, 'Cushion his fall.'

With the panic in Niamh's voice, Nervoria grabbed for Elenni and so the three formed a circle between them. Niamh ran to the edge of the parapet and watched in horror, her hands over her mouth as Alistair fell. The mages were not strong enough to stop the fall, Niamh could see that at once. The boy's descent slowed a little, but not enough. Niamh felt tears explode from her eyes, but then all of a sudden, another dragon appeared, a huge white with scales that gleamed silver and vast wings that must have each stretched out taller than she was. The dragon swooped, gripped Alistair in its claws, and then pushed up with a roar, bellowing fire in the direction of Helligan's opponent. The blue dragon screamed in the flames, batting its own wings to raise it up. As Niamh watched, her hand gripping tight to the stone of the parapet, the other blue rose up and filled its gullet again. It might have breathed the flames at the newcomer, effectively ending Alistair's life, if not for Helligan's throwing himself bodily at the beast, managing to grab a hold of its back leg with his claws and throw it off balance. The other blue roared again, and then turned tail and flew away, begging a retreat.

Niamh felt her shoulders slump, her whole body sagging. She turned about to look upon her companions. The three young mages were slumped too, all linked still by the hands but no longer upright. The sages were stirring and the corpse of Magda lay still on the ground, Niamh's arrow still through her throat. Niamh felt for a moment like she would stumble but sheer determination kept her upright. She had no idea where the others were. Jedda and Lorne should have fled with Jess, but Josynne was missing too now and she'd seen nothing of Kilm since the beginning of the battle. Niamh stooped to unlink the hands of the children in an effort to break the link to the magika which she could still feel buzzing about her. On the other side, the three white dragons had landed and Niamh could just about make out Alistair's shape. It seemed fitting for her boy to be amongst the dragons but still she feared the worst. The biggest of the three, the newcomer, began to flap his wings again, and as he rose up Niamh saw he had an unconscious Helligan clutched by the belly in his claws. He moved across the distance quickly, and then Niamh saw Alistair clamber up onto the back of one of the others.

The white dragon was even bigger up close. The flapping of his wings was enough to move the dust and dirt about, almost to knock her from her feet with it! Sage Tamm who until that point had been so still Niamh had worried for his life, moaned at the sensation and lifted his head, his tree-bark lips sagging open. The dragon dropped the unconscious form of Helligan at Niamh's feet, then landed at her side. Helligan was badly burned and barely conscious, his great yellow eye dim where it was set into his blue scales, open but unseeing. Niamh repressed more tears, there would be time for those, later.

A white mist formed then, cool and soft, comforting. Niamh recognised well the sight of a dragon returning to human form as the mist curled and coiled, then dissolved into a haze of fresh comfort. As he changed form, Niamh was distracted by the other one landing too and Alistair jumping down from the wall – amazingly unharmed, if a little mussed for his adventures. Her son looked pale but also empowered, his young eyes were dark and his lips pressed very tight just as his father did when in his more serious of mindsets. Alistair ran to Niamh and she crushed him to her. He did not weep though, merely pressed her closely and then stepped aside. In a handful of minutes, her son had aged by years!

'My good lady,' a voice made Niamh look up to view the oldest man she'd ever seen. He was bent with hair which was a mix of both white and grey streaks, ancient eyes which were of a grey which seemed to be tinged with red. He was nude, as were all draconis after the transformation, but his hair was long enough to hide his dignity and he showed no shame for it. Niamh clutched Alistair a little closer as the third of the white dragons landed next to Helligan and laid down her head on his. For the first time, Niamh realised that both of the smaller white dragons had red eyes too. The old man had in his hand one of the strangely carved Draconis essence vials, this he passed to Niamh.

'You will need this,' he said. 'It is not his own but it will suffice.'

'Thank you. Who are you? What… what just…'

'A long story, for perhaps another time. I fear a war is beginning this day though, one of my kingdom, rather than yours.'

'That was…'

'Argosus, Helligan's brother. He is the leader of the clans now. I am afraid he saw my daughters leave Zaikais and sought to interfere! I am sorry it delayed us to the point that it did.'

Niamh nodded, and then put out her hand. The old man took it and rubbed a thumb over her fingers. At once Niamh felt clearer, more level-headed.

'No matter the events taking place in our city as we speak, my children and I are now outcasts,' the old man said, 'Might we find shelter in your kingdom?'

Alistair turned about to face them, his young shoulders firm and his eyes bright, 'You will ever have a home here,' he said, before Niamh could respond, 'won't they, Mother?'

'I… yes, of course…'

The old man smiled at Alistair, and Niamh saw a glimpse of something in his eye. Could that be pride? She shook it off. The old man moved to bend over Helligan and there he put a hand over his heaving side. That same white light from before seemed to bloom, growing in intensity until it was almost blinding, but then fading away. As Niamh watched, the burn on Helligan's throat began to fade away.

'That is the best I can do,' the old man said, 'he will need more than healing to remove the curse he is under.'

'Curse?' Niamh murmured.

'Indeed, the curse put upon him by his brother…'

Niamh's eyes filled with water again although she didn't cry. She swallowed the suddenly plentiful saliva in her mouth and then nodded, 'I'll take him to Morgana,' she said.

The old man said nothing at first, his eyes still on Helligan, but then straightened up, 'This Morgana, she is a shaman?' he asked.

'Of a sort, she is a witch.'

'Then she might be able to help. I suggest you move quickly though…'

Niamh nodded again but the two smaller white dragons were already moving their wings in unison, rising up into the air. The old man stepped backwards and lifted his own vial from where it lay against his naked chest.

'My daughters and I shall make our home in the mountains of the whites,' he said, 'our ancestral home…'

'T-take them… then, as… as my gift to you,' Niamh whispered, 'and… and make them as once they were… so long as you spare the inhabitants…'

The old man half-smiled and nodded. 'Fare well, Queen Niamh,' he said, and then his eye twinkled more so, 'and get my son to your witch before that curse spreads to his heart.'

'Your son?' Niamh gasped, but the old man had already lifted his focus and so there was nothing to see but a cloud of white as he was transformed back into form. Alistair moved forward as the dragon once more stood on the parapet, and put up a hand to touch its chest. The great beast bowed its head, and then began to flap its wings once more.

Niamh stood for a long moment, but then was pulled from her daze by Josynne's re-emergence from the other turret. He ran up the steps but then paused at the sight of the unconscious dragon, the similarly affected children behind.

'What the devil happened?' he asked, he was covered in soot, and stinking of the cloying smell of smoke.

'No time,' Niamh whispered, 'Jess…'

'Is fine, she is with Lorne and Jedda in the great hall. The horde got into the keep but those not decimated by the flames have been taken out by Kilm and his men!'

'It… it is over, then?'

'It is over, yes. I have sent orders for a man to put a sword through Laurin's heart – just to be sure, and I will see if we can locate your nephew too.'

Suddenly the weight of the world took Niamh to her knees. She sat for a moment, allowing the relief of that at least to wash through her, but then looked over at the still and silent form of Helligan.

'Is he… dead?' Josynne asked softly.

Niamh shook her head. She pulled the stopper on Helligan's vial, and then repeated the incantation Mother Morgana had given to her in a time which felt like a millennia ago. As the blue haze began, Josynne moved past Helligan, and her too, to see to the injured and depleted people beyond. Alistair went to join him but Niamh sat on the hard stone with water in her eyes, Helligan her only focus. At last the mist cleared and there he was. Still and silent, naked on the stones. Niamh shuffled forward and pulled his head into her lap. Helligan's lips parted and he moaned, then, before Niamh's very eyes, the lines of the curse moved, twisting and sliding their way over his shoulders, up onto his face.

'Helligan?' Niamh's voice was high-pitched – frightened.

Helligan's eyes rolled open, not quite comprehending, but open at least. Niamh gasped, her hand going up to clutch over her lips. Even the whites of his eyes were changing, the black smoke of the curse moving onto the surface of them, making the illusion of complete darkness. Helligan moaned again and then closed his eyes, unable to maintain consciousness.

Josynne came back to her side. His hand moved to caress her shoulder. 'Alistair and I will cope here,' he said gently, 'there is no danger now, and much to be straightened out. Jess and Jedda are well, they are in the room beyond, and so you might take him with an easy heart. We'll do this, you go…'

Niamh nodded and then forced herself back to her feet. she was dizzy with hunger and exhausted beyond belief, but she knew there was no time to dally for food and rest.

'W-will you… is there a horse l-left alive?'

Josynne let his arm slip around her and pulled her in for a quick embrace, then took off shouting for aid, for a horse and somebody to carry Helligan to it.

Epilogue

The day broke bright and crisp as the broad beams of sunlight slipped through the thick woodlands of the forest. Niamh felt as though she were walking through a sea of mud. She had managed a few bites of bread on route, but she had not slept. Her horse was bound to the tree on which she leaned, strong and firm in her back, holding her up. Helligan was so weak now, and the black lines covered his entire form. Agamariss would not take him though, not for the time-being at least, not if she had to beat death away with a sword herself!

Niamh sat for a long moment basking in the sunshine and allowing the goddess to warm her, to strengthen her. Once, whilst courting, Helligan and she had made love under these very trees. It seemed a lifetime ago now. Niamh stood and unhooked her water skin from the saddlebag and knelt beside Helligan. His face was a little burned by the sun for having been laid in the bundle pack which her horse dragged behind it. He was well lashed in though and the pack was secured in a manner that disallowed it to be turned over. Despite this being the best way to transport him, Niamh worried that he was going to burn up or suffer heat exhaustion from the bright sunlight. She opened her waterskin and allowed a few dribbles to fall onto his dry lips. Helligan did not stir, not even to taste the water but Niamh preserved long enough to ensure he was hydrated before covering his face as best she could without smothering him and moved back to the saddle. Her whole body ached, protested, but she repressed it. She could sleep when Helligan was safe!

The journey seemed never-ending, especially alone. Niamh had refused a guide, refused guards and maids too. The Wolder had very few secrets left, but Havensguard was one of them and Niamh wasn't prepared to reveal the little village up in the mountains to what was left of her court. Finally, the trees thinned though and they approached the village of the witch, Morgana. Niamh, as ever, felt her pulse race faster as they approached the run-down little hut, even more so now after so many years past.

'*Please, Morgana, still be alive,*' she repeated over and over inside her head. The old woman had seemed to be pushing a hundred for the fifteen years or so that Niamh had known her at least. She glanced behind, to where Helligan was being drawn behind the steady old horse. If Morgana was gone, then Niamh was out of ideas.

'Not much longer my darling,' she murmured, guiding the horse out past the edge of the path to the village.

If anything, the village of Havensguard actually seemed to have prospered since last Niamh set foot there. Several children were playing out in the streets and there was a new row of hut-houses moving out further from the trees. Some of the houses had gardens now, mostly brimming with foodstuffs rather than flowers but beautiful still in their own way. The sunshine which cast its brightly warm glow into the village now that the trees had broken played its part in making the place look brighter, more welcoming. Niamh paused and glanced about, then caught sight of a face she recognised well.

'Morkyl! Morkyl Greashion!' she said, her voice ringing out oddly despite the general noise and clutter of village life. The old man was standing looking up at the roof of one of the houses, a lad by his side. He was dressed in the fur and rags of the rest of the villagers and his once black hair was mostly greyed, his stature more stooped than Niamh remembered. Nobody would have believed that this man had once been one of the most accomplished warriors in Niamh's army. She'd not lain eyes on him in many years though, as despite her offers of a place at her side, Morkyl had instead chosen retirement to the village of his youth.

At Niamh's uttering of his name, Morkyl turned. His eyes lit up upon seeing her and his grin widened. The pair had parted on good terms, and only time had distanced them.

'Well, In't we honoured,' he said, still smiling, 'If it's not the queen herself come to visit with us wild men, eh?'

Niamh dropped the horse's rein and ran to Morkyl. She paused for half a moment, decorum fighting joy, but the joy won out and like an errant child, she embraced him.

'Uff! Now there's a greeting! I heard rumours that you've been somewhat occupied of late? Necromancers and the like!…'

'I have, Morkyl… I can explain more later but I need… I need Morgana's wisdom, is she…'

'Aye, yes child, she's still here. What's the bother?' he glanced up at her horse again, his eyes wondering to the bundle of rags attached to the cart behind and then widening as he realised that those were no rags.

'It's Helligan,' Niamh said quickly.

'Helligan? I heard he was back! He's injured?'

Niamh nodded and moved back to the horse, taking Morkyl with her, 'He is… ailing, see…' She knelt to reveal Helligan's unconscious form, then pulled up the shirt she'd dressed him in to reveal the odd black lines on his skin. Morkyl wrinkled his old eyes up to view the diseased skin, then stood back up looking grim.

'Let's get him in to see Mother,' he said.

Morgana looked exactly the same as she had the last time Niamh had seen her but for the whiting of one of her eyes, a blindness which had not ailed her before. Her old back was bent but no more so than it had been and her good eye looked out from brows which were almost as bushy as Morkyl's. As ever, nobody knocked at Morgana's, they just entered, and she was already brewing tea for the party. The hut was very dark with a fairly low ceiling, not enough to bother Niamh but ever Helligan had had to stoop, there. There was a fire lit, and a cauldron upon it, bubbling away. Morgana's bed was just a bundle of blankets on a frame in the corner, and her chair by the fireplace was the very same in which she'd sat when first Niamh had happened upon her, so many years earlier. Morgana turned as Niamh and Morkyl entered the hovel.

'Mother,' Niamh said, bowing her head.

'Hmmm, an errant child returned… with a burden too. Where be my broken son?'

'He is without, Mother. He is…'

'He ails.'

'Yes, Mother.'

'A curse which burns deep within im, I feel the stench of it even now w'in my bones. He's fading fast, can ye sense it?'

'I can. That is why I have come to you!'

Morgana handed Niamh a cup of heavily stewed liquid. Not quite tea, but fragrant and sweet where she sipped it. At once a calm seemed to steady her jangled nerves.'

'Come,' Morgana said, and hobbled to the door. She moved out of the hut with limping steps to where Morkyl knelt before the prone Helligan. Niamh followed but stayed back as Morkyl showed the mottled skin to Morgana. She merely stood and looked, then turned to Niamh.

'How long?'

'Some weeks since it began. It was… was mild to begin…'

'But he weakened fast, mmm?'

'Y-yes. It seemed to… to worsen when he used his dragon magic but… but…'

'But the fool would not stop using it?' Morkyl said, the question more a statement – he knew his old friend well.

'Indeed…'

Morgana put a finger down on Helligan's back. 'Great evil has been done ere,' she said. 'A curse, yes, an placed by his own kin, if I'm not mistaken.'

Niamh reeled to have it confirmed so matter-of-factly, but after the way Argosus had attacked Alistair, nothing surprised her anymore. 'You are sure? It was Argosus?'

'I deal not in details, I know only that this is a brother's hand that laid this upon im. A fire imp as vessel, but a brother's curse'

'Can… can you save him?'

'Aye. Shame of it bein kin to im.' Morgana said, looking down at Helligan again, 'Harder to repress that way, but there is still time… Morkyl take Helligan up into the glade! Niamh, I need you to go gathering for me. Pommel, whimswhipple, clouster and gale-flower. As much o' each as you can git.'

Niamh knew better than to argue despite her tumultuous thoughts and nodded, moving back to Morkyl's side.

'One other thing…'

'What, what is it?'

'I…' Niamh had never seen the old woman at a loss before, but her lips pressed and her chest heaved with worry. 'I won't be able to save his dragon essence from the curse, ee's too far gone. I will have to sever them.'

'I don't understand – what does that mean?'

'It means Helligan will live, but he will be human. No more dragon-essence, body or form. No more magic. He would age and he will be as vulnerable as any other – more so, perhaps, as he knows no caution.'

Niamh's heart took up banging. The choice was not hers but then Helligan was in no fit state to make it. She looked down on his unconscious face. There was no reprieve, she'd have to choose. A dead dragon, or a living human Helligan. In the end, the choice was simple.

'Do it,' she whispered.

The End

(for now...)

About the Author

Ever since I was a kid, I wanted to write for a living! Sure, all authors say that, but in my case it was very true. From the poorly structured short-stories of my final years at school, to my days as a performance poet in the early years of university. I always knew where my true love lay, though, in the rewarding pursuit of novel writing. I finished my first at about nineteen years old. Ok, it was pretty dire but hell, it was a start. That one I put aside and tried again, and again and again. After the fifth novel, I had something even I knew was a bit good! Perfected and polished!

That novel was Ella's Memoirs.

Ok, so I had a book to publish. There was a slight problem though, I had no idea where to start! Traditional publishing was a scary thought, and "indie publishers made no money" or so I was told, and so had to put writing on a back-burner whilst they maintained a "normal" person job. So, like any good ostrich, I turned my back on the idea of publishing, buried my head in the sand, worked whatever jobs I could get and just wrote books in my spare time.

Lots of books!

In May 2014, with a backlog of nine novels, about five of which were publishable, I finally decided to look fate in the eye and give it a shot. I chose to indie publish as one thing I have never wanted to do was to take away the pleasure of writing by running my ever so crinkled, non-conforming babies of literature through the heavy press of traditional publishing.

And here I found success. More success than I had thought possible!

Ella's Memoirs was a hit – I tried a 2 day free promotion on the guidance of some wonderous guru of internet forum fame, and then suddenly I was in the top 1000 free ebooks of that particular week. I was astounded, befuddled and just happy to soak it all in.

As many indie authors can attest to, these things don't always last, and whilst it is true that my next two books were both still well received, that little wave did reside somewhat. I became busier with university, moving on from my Psychology Degree and MSc to start, and then complete, my History Masters. Then to PhD which is still ongoing. The Blood of the Poppies was my second novel, released whilst I was still studying for my Psychology Msc – and to this day remains one of my favourite that I have ever written. Poppies was followed by The Black Marshes in 2018. Both might perhaps be best described as "a moderate success".

My fourth novel, then, The King's Idiot, was released in 2019 and was my first in a new genre, being historical fantasy. Here, suddenly, it all came rushing back. The book signings, the interviews, people leaving fab reviews and asking me almost relentlessly for book two! I was contacted by subscription services with a view to distribution and finally, the dream seemed to be coming true.

I guess you could say – to be continued….

https://www.facebook.com/EmmaBarrettBrown/

Also by this Author:

Ella's Memoirs
The Blood of the Poppies
The Black Marshes
The King's Idiot
Donor
The Man Who Painted a Fairy

Printed in Great Britain
by Amazon